Heidi was Johanna Spyri's first book. It was originally published in 1880 and has since been enjoyed by generation after generation.

   Now author Anne de Graaf has rewritten this delightful story in simpler language for today's children. She replaces outdated terms with more clearly understood phrases, while still capturing the charm of the original *Heidi*.

   This version also highlights the moral messages of a story about a little girl and her loss and love and life. Here is a children's classic taken from the past . . . made readable for the present.

To Erik

Heidi.

Text copyright © 1989 by Anne de Graaf and Scandinavia Publishing House.

Illustration copyright © 1989 by Chris Molan and Scandinavia Publishing House.

Published by Crossway Books, a division of Good News Publishers, Wheaton, Illinois 60187.

First U.S. printing, 1990 / Printed in Hong Kong

Library of Congress Cataloging-in-Publication Data

De Graaf, Anne.
    Heidi / retold by Anne de Graaf from Johanna Spyri's classic story : illustrated by Chris Molan.
       p. cm. — (Classics for children)
    Summary: A Swiss orphan is heartbroken when she must leave her beloved grandfather and their happy home in the mountains to go to school and to care for an invalid girl in the city.
    [1. Grandfathers—Fiction. 2. Mountain life—Fiction. 3. Orphans—Fiction. 4. Switzerland—Fiction.]
I. Molan, Chris, ill. II. Spyri, Johanna, 1827-1901. Heidi. III. Title. IV. Series: De Graaf, Anne. Classics for children.
PZ7.D33946He 1989   [Fic]—dc20   90-46732
ISBN 0-89107-600-X

99	98	97	96	95	94	93	92	91	90
15	14	13	12	11	10	9	8	7	6	5	4	3	2	1

Classics for Children

Heidi

Retold by Anne de Graaf
from Johanna Spyri's classic story

Illustrated by Chris Molan

CROSSWAY BOOKS • WHEATON, ILLINOIS
A DIVISION OF GOOD NEWS PUBLISHERS

CHAPTER 1
Up the Mountain

About a hundred years ago there lived a little girl named Heidi. Heidi was five years old. For most children, five is the age when mothers and fathers say, "You're getting so big!" But Heidi had no parents. They were both dead. So Heidi's aunt took care of her instead. But not really.

Heidi's aunt had found a good job in Germany. Although she and Heidi were from Switzerland, her aunt decided to take the job and find someone else who could take care of Heidi. Poor little Heidi. She had no Mommy and Daddy, and she had no home.

This is how it happened that one sunny summer morning Heidi was following her aunt, who was called Detie, along a path which led up a mountain. They were in the little Swiss village of Dörfli, where Heidi's parents and aunt had grown up.

Dörfli was nestled in a valley at the foot of great, tall mountains. The air there was sweet from wildflowers growing on the slopes higher up.

Heidi had no choice but to follow Aunt Detie as she tugged on Heidi's hand, pulling her along. Heidi was so hot, she could hardly breathe. She wore two dresses, one on top of the other, and had a red scarf wrapped round and round her. Her aunt had not wanted to carry the clothes, so Heidi had to wear them.

As Aunt Detie led her through the village, people called to the young woman.

"Detie, you're back!"

"How are you?"

"Who is the child?"

But Aunt Detie did not say much. She kept walking until she reached the last house. There a woman said, ""Half a minute, Detie. I'll come with you if you're going any farther."

Aunt Detie stood still. Heidi let go of her hand and sat down on the ground. "Tired, Heidi?" Aunt Detie asked her.

"No, but I'm roasting hot," the child said.

"We'll be there soon. Try to keep going. See what big steps you can take."

Just then a large, smiling woman came out of the last house and joined them. Heidi got up and followed as the two women talked away. After a little while, the village woman looked at Heidi and asked, "Where are you going with the child, Detie? Isn't she your sister's little girl?"

Aunt Detie nodded. Heidi's mother, who was Aunt Detie's sister, had died a year after Heidi was born. "Yes. My mother and I have been taking care of her. But now my mother is dead, and I want this job in Germany, working for a family I met last summer. So Heidi must go to live with her grandfather."

The village woman was so surprised, she stopped walking. "What?" she cried out. "You're bringing this little girl to live with him?" Then she lowered her voice and glanced behind her to make sure Heidi had not heard. But Heidi was much farther down the path. She had stopped to take her scarf off, because she was so hot underneath all those clothes.

The village woman said more softly, "But, Detie, you must be crazy! How can you think of such a thing?"

"And why not?" Aunt Detie asked. "He's her grandfather, and it's high time he did something for her. I've looked after her so far. Now her grandfather must do his duty."

"If he lived like other people that might be all right," Aunt Detie's friend said. "But he

2

lives all alone on top of the mountain. He hardly ever comes into the village. And when he does, carrying that big stick and looking so wild with those bristling gray eyebrows and that dreadful beard, everyone stays out of his way. What does he know about taking care of a little girl? I just wonder what terrible thing he has done that he feels he cannot live a normal life with other people." The village woman paused to catch her breath. She liked nothing better than to talk about other people. "I bet you know why he lives up there all alone, don't you, Detie?"

Aunt Detie nodded. "He is a sort of uncle to me. My sister married his son. But if he finds out I told you, I would be in a lot of trouble." Detie looked around for Heidi. She must not overhear them.

But while the two women had been climbing up the path, Heidi had made a new friend. Peter the goatherd was taking his goats up the mountain. Peter was eleven, and every morning he went to the village to get the goats. Then in the evening he brought them back again. The goats were gentle animals and easy to take care of.

He did this every day so the goats could visit the higher pastures where the wildflowers grew. Heidi had joined him, and the two women could see the children chattering away as they ran to keep up with the goats.

The village woman said, "Oh, she's with Peter. He'll take good care of her."

"Peter doesn't have to. Heidi can take care of herself. She's a big girl for five, which is just as well since she'll be living with an old man now who has nothing but his hut and two goats."

"But a long time ago he must have had more?" prodded Aunt Detie's friend.

"Oh yes. Uncle had one of the best farms around. And since he was the eldest son in the family, the money and land were his. But he went off and spent the money in bad ways. He pretended to be someone very important and ate and drank and threw

good boy and everyone liked him, even if they stayed away from his father.

"When Tobias grew up, he married my sister Adelheid. They were very happy for two years. And then a huge piece of wood fell on Tobias and killed him while he was building a house. My sister died a few weeks later of a broken heart."

The village woman dabbed her eyes to wipe away a few tears. "So sad, so sad," she muttered.

But Aunt Detie went on, "It seems like we are all related here in Dörfli, so that's why everyone calls him 'Uncle.' But it's also why people just wouldn't leave him alone. The village said Uncle lost his son as punishment for the bad things he had done. They even told him so. And he became so angry he went way up onto the mountain, and we heard he wasn't coming down any more. He's actually stayed up there ever since, fighting God and man, as they say."

"And Heidi?" the woman asked.

"Heidi was just a tiny baby when her parents, Tobias and Adelheid, died. My mother and I have taken care of her. Now it is Uncle's turn because there just is nobody else." Aunt Detie looked like she was not about to change her mind.

"Oh, Detie, how can you just hand her over to someone like that?" the woman asked.

"Well, what else can I do?" demanded Aunt Detie angrily.

The village woman shook her head. Then she turned off the path and headed toward a little hut which nestled under a few trees. "Where are you going?" Aunt Detie asked.

"I want to see Peter's mother. So this is where I leave you. Good-bye, Detie, and good luck."

Aunt Detie turned to go up the rest of the path to Uncle's hut. She was almost halfway up the mountain now. As she passed Peter's hut, she shook her head at the little house. It was almost ready to fall over, and looked so flimsy and old. "How does it ever keep standing during the winters?" she wondered.

Aunt Detie looked around for Heidi again. Seeing Peter's home had reminded her the little girl was with him. "Now where could those children be?" she sighed.

wild parties. Before long there was no more money left.

"His parents died of the sadness and shame he brought upon them. Uncle had nothing left but a bad name. So then he joined the army, and no one heard of him for years and years until he came back with a little boy named Tobias.

"His wife had died, and Tobias was all he had left. When he asked people to help him raise his son, though, everyone said no. Nobody would have anything to do with Uncle, especially after they heard that he was thrown out of the army for causing trouble. Well anyway, little Tobias was a

Peter and Heidi had taken a different way up the mountain than Aunt Detie and her friend. Peter always led his goats where they could find the tastiest bushes and most tender grass. At first Heidi had scrambled up after him, puffing and panting. She was sweating because of all the clothes she wore. Although Heidi did not complain, she did wish she could wear clothes like Peter. He looked so cool and comfy, running up the slopes in his bare feet and pants.

Then suddenly she sat down and pulled off her boots and socks. She quickly unbuttoned both dresses, pulled them off, and stood there in nothing but a little white petticoat. Heidi waved her bare arms in the air with delight. Then she put all the clothes together in a neat pile and danced off to catch up with Peter and the goats. He had been watching and grinned from ear to ear as she ran up to him. But he was careful not to say anything about it. Heidi felt much happier, and free as a bird. She started asking him all sorts of questions—how many goats he had, where was he taking them, and what was he going to do when he got there.

And that was when Aunt Detie saw them. "Heidi!" she shrieked. "What have you done, child? Where on earth are your clothes?"

Heidi calmly pointed at the neat little pile farther down the slope. Her aunt could see something lying there all right, with a red spot on top. That was the scarf.

"Oh, you are a naughty little girl," she cried. "Why did you ever do such a bad thing?"

"But I didn't need them," replied Heidi.

Aunt Detie frowned as she thought of an even worse idea. "And who do you suppose will go down and bring them up here? Certainly not me. Peter . . ." The young woman pointed at the boy. "Peter, you run down and get them for me."

But Peter just stood there with his hands in his pockets. "I'm late as it is," he mumbled.

"Oh, very well," Aunt Detie said. She rummaged in her pocket and held out a shiny coin. "Here, you can have this if you help me."

In a flash Peter darted down the hill and was back in no time. As he tucked the coin away deep down in his pocket, he grinned. It was not every day that such treasures came his way.

Aunt Detie set off up the slope again. This time Peter followed obediently behind her, carrying Heidi's little bundle. Heidi skipped next to them both, talking nonstop about the mountains and trees and village down below which seemed to grow tinier and tinier with every step.

On that seat there was a man smoking a pipe. Although his hair and beard and eyebrows were a bushy white, the man sat straight and tall. He did not look like an old man, but rather like a strong man enjoying the view.

Peter and Heidi ran ahead of Aunt Detie for the last part of the way. Heidi was actually the first to reach the man. She did not even stop to think, but right away held out her hand. "Hello, Grandfather," she said.

"Hey . . . what's that?" he growled. But he took her hand all the same.

"Good morning, Uncle," Aunt Detie said. "I've brought you Tobias's daughter." Now although Aunt Detie acted like she knew what she wanted to do, she really was not so sure of herself. All she could think about was, the sooner Heidi was left with Uncle and all this unpleasant business was over, the better. So she got right to the point. "She's come to stay with you, Uncle. You haven't seen her for four years. I've done all I can for her, and now it's your turn."

The old man snapped back, "My turn, is it? And when she starts to whine and cry for you, what am I supposed to do then?"

"That's your problem," Aunt Detie said. "You're the child's grandfather. If you can't take care of her, then find someone else who can. But if she gets hurt while you're taking care of her, it'll be just one more thing for you to feel guilty about." Aunt Detie had not meant to be so nasty, but the old man made her nervous.

"Out of here!" he shouted at her as he stood up. "Go back where you came from, and don't come here again!"

Aunt Detie turned to Heidi and said, "Good-bye then." She fairly ran all the way back to the village. And as she walked past the row of houses, all the women leaned out of their windows and said, "What have you done with Heidi?"

"You didn't leave her with the old man, did you?"

"Oh, Detie, how could you leave that little helpless creature with that man?"

But Aunt Detie walked by them all without a word. She wasn't going to give anyone the chance to change her mind.

After another hour, the little group came to a high pasture where three fir trees stood behind a cabin. "There it is," Aunt Detie said.

Heidi looked up and saw the little house which seemed to perch right on top of the world. It was surrounded by green pastures dotted by yellow and white flowers. Beyond the fir trees rose gray granite cliffs. There were no trees up that high. A little wooden bench stuck out of the side of the house, looking over the valley. The view was glorious!

6

CHAPTER 2
At Grandfather's

When Aunt Detie left, Grandfather sat back down on the bench and started puffing great clouds of smoke from his pipe. Heidi watched him for a few moments, then ran off to explore her new home. She visited the goats' stall, which was empty. Then she ran through the fir trees and stopped to listen to the wind singing through their branches. The pine scent drifted like perfume all around her, and she raised her arms and did a little dance underneath the great branches.

Heidi went back to Grandfather then and waited for him to stop puffing so furiously before she asked, "Please, Grandfather, may I see the inside of the hut?"

The old man was not all that happy with the way things had turned out. He said roughly, "All right," then led her through the door. Inside, Heidi saw one big room, with a ladder that went up to a loft. There was a small table with one chair in the corner near the fire, and cupboards lined the opposite wall.

"Bring your clothes in," Grandfather said, pointing to the bundle outside.

"But I don't need them anymore," Heidi said. She stuck out her chin stubbornly.

Grandfather noticed Heidi's sparkling black eyes. "She's a clever one," he said aloud to himself. "There's something on her mind. And why is that?" he asked.

"Because I want to run around like the goats do," she said softly.

"Well, so you can, but bring the clothes inside anyway. You can put them in the cupboard."

Heidi did as she was told. After spending a few moments exploring all four corners of the little cabin, Heidi asked, "Where is my bed, Grandfather?"

"Wherever you want," he said.

Heidi climbed up the ladder then and discovered a sweet-smelling hayloft. "Oh! I want to sleep up here, Grandfather. Look!" Her voice squealed even higher. "There's even a little round window so I can see the stars at night."

Heidi set to work arranging the hay into a bed. She pulled and piled it into one mound, and at the head of the hay bed she made a hay pillow. Grandfather brought her a heavy sheet to tuck around the hay so it would not tickle her at night.

"But, Grandfather, where is the blanket which will cover me and keep me warm?" Heidi asked.

"What makes you think I have an extra blanket?" he grunted.

But Heidi said happily, "Oh, that's all right. I can always throw hay on myself to stay warm." And she started to do just that. But Grandfather went back down the ladder

and got a heavy sack which had covered his own bed.

He threw it over Heidi's new bed and said, "There, that will keep you warm." The bag of blankets was just like a giant pillow. Heidi was so pleased with her new bed she said, "I almost wish it were time to go to sleep now."

"Don't you think we should have something to eat first?" Grandfather asked.

"Oh yes!" Heidi cried. She had completely forgotten about food, what with all the excitement. All she had eaten that day was a piece of bread and a cup of weak coffee in the morning when she and Aunt Detie began their journey. She climbed down the ladder and watched as Grandfather took some bread and cheese out of the cupboard.

Then he built up the fire and hung a pot of milk over the flames. He stuck a huge chunk of cheese on the end of a long fork and held it near the glowing wood. As he

turned it, slowly but surely a golden crust appeared on the cheese.

Meanwhile, Heidi had an idea. She ran back to the cupboard and set the table with things she had seen there when she was exploring. By the time Grandfather brought the cheese and steaming milk back to the table, Heidi was all ready. "Well, I'm glad you're the type who sees what needs to be done," he said.

Then Grandfather cut two thick slices of bread and put one on each plate. He covered these with the roasted cheese and scooped out two hot mugs full of the creamy milk. "There," he said. "But there's one thing missing. Where are you going to sit?"

Heidi looked around and ran to get a little stool she had seen in the corner. But when she sat on it, she was still too small.

"Here," Grandfather said, "sit on the stool and use my chair for a table." Then he perched himself on the corner of the table and ate his meal.

Heidi drank down the warm milk as fast

as she could. "Oh, that was good," she said, wiping her mouth with the back of her hand.

"You like it, huh?" Grandfather said. "It's goat milk and good for you." He refilled her cup, then watched as she ate the bread and cheese, pulling the strands of sticky cheese from finger to finger. She looked as happy and content as could be.

When they had finished, Heidi helped Grandfather clean up. Then she followed him around as he swept out the goats' stall, then hammered a nail here, tightened a screw there. Once he had set the little cabin in order, they went into the shed, which was built onto the side of the house. Grandfather sawed off several round sticks of wood. Then he drilled holes to fit them in a flat piece of board. Once they were all fitted together, he asked, "Do you know what this is?"

Heidi had been watching the whole time, her mouth hanging open. "It's a chair just for me," she said, amazed. "And how quickly you made it!"

Grandfather said out loud to himself, "She's got eyes in her head and knows how to use them."

No sooner was the chair finished when Heidi heard a high, shrill whistle. "It's Peter! He's come back with the goats!" She ran to meet him, and Peter grinned when he saw the little girl running in his direction.

Two goats left the rest and went up to Grandfather. He gave them each a little salt and they stood by him, licking his hand. "Oh, Grandfather, are these our goats?" Heidi asked. She turned to wave good-bye to her new friend. "See you tomorrow, Peter!" Then she followed Grandfather back to the cabin.

He had her mug and said, "Watch this now." He bent over and filled the cup with foaming milk from the white goat. The brown goat looked on with big, brown eyes. "Drink this," he told Heidi. After she had done so, he gave her some more bread and cheese and told her to sit on the bench and eat while he settled the goats down for the night.

Heidi ran after him. "But, Grandfather! What are their names?"

"The brown one is Dusky. The one who gave you her milk is Daisy."

"Good night, Dusky! Good night, Daisy!" Heidi called after them. Then she climbed up on the wooden bench and watched the fir branches bend and bow in the evening wind. As soon as she finished, she ran inside, climbed up the ladder, and slipped under the pillow-quilt on her bed. As soon as her head touched the hay pillow she fell sound asleep.

Later that night a fierce windstorm knocked some of the fir branches onto the roof. Grandfather thought to himself, "The noise may scare the child." So he climbed the ladder to check on her. Just then the moon came out from behind the clouds and shone through the little window, straight onto Heidi's little face. Grandfather saw her eyes were closed. Her head rested on one chubby arm, and she was snoring softly. As he stood and watched, a small smile twitched over her lips. Then the clouds covered the moon again, and Grandfather went back to bed.

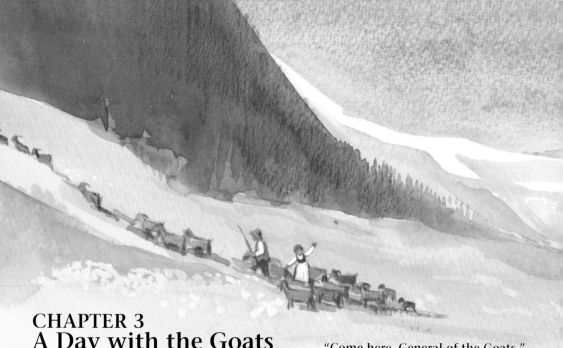

CHAPTER 3
A Day with the Goats

The next morning Heidi woke up to the sound of a shrill whistle. She opened her eyes and looked around. A shaft of sunlight shot through the little hole in the loft and turned the straw into strands of gold. "Where am I?" she wondered as she sat up and stretched.

Then she heard her grandfather's deep voice outside and remembered joyfully that she had come to live in the mountains. Always before, she had been told, "Heidi, stay inside. Heidi, don't run about so." That morning, though, as she climbed down her ladder, she said to herself, "From now on I can play outside every day."

She fairly flew out the door to where Grandfather was talking with Peter. She ran over and gave them both hugs. "Good morning, Grandfather! Good morning, Peter!" Then she ran over to Daisy and Dusky, who had joined the other goats, and gave them hugs too.

"Do you want to go up to the pastures with Peter?" Grandfather asked. Heidi jumped up and down and clapped her hands. "All right," Grandfather said, "but you'll have to wash up first. Otherwise the sun will laugh to see you looking so black."

He pointed to a tub full of water, standing in the sun beside the door, and Heidi went over to it at once and began splashing and splooshing.

"Come here, General of the Goats," Grandfather called to Peter. He put a thick piece of bread and huge chunk of cheese into Peter's small backpack. Peter's eyes grew round. This was far more food than he was used to seeing.

When Heidi came bouncing over to them after her bath, Grandfather had to smile. She had tried so hard to make sure the sun would not laugh at her, Heidi had scrubbed her face until it glowed red and shiny, like a lobster's. "That's right," Grandfather said. "And this evening when you come back you'll need to do the same because your feet will be black from running after the goats all day. Now off you go. And, General," he said to Peter, "make sure she doesn't fall into the ravine."

As Heidi followed Peter she was so excited, she skipped and hopped, crisscrossing the slope. She had never seen so many colors at once. The sky was a rich blue. The dew-covered grass twinkled like so many emeralds. And everywhere there were wildflowers of as many different colors as the rainbow. Heidi dashed here, then there, filling her apron with flowers. She wanted to bring them back to her loft and sprinkle them over the hay. Then at night she could pretend she was sleeping in a meadow.

Peter had quite a job trying to keep track of her and all the goats. At one point he called out, "Try not to run around so much,

Heidi. Uncle said I should take care of you, but you don't make it easy. And maybe you should stop picking flowers or there won't be any left for tomorrow."

This made good sense to Heidi, so she settled down a bit and followed Peter to the top of the ridge. It was a steep slope which looked down, down, down into a rocky hole. That was the ravine. Peter put their lunch into a little hole so the wind would not blow it away, and Heidi hid her flowers there too. Then she sat down to watch the goats as they sniffed out the sweet herbs which only grew high up on the mountainside. For the goats, these tender plants were as sweet as chocolate is for children.

Peter lay down to sleep on the soft grass. Heidi hugged her knees. There before her stretched a wonderful sight. The valley below was bathed in sunlight. In front of them rose a snowcapped mountain, looking out like some king watching over his kingdom. Everything was very still; only a soft breeze pushed the blue and yellow flowers all around them. Now and then one of the bells around the goats' necks tinkled. Heidi pinched herself to make sure she was not dreaming, it was all so lovely.

Suddenly Heidi heard something scream in a croaking voice. She looked up and saw a huge bird circling above them. He swooped down, then disappeared behind the mountain. "Peter, look! What was that big bird? Did you see him? Why is he on the mountain now?"

Peter sat up and rubbed his eyes. "That's just the hawk. He built his nest up there."

"Oh, let's go see!" Heidi jumped up and began to run toward the edge of the slope.

"Oh no you don't!" Peter called after her. "Not even the goats can climb way up there. You might fall into the ravine. Now come here and we'll eat lunch." Heidi watched as Peter spread a small cloth on the grass and put their bread and cheese on it. Peter filled her mug with milk from Daisy. Then the two settled down to eat.

Only a few bites later, though, Heidi said, "I've had enough. Would you like the rest of my bread and cheese, Peter?"

Peter thought Heidi was joking. Peter had never been so full that he did not want more to eat. When Heidi set the cheese on his lap, though, he knew she meant it. He nodded his thanks.

Then Heidi went off to play with the goats. She noticed each goat was different, just like people are. They all had their own way of smiling and playing. Daisy and Dusky had the shiniest coats. They seemed like the king and queen of the herd. But one little white

11

goat
did
nothing
but stand and
cry, "Baaaa!
Baaaaaaaa!" Heidi went
up to the baby goat and put
her arms around her. The goat
buried her nose in Heidi's arm and
finally stopped crying.

Then Heidi ran back to Peter, who was
just finishing his lunch. She was brimming
over with questions. "What are they all
called, Peter? Why is that big brown one so
bossy to the others? Why does that little
white goat cry all the time? Why are Daisy
and Dusky so clever-looking?"

Peter was usually not very good at
answering questions. But the one thing he
did know something about was goats. He
told Heidi all the animals' names, pointing
them out to her. "The brown one is Big
Turk. You're right, he is always trying to
boss the others. But little Finch there is the
one who's always trying to get into trouble
and pick a fight with Big Turk. Daisy and
Dusky look so fine because Uncle takes such
good care of them. They have a warm stall
and fresh hay every night. And that little
Snowflake you were petting just lost her
mother a few days ago when her owner sold
her to someone else. . ."

Heidi interrupted, "But what about her
grandfather—can't he take care of her?"

"She doesn't have anyone else," Peter said.

"Oh, poor Snowflake!" Heidi ran back
down to give Snowflake another hug.

All at once Peter jumped up and ran
down the slope toward the ravine. Finch
had strayed clear to the edge. Peter lunged
and grabbed hold of the little goat's leg. But
Finch struggled against the grip and kicked
and kicked. Peter could not get up without
letting go. "Help, Heidi, come and help!"

Heidi saw right away what she must do.
She quickly grabbed a handful of the sweet
grass and shoved it under Finch's nose. The
little goat stopped fighting and followed
Heidi as she backed away from the edge.
Then both Peter and Heidi took hold of the
goat's collar and led him back to the others.
12

On the way
Peter grabbed a long
stick, and once they were
away from the edge he raised
his arm to give the goat a spanking for being so naughty. "No! You
can't hit him!" Heidi shrieked.

"But I have to teach him a lesson." Peter's
heart was still pounding from the fright
Finch had given him. It was Peter's job to
look after the goats. If anything should happen to one of them, he would be blamed for
it.

"No! Promise me you won't ever beat
them, and I'll . . . I'll . . ." Heidi stopped to
think of something which would change
Peter's mind. "I'll give you my cheese and
some of my bread every day."

"If you want," Peter agreed. Anytime he
could get some extra food, it was worth it.
He let Finch go, and the goat bounded back
to the herd.

It was getting late, and the sun went down
behind the big mountain. Heidi watched for
a few moments and then let out a squeak of
surprise. "The mountain's turned red! Look,
Peter, the mountains are on fire, and the trees
and rocks too! Why is it all on fire?"

"It's always like that in the evening,"
Peter said. "It's not a fire. It just happens."
When Heidi asked him what the names of
the mountains were, he shook his head.
"They don't have names."

Heidi stood still, soaking in the sight. But
after a few more moments, her smile turned
to a frown. "Oh, now look. The colors are all
gone, and everything has turned gray! Oh,

tell him. Later Heidi sat in her special high chair, nibbling the sweet cheese melted on toast and sipping the steaming milk. She asked again, "What does the hawk say as he goes around in circles so high in the sky?"

Grandfather's answer was so rough, he almost sounded like the hawk croaking. "He's laughing at all the people who live in the villages and make trouble for each other. 'Mind your own business and climb up to the mountaintops as I do. You'd be a lot better off,' he says."

Heidi asked, "And why haven't mountains got names?"

"But they have," Grandfather told her. "If you can describe one to me, I'll tell you its name."

So Heidi told him about the mountain with two peaks and described it very well. Her grandfather was pleased. "That's called Falkniss," he said.

Peter, why did it go away?" Heidi was all ready to cry, but Peter told her the colors would come back tomorrow evening, and that helped a little at least.

As they walked downhill, Heidi was so busy thinking about all she had seen and heard that before she knew it, they were within sight of Grandfather's cabin. Heidi ran up to him and showed him the flowers she had collected in the morning. But they were dried and shriveled and looked like hay. "Grandfather, what happened to them?"

"They wanted to stay in the sun and didn't like being shut up in your apron."

"Then I'll never pick any more." Then Heidi started asking one question after another.

"Wait a minute, wait a minute. Not so fast," Grandfather said. "First you take a bath, then over dinner you can tell me all about it. You did have a good day, didn't you?"

Heidi nodded, hardly daring to open her mouth, there was so much she wanted to

Heidi had one more question. "Grandfather, why were the mountain and snow and plants and rocks and trees on fire in the evening?"

"It's the sun's way of saying good night to the mountains. He spreads that beautiful red light on them so that they won't forget him until he comes back in the morning."

Heidi said, "Ohhhh" and smiled. She liked that answer very much. After she climbed into her hay bed and closed her eyes, her dreams were all about mountains and flowers and Snowflake hopping happily through the grass.

13

CHAPTER 4
A Visit to Grannie

All during that summer, Heidi went up to the pasture with Peter and the goats. Her skin turned a toasted brown. She grew strong and healthy and happy as a bird. But when autumn came, the mountain winds grew strong. Then more often than not Grandfather said Heidi must stay with him or else she might get blown clear off the mountain.

Peter did not like going alone. The goats were that much harder to keep track of. Without Heidi, they seemed to wander around looking for her. But Heidi was happy wherever she was. And she helped Grandfather get the cabin ready for winter. She followed him around like a little puppy, helping where she could, asking an endless stream of questions, and enjoying every minute of her time with him.

Before long the wind became quite cold. One morning Heidi woke up and saw that her beloved fir trees had become part of a winter wonderland. As she peeped out of the round hole in her loft, she could hardly believe what she saw. Snow! It covered everything, even the little bench on the side of the hut. All that day it snowed. And Peter did not bring the goats up, for it was far too cold. Heidi stayed inside. She could not dance under the trees, listening to the branches sing to the mountain breezes.

Late that afternoon Grandfather went outside and shoveled the snow away from the door. Otherwise it would not be long before their cabin would be buried under the snow. He had just finished and come inside to sit by the fire when there was a ferocious banging at the door.

It opened, and there stood Peter, looking like some sort of snow monster. He stamped his boots to get the snow off, came inside, and stood by the fire. Heidi giggled as the snow melted into a puddle around Peter.

"Well, General of the Goats," Grandfather said, "how did you like your first day back at school?"

"What do you mean?" Heidi asked.

Grandfather explained that in the winters, when the bad weather kept Peter from bringing the goats up to pasture, he went to school and learned how to read and write. "But I can tell by Peter's frown that he's not too happy about it," Grandfather said. Peter grunted.

The three had a good time talking together. Peter stayed to have dinner, and ate more and more and more. Then Peter got ready to go since it was almost dark.

"Good-bye," he said, "and thank you. I'll come again next Sunday. Grannie says she would like you to come and see her."

Heidi was delighted at the idea of going to visit someone. That was something new! So the next morning the first thing she said was, "Grandfather, I must go and see Peter's Grannie today. She'll be expecting me."

"The snow is too deep," said Grandfather, trying to put her off. But the idea of visiting

Peter's mother, and especially his Grannie, was stuck in Heidi's head.

Over and over again each day she reminded Grandfather, "I really must go or Grannie will be tired of waiting for me." Four days after Peter's visit the snow froze into a hard crust. It was still cold, but the sun was bright. Again Heidi said, "Grandfather, I really must go and see Grannie today, or she'll think I'm not coming."

Grandfather nodded, and Heidi let out a squeal of delight. In no time at all she was dressed warmly and standing outside, listening to the snow crunch as she walked on it. Grandfather brought the blanket bag down from Heidi's bed, then carried a big sled out of the shed.

He told her to climb on, then wrapped her in the covers so that only her face felt cold. The rest of Heidi was all nice and warm. He sat down behind Heidi. Then, with one arm holding her tightly, Grandfather pushed off down the hill.

Whoosh! They fairly flew as Grandfather guided the sled by leaning first this way, then that way. Heidi closed her eyes and

yelped out loud, they went so fast. When she did peek a little, the white trees and rocks were moving by so quickly, she could hardly catch a glimpse of them.

With a jerk Grandfather stopped the sled. Heidi looked around and saw the little house by the trees which she had first seen when Aunt Detie had walked her up the mountain. Grandfather helped her get out of the blankets, then told her, "Now, when it starts to get dark, come outside and I'll be waiting to bring you back home."

"Yes, Grandfather," Heidi said, but her words were lost to the wind as she scurried into the little house.

Heidi stopped to look around. This cabin was much smaller than Grandfather's. Every corner seemed full of something. It was crowded, and darker too. Heidi saw a woman sitting at a table, patching what looked like Peter's coat. In one corner a white-haired woman sat bent over her spinning wheel.

Heidi went straight over to her and said, "Hello, Grannie. Here I am at last. I bet you thought I would never come to see you."

Grannie raised her head and felt for Heidi's hand. When she had found it, she held it tight for a few moments. Finally, she

said, "Are you the child from Uncle's? Are you Heidi?"

"Yes. I just came down on the sled."

"How can that be? Your hands are so warm," Grannie said.

"He wrapped me in my blanket, and we flew down the mountain!" Heidi showed with her hands how fast the sled had gone, but Grannie seemed not to notice. Heidi looked around the little room.

"Grannie, that shutter is hanging loose and could break the window." She had learned a lot from being Grandfather's helper. "Look, Grannie, see how it bangs back and forth."

"I can't see it, dear, but I can hear it. And you're right. Sometimes at night this little hut creaks and moans so much I'm afraid the wind will knock it right down. There's no one to fix these things for us. Peter is too young."

"But why can't you see it?" Heidi asked. "Look, there it goes again." Heidi pointed at the window.

"I can't see at all, child. It's not just the shutter," said the old woman with a sigh.

"But if I go and open the window wider, so there is more sunlight, then you'll be able to see, won't you?"

"No, not even then. Light or dark makes no difference to me."

"But if you come with me outside and see the bright snow shining in the sun, I'm sure you'll see then. Come and see!" Heidi grabbed Grannie's hand and tried to pull her up.

"Leave me alone, child. I won't see any better even in the light of the snow. I'm always in the dark."

"Even in the summer, Grannie?" Heidi cried. "Surely you can see the sunshine and watch it say good night to the mountains and make them all red like fire, can't you?"

"No, child. I'll never see them again."

"Oh, Grannie!" Heidi wailed. And the tears fairly jumped out of her eyes. It was a terrible thought for Heidi, but she knew it was true: Grannie could see nothing but darkness. Heidi did not cry very often, but when she did, it was hard to stop her.

She cried and cried, and nothing Grannie or Peter's mother could do would stop her. Finally Grannie said, "Dear child, I may not be able to see, but I can always tell a friendly voice, and you have one. I don't mind being blind half so much if I have someone beside me who can tell me stories and keep me company."

At this, Heidi calmed down and wiped away her tears with the back of her sleeve. She pulled up a stool and sat down again next to Grannie, holding her hand. "What do you want to hear?" she asked in a small voice.

"Tell me what you and your grandfather do up on the mountain all the time."

It did not take long for Heidi to forget about how sad she was. She told all about

17

Grandfather, and her bed in the loft, and the goats, and dancing under the fir trees. "And Grandfather is so very clever with his hands, Grannie. I'm sure he could fix your hut in no time. Why, I've seen him build chairs and tables and the goats' winter stall, and even spoons and plates out of wood."

"Did you hear that?" Grannie asked Peter's mother. "It sounds like all of Peter's stories were true, after all."

Peter's mother was named Bridget. She was Grannie's daughter. Bridget nodded. She had not missed a word of what Heidi had said.

Then, right on cue, the door banged open and Peter came in. A gust of cold air swept through the little house as he shut the door. He saw Heidi smiling at him from Grannie's side. "Hello!" she said. He smiled a big, wide grin.

"Oh!" Grannie said. "Is the afternoon over already? How quickly it passed by with you here, Heidi. Peter, how are your reading lessons coming?"

"Just the same," he said quietly.

"Oh dear," she sighed. "I had hoped you might have something different to tell me by now. You'll be twelve in February."

"Something different to tell you? What do you mean?" asked Heidi.

"Only that he'd finally learned how to read. There's a beautiful old songbook on the shelf with lovely hymns in it. I keep hoping Peterkin will be able to read them to me. But he just doesn't seem able to learn, and Bridget never went to school."

Peter's mother said, "I think I had better light the lamp. It's getting dark."

"Oh!" Heidi jumped up. "If it's getting dark, I need to go. I promised Grandfather I would leave then. Good-bye, Grannie." She said good-bye to the others, then ran outside.

Grannie sent Peter after her with a shawl, but no sooner did he reach Heidi than he saw Grandfather walking towards them.

"Good girl, you did as you were told," he said. Then he wrapped her up in the blanket again, picked her up in his arms, and turned for home.

Bridget had watched it all from the window. She told her mother about how tender and careful Grandfather was with Heidi.

Grannie nodded. "I always knew he was a good man. Oh, but I do hope he lets Heidi visit me again. She has done me a world of good. And what a kind heart the little one has."

On the mountain, Heidi chattered away inside her blanket bag, but all Grandfather could hear were muffled sounds. When they got home, he unwrapped her and set Heidi before the fire. Right away she told him all over again all about the visit.

"And tomorrow we must take a hammer and some big nails down to Peter's house, so that you can fix Grannie's shutter and all the other things which creak and rattle."

"Oh we must, must we? Who told you to ask that?"

"No one. I just know because all the shutters and doors are loose and banging. Grannie gets afraid and cannot sleep sometimes. And she can't see, and she says no one can make her better, but I bet you can, can't you, Grandfather? We'll go tomorrow, won't we, Grandfather?" She stopped to catch her breath.

Grandfather said nothing about Grannie being blind. But he did say, "Well, the least we can do is stop the banging, and we'll do that tomorrow."

Heidi was so happy, she went skipping round the hut, singing, "We'll do it tomorrow! We'll do it tomorrow!"

Sure enough, the next day when Grandfather brought Heidi down on the sled again he carried a hammer and a bagful of nails with him. When he set her off at the doorstep, he said, "Now you go on inside. I'll stay here and work until it starts to get dark. You come outside then and I'll take you home."

Heidi had hardly set foot inside when Grannie called out from her corner, "Here she comes again!" Heidi ran and gave her a hug, then pulled up the stool and started chattering away. Suddenly there was a terrible banging sound, and the little house trembled.

"Oh! This time it really will fall on us!" Grannie cried.

Heidi took her hand and said, "It's all right, Grannie. It's just Grandfather fixing your shutter. He's going to fix everything so

18

you won't have to be
afraid of the banging
and rattling anymore."

"Is it true? Then God has not forgotten us
after all. Can you hear it, Bridget? Oh, run
outside and thank Uncle for us."

Peter's mother went around the outside of
the house to where Grandfather was hammer-
ing on the shutter. She started to thank him,
but he sent her away with a rough "That's
enough. Go indoors. I can
see what needs to be done."

By the time it started
getting dark,
Grandfather had used
up all his nails. Heidi
came outside, and just
like the day before
Grandfather bundled her
up and carried her up the
mountain.

All that winter
Grandfather brought Heidi to
visit Grannie whenever the sun
was shining. And every afternoon he
did a little more to the tiny hut, straight-
ening this, fixing that, even making sure
the roof would not leak anymore.

Heidi and Grannie became special friends.
Once Heidi knew for sure that no one could
help Grannie see again, she was very sad. But
Grannie made it a little better when she told
Heidi her visits brightened her days as much
as if she could see the sunshine.

"May God keep the child safe and help
her grandfather to smile," Grannie prayed
every night. Thanks to Heidi and
Grandfather, she could fall asleep without
being afraid of the moaning and groaning of
her little house.

19

CHAPTER 5
Two Unexpected Visitors

A winter passed, and then another happy summer, and now Heidi's second winter on the mountain was nearly over. She could hardly wait for the spring, when warm winds would melt the snow, and all the blue and yellow flowers would bloom again.

Twice during the winter Peter had brought Grandfather messages from the teacher, saying he should send Heidi to school in the village. Both times Grandfather said, "I won't send the child to school."

One spring day, as Heidi was outside playing, she saw an old man coming up the hill toward Grandfather's cabin. He was dressed in black and looked very serious. "Hello," he said. "You must be Heidi. Where is your grandfather?"

"He's indoors making wooden spoons," she told him. Then she showed him in.

He was the old pastor from Dörfli and had been Grandfather's neighbor when he still lived in the village. "Good morning, my friend," he said as he went up to him.

Grandfather looked up in surprise. "Good morning, Pastor," he said.

"I haven't seen you for a long time," the pastor said.

"And I haven't seen you for a long time, Pastor."

The pastor looked over at Heidi. "I need to talk to you about something important, friend."

Grandfather told Heidi to go give some salt to the goats. She did as she was told right away. Then the pastor said, "Neighbor, that child should have gone to school last winter, and the winter before. She needs to learn how to read and write."

"I'm not going to send her to school," Grandfather said.

"But what will happen to her then?"

"She'll grow up with the goats and the birds. They won't teach her any bad ideas, and she'll be very happy."

"She's not a goat or bird, though," the pastor said. "She's a little girl. Surely after all you've seen of the world, you know how important it is for her to learn how to read and write."

Grandfather just shook his head stubbornly. "I can't let a little girl like her go up and down the mountain during the winter. It's hard enough for a grown man to make the trip through the snow and against the wind."

"Oh, you're right about that," the pastor said. "And that's why I'd like to ask you to come back down to the village and live with us there. Make your peace with God, then come make your peace with your neighbors." The pastor held out his hand to Grandfather.

Grandfather shook his head. "The people of Dörfli don't want to see me any more than I want to see them. No, Pastor, I know you mean well, but I just will not send the child to school." But Grandfather did shake the pastor's hand.

"Then may God help you," the pastor said, and he went sadly out of the cabin and down the mountain.

Grandfather was not very happy after the pastor left. He wandered around the cabin with a big frown on his face. When Heidi asked, "Can we go visit Grannie today?" he just shook his head and walked away.

The next day Heidi asked again about visiting Grannie. Grandfather mumbled, "We'll see." But just an hour later there was another visitor at the door. This time it was Aunt Detie! She wore a fancy hat with a feather and a long dress which looked silly as it dragged over the cabin floor. Grandfather looked her up and down and frowned. He did not say a word. But Aunt Detie talked and talked and talked.

"Doesn't Heidi look wonderful! I must say, Uncle, you've taken good care of her. Of course I always meant to come back for her because I know she must be in your way. That's why I'm here now, actually. The family I work for in Germany, they know another family. They are very rich and have a little girl who is quite sick. These rich people are looking for another little girl to live with them and be a friend to their daughter. They wanted someone a little unusual, so ight away I thought of Heidi. Besides, if their little girl dies, who knows, they might even let Heidi take her place and . . ."

Grandfather interrupted, "Are you almost done?"

"Well!" Aunt Detie was hurt. "You act as if I'm not saying anything important. Well, let me tell you, I hope you don't try to keep Heidi with you because I've heard in the village how you won't let her go to school. And if you take this to court, you'll find yourself hearing stories which you would rather leave forgotten."

"That's enough!" Grandfather thundered. "Take her away then and spoil her. But don't ever bring her back to me. I don't want to see her with a feather in her hat or hear her talk as you have today." And he walked out of the cabin.

"Now look what you've done," Heidi said in an unfriendly way. "You've made Grandfather angry."

"Oh, he'll get over it," Aunt Detie said. "Now come on, where are your clothes?"

"I'm not coming," said Heidi.

"Don't be silly!" Aunt Detie snapped. "You're going to have such a good time in your new home. Besides, you heard Grandfather say he didn't want to see us again. He wants you to go with me, so you'd better do as he says or you'll make him even angrier." Aunt Detie grabbed Heidi's hand and started pulling her down the path.

"But I don't want to go!" Heidi yelled.

Aunt Detie said in a nicer tone, "Besides, if you don't like it, you can always come back. Grandfather will be in a better mood by then."

"Can I come back tonight?"

"Well, no . . . but soon." So in this way Aunt Detie managed to make Heidi walk down the mountain with her.

But as they passed Peter's hut, Peter was bringing in some firewood and saw them. "Where are you going?" he called out.

"I'm going with Aunt Detie to visit Germany," Heidi called back. "But I need to say good-bye to Grannie first," she said to Aunt Detie.

Aunt Detie was afraid she would never get Heidi to leave if she stopped to see Grannie. So she just pulled her along and said, "There's no time for that."

As they hurried on, Peter came into his house and banged the door. The wood clattered onto the ground as he dumped it down. "What's that?" Grannie called out.

"She's taking Heidi away," he said.

"Who is?" Then Grannie remembered that Bridget had told her Detie was back, and she guessed what had happened. Grannie stood up and felt her way to the window. "Wait!" she called out. "Don't take the child away from us, Detie!"

Aunt Detie and Heidi could barely hear Grannie, and did not know what she said. "I have to go back, she's calling me," Heidi said.

"We can't stop now or we'll miss the train. Besides, you can always bring a present back for her."

"Can I really?" Heidi asked excitedly. "What could I bring back for her?"

"Oh, something nice to eat perhaps. She would probably like the soft, white rolls they have in town. The black bread must hurt her teeth."

"Oh it does," said Heidi. "Just the other day I saw her give her bread to Peter because it was too hard for her to chew. Oh, let's hurry, Aunt Detie. Can we get to Germany today? Then I could come back right away with the rolls." She started to run so fast, Aunt Detie could hardly keep up with her.

And when they reached Dörfli, the villagers saw Heidi running ahead of Detie. They called out, "Detie, where are you taking the child?"

Aunt Detie said, "We must catch a train, so we don't have time to talk." She hurried past them, afraid that once they stopped, Heidi would not want to go on. But Heidi said nothing.

The villagers said to each other, "See how quickly the little girl wants to get away from her grandfather? It must have been terrible for her to live up there with him."

And as if to prove them right, from that day on Grandfather became a grumpy man, angry at the world. Whenever he did come into the village to buy supplies or sell the goats' cheese he made, he hardly spoke to anyone, and he never smiled.

Whenever anyone visited Grannie, though, she told him how kind he had been to fix her house. The villagers found this hard to believe. They decided she did not know what she was talking about, being blind and probably deaf too. Grandfather never went near Grannie's house again, but he had done his work well, and her house no longer moaned or groaned. Without Heidi's chatter, Grannie found the days long and empty, and she was very sad. She would often say, "I would like to hear that dear child's voice just once again before I die."

CHAPTER 6
A New Life Begins

The house in Frankfurt, Germany, where Aunt Detie was taking Heidi, belonged to a rich man named Mr. Sesman. His little girl Clara was so sick, she could not walk. Clara spent all day in a wheelchair and had to be pushed wherever she wanted to go. Clara's mother had died a long time ago. Because her father was often away on business, Miss Meyer, the housekeeper, was in charge of telling the servants what to do. Her job was to make sure Clara always had whatever she needed.

On the day Aunt Detie was supposed to arrive with Heidi, Clara sat in the study with Miss Meyer. Clara kept looking at the clock, wondering why it went so slowly. Finally she said, "Miss Meyer, shouldn't they be here by now?" It was not like Clara to complain, despite her sickness. She usually was very quiet and only smiled when her father was home.

Just then the doorbell rang. The maid opened the door and saw Aunt Detie holding on to Heidi's hand. She had them come in, then went to tell Miss Meyer. When Aunt Detie and Heidi were finally brought into the study, Clara was so excited she thought she would burst.

Heidi looked at Miss Meyer with big eyes. She had never seen such a strange-looking hat before. Miss Meyer stared back at Heidi. She had never seen such a strange-looking child before. Heidi's dress was crumpled from the long trip. Her straw hat was dirty and about to fall to pieces.

"What's your name?" Miss Meyer asked. She did not smile. Heidi told her in a nice clear voice. "That can't be your real name. Now speak up—what was the name you were given when you were a baby?"

"I don't remember," Heidi said.

"That's no way to answer! What's the matter with her?" Miss Meyer asked Aunt Detie.

"Oh, she's just not used to a big house like this, ma'am," Aunt Detie explained quickly. "She doesn't know how to answer questions very well, but there's nothing wrong with her. She's smart enough, and if someone will just take the time to teach her how to act, she'll learn fast enough. Her proper name is Adelheid. She was named after her mother, my dead sister."

"But she looks much younger than what I had in mind," Miss Meyer said. "We were looking for someone around Clara's age. She is twelve. How old is Adelheid?"

"I don't remember," Aunt Detie lied.

"Grandfather told me I'm almost eight," Heidi said proudly. Aunt Detie pushed her from behind, but Heidi did not know why.

"What?" Miss Meyer shrieked. "Why,

hat's at least four years too young! And what books have you been using in your lessons?"

"None," said Heidi.

"What do you mean? How did you learn how to read then?"

"I don't know how to read," Heidi said. "Peter doesn't know how either."

"But . . . but that's impossible!" Miss Meyer sputtered. "What have you learned then?"

"Nothing," said Heidi.

Now Miss Meyer turned to Aunt Detie. "Oh really, Detie. This is not at all the kind of child we wanted. I don't know what you were thinking when you brought her here."

But Aunt Detie was not going to give up very easily. She said brightly, "But I thought you wanted an unusual child. And there's nothing unusual about older children. Heidi is different. I'm afraid I have to get to my job now, so I will leave Heidi here and come back in a few days to see how she's doing." Aunt Detie curtsied, then ran out of the room and out of the house as fast as she could. There wasn't very much Miss Meyer could do about it. But she chased after Aunt Detie all the same.

The children were left alone. Clara turned in her wheelchair to look at Heidi. "Do you want to be called Heidi or Adelheid?" she asked.

"Everyone calls me Heidi. That's my name," she said.

"Well, I'll call you that too. Are you glad you've come here?" Clara asked.

"No, but I'll go home again tomorrow, and then I can bring some nice rolls for Grannie."

Clara smiled. "You are a funny child. But we might have some fun since you can't even read. Whenever my teacher comes to the house to give me my lessons, I get awfully bored. Mr. Usher is nice, Heidi. You'll like him. Just don't ask too many questions, otherwise he'll give you an answer which lasts forever. It will be fun watching him teach you how to read."

Heidi shook her head doubtfully. Clara said, "Oh, you'll learn sure enough. It's not that hard . . ."

Just then Miss Meyer came back into the room. She was out of breath and terribly angry because she had not caught up with Aunt Detie and she did not want to take care of Heidi. But now she had no choice. She said nothing to the children, but stormed out of the room to make sure dinner was ready. In the dining room she snapped at Sam the butler and told him to bring Clara to dinner. Then she ordered Tina the maid to make sure Heidi's room was ready.

As Sam pushed Clara's chair into the dining room, Heidi walked beside him and decided he looked a little like Peter. Once Miss Meyer and the children were seated, Sam brought in a plate of baked fish and held it out to Heidi. She hardly noticed, though. All Heidi could see was the fresh, soft roll sitting by her plate. She whispered to Sam, "May I have this?" and pointed at the roll.

Sam knew no one was supposed to talk to him while he was serving. He nodded yes, then struggled not to laugh as the little girl slipped the roll into her pocket. He waited with the fish for several moments. He was not allowed to say anything to Heidi. Finally Heidi asked him, "Is this for me too?"

Sam did not trust himself to open his mouth. He was afraid he would burst out laughing. So he nodded again. But his mouth twisted with the effort not to laugh.

Miss Meyer was not very happy about all this. She told Sam to just leave the plate of fish on the table and please leave the room. Sam ran for the door and barely got into the kitchen before he burst out laughing. "Oh, we will have fun with the little miss in our house now," he said to himself.

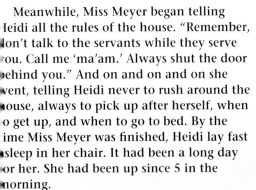

Meanwhile, Miss Meyer began telling Heidi all the rules of the house. "Remember, don't talk to the servants while they serve you. Call me 'ma'am.' Always shut the door behind you." And on and on and on she went, telling Heidi never to rush around the house, always to pick up after herself, when to get up, and when to go to bed. By the time Miss Meyer was finished, Heidi lay fast asleep in her chair. It had been a long day for her. She had been up since 5 in the morning.

"Now, Adelheid, do you understand what I've been saying?" Miss Meyer asked.

"Heidi's asleep," Clara said with a smile. She could not remember ever having so much fun at dinner. Miss Meyer was very

annoyed though. She rang the bell for Sam and Tina. They both scurried into the room, wondering what had happened now. But Heidi stayed fast asleep. In fact, Sam had quite a time waking her up enough to get her into her room. There she quickly fell asleep again, in her new bed in her new home.

CHAPTER 7
A Bad Day for Miss Meyer

When Heidi woke up the next morning, she did not know where she was. She lay in a big white bed in a room with white curtains, two chairs, a couch, and a sink in the corner. Then Heidi remembered what had happened the day before. But she could not quite remember what Miss Meyer had said about the rules for getting up in the morning.

She jumped out of bed and got dressed. Then Heidi ran to one window and tried to look through it. There were heavy curtains in front, but she crawled under them. When she finally managed to peep out, all she saw were walls and windows of more houses. She was too short to see more, and with the windows closed she could not lean out to get a better view.

At Grandfather's the first thing she did when she got up was run outside to have a good look around. She had always checked to see if the sky was blue and the sun shining. Then she said good morning to the trees and flowers. But here it was different. Frightened, Heidi ran from one window to the next like a wild bird in a cage, looking for a way out. She thought, "If only I could see what is outside, I'd see the snow melting on the grass." But no matter how hard she tried, she could not open the windows even a tiny bit.

Just then there was a tap at the door, and Tina snapped, "Breakfast is ready."

Heidi did not know what Tina meant, but she had sounded so angry, Heidi thought she had better stay put. Before long Miss Meyer came in and said, "What is the matter with you, child? Don't you even know what breakfast is? Now come along!"

This was something Heidi could understand. She meekly followed Miss Meyer to the dining room. Clara had been waiting for some time, but she smiled at Heidi when she entered the room. She had an idea this would be quite an interesting day.

Breakfast passed without any problems. Then the children were brought to the study to wait for Mr. Usher, the teacher. Once they were alone, Heidi asked Clara, "How can I

pen the window so I can see what's out-
ide?"

"You have to ask Sam to open it for you.
He'll do it for you."

Heidi was relieved to hear that. Then
Clara began to ask about Heidi's life at
home. Soon the little girl was chattering
away about the mountains and the goats
and the fir trees and all the other things she
loved so much.

When Mr. Usher arrived, Miss Meyer tried
to use him as a way to get rid of Heidi. "She
doesn't know how to act properly and cannot even read," Miss Meyer said. "So if you
tell Clara's father it is too hard to teach such
a child, I'm sure he will send her back to
Switzerland where she belongs."

Mr. Usher was a fair man. He could guess
Miss Meyer might not have given Heidi a
chance. "Well, you never know. Sometimes
children who are not good at one thing are
very good at doing other things." This was
not what Miss Meyer wanted to hear. Mr.
Usher went into the study.

Miss Meyer could not stand the sight of
Heidi learning her alphabet, so she stayed in
the dining room. But suddenly she heard a
terrific crash and clatter. Someone called for
Sam. When Miss Meyer went into the study
again, she found it was a huge mess! Books
were all over the floor. The tablecloth was
crooked and covered with ink stains, as was
the carpet. And Heidi had disappeared.

"Goodness! What has happened?" Miss
Meyer shrieked.

Clara smiled. "It was Heidi, but she didn't
know she was doing it."

Mr. Usher still looked surprised. "Er . . .
yes . . . It seems the little girl heard the carriages outside and rushed first to the window, then out the door to see them. I don't
suppose she's seen carriages before." He
scratched his head.

Miss Meyer ordered Sam and Tina to
clean up the mess. Mr. Usher went home
since there could be no more lessons that
day. And Clara thought to herself that she
had never enjoyed her lessons so much.

Heidi, meanwhile, stood on the street, in front of the door, looking up and down the street with a confused look on her face. When Miss Meyer found her, she said, "What is going on, young lady?"

Heidi said, "I . . . I heard the fir trees rustling in the wind and I ran outside to see, but there was nothing."

"Fir trees? Does it look like we live in a forest? Now get inside and I'll show you what trouble you caused."

Miss Meyer marched Heidi back into the study, and Heidi was most surprised when she saw the mess which Sam and Tina were busy cleaning up. Miss Meyer yelled at Heidi, "Don't ever do anything like this again! When you are having your lessons, you stay in your chair and listen. If you can't do that, I will have to tie you down. Do you understand?" Heidi nodded. It was one more rule for her to remember.

In the afternoons Clara always took a nap, and Miss Meyer told Heidi she could do what she wanted. This was the chance Heidi had been waiting for. She found Sam carrying a heavy tray of plates into the dining room. "You there, could you help me?" She said this because after Miss Meyer's speech the night before, she did not know what she should call Sam.

He was feeling grumpy and answered, "What do you want?"

Heidi said as nicely as she knew how, "Could you please help me open a window?"

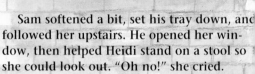

Sam softened a bit, set his tray down, and followed her upstairs. He opened her window, then helped Heidi stand on a stool so she could look out. "Oh no!" she cried.

"What's wrong?" he asked.

"There's nothing out there but more houses and windows and stony streets. There's no grass or trees at all!" Heidi looked as if she were going to cry. "There must be more. How do I look out over the whole valley?"

"You'd have to climb up high somewhere like a church tower. You could see very far from there."

Before Sam could say any more, Heidi ran downstairs and out the front door. But the churches she had seen from her window could not be seen from the street. She did not know which way to go and wandered from street to street. All the people were walking by so fast, they looked too busy to answer Heidi's questions.

Then Heidi saw a little boy playing a hand organ. He turned the handle, and music came out of the box strapped to his shoulder. His clothes were too small for him and needed to be washed. A turtle stood next to him, tied to a string. There was a shiny metal cup on the ground containing a few pennies. Heidi waited until he had finished, then asked, "Do you know where I can find a church tower?"

The boy stared at her. Because Heidi was from Switzerland, she spoke German a little differently than the people in Germany. Still, he understood her easily enough. "Yes," he said.

"Will you show me where it is?"

"Will you give me two pennies if I do?" asked the boy.

"I don't have any money," Heidi started to say. "But Clara must have two pennies, and she will pay you."

This was good enough for the boy, and he and Heidi set off down the street. The way twisted and turned until they came to a long street. There at the end rose a tall church.

The tower seemed to touch the sky. When the children reached the door, though, it was locked. Heidi rang the bell.

"Hey! You there!" a voice shouted from a window just above them. They waited a few moments, and then an old man opened the door. "What do you children think you are doing, ringing the bell like that? Can't you read?" The little man pointed at a sign next to the door. *Ring if you want to visit the tower.*

"Oh, but that's me," Heidi said. "I want to go up high and look out over everything." She did not say that she hoped to see forests and mountains beyond all the tall houses.

"I can't take you up there," the man said angrily and started shutting the door.

"Oh, please, please, let me go up, just this once," Heidi pleaded.

He looked down at her. She looked so eager, he took her by the hand and grumbled, "Oh well, if it means that much to you, come along."

Before they disappeared up the stairs, though, Heidi asked the boy to wait for her.

Then he could show her the way back home. He agreed when she promised to pay him another two pennies. Heidi and the old man climbed and climbed and climbed. Heidi had never seen so many stairs!

Suddenly they were at the top, and sunshine poured through a little window next to a great big bell. The man lifted Heidi up and she had a good look around. But still she saw nothing but a sea of roofs, chimneys, and towers. After a minute she turned to him and said sadly, "It isn't the least bit what I expected."

"Well, what does a little thing like you know about views? Come along now, and don't ring any more tower bells."

Heidi followed the tower keeper down the stairs. Once they reached the bottom, though, she noticed a door on the left, leading to a room. There in a corner lay the biggest cat Heidi had ever seen. And on a chair next to the cat was a basket overflowing with kittens! Heidi stood and stared in wonder.

The keeper noticed and said, "Come and look at the kittens." Heidi went up to the basket.

"Oh, aren't they sweet! Oh, just look at how tiny they are!" Heidi's eyes sparkled as she watched eight little kittens climbing all over each other.

"Would you like one?" the man asked.

"To keep for myself?" gasped Heidi.

"Of course. You can have more than one if you like, or all of them if you have enough room," he said. The tower keeper was glad to get rid of the kittens. Heidi jumped up and down, she was so excited. There was plenty of room in the big house, and she was sure Clara would love to have them.

"How can I carry them all though?" Heidi asked.

"If you tell me where you live, I'll bring them by," the keeper said.

"Bring them to Mr. Sesman's house. The front door has a big golden dog's head with a ring in its mouth."

The old man knew exactly which house Heidi meant and nodded. "You'd better get back there now," he said.

But Heidi had a hard time tearing herself away from the kittens. "Oh, please, do you think I could take just two with me now? One for Clara and one for me?"

"Wait a minute then." The man picked up the big mother cat and put her in another room. After he had closed the door, he said, "Now you can take them."

Heidi's eyes were shining. She chose a white kitten and an orange-striped kitten. She stuffed them into her pockets, then followed the old man outside. There the little boy still sat on the step, waiting for her. "Now, which way is it to Mr. Sesman's house?" she asked him.

The boy shrugged his shoulders. "Don't know," he mumbled. So Heidi described the front door for the boy in the same way she had for the tower keeper. The boy ran off in the direction they had come, with Heidi following close behind.

They soon arrived at the right door. But when Heidi banged the ring in the dog's mouth against the door, the door opened right away. "Hurry inside, Miss," Sam whispered. He looked very worried, pulled her

inside, and shut the door without even
noticing the little boy.

Heidi went into the dining room, where
dinner was about to be served. There was an
awful silence as Miss Meyer glared at her. "I
will speak to you later, Adelheid," she said
angrily. "For now, though, I will only say it
was very, very naughty of you to go running
out without telling anyone where you were
going, then coming back so late. You are a
bad little girl."

"Meow," Heidi's pocket said.

"How dare you make fun of me?" Miss
Meyer's face turned red.

"i didn't," began Heidi. But before she
could finish, there was another "Meow,
meow!" Sam almost dropped the plate he
was carrying and had to rush from the room
again to keep from laughing.

"That is enough, I say!" Miss Meyer was
now so angry she could hardly see straight.
"Leave this room right now."

Heidi stood up, very scared. She tried to
explain again, but the kittens both started
crying, "Meow, meow, meow!"

"Heidi," Clara said, "why are you being
so rude to Miss Meyer?"

"But it's not me, it's the kittens," Heidi
finally managed to say.

"What! Kittens! Here?" screamed Miss
Meyer. "Sam! Tina! Come here at once and
get rid of these miserable little creatures!"
And with that, Miss Meyer picked up her
skirts and ran as fast as she could out of the
dining room. Miss Meyer hated cats so
much, she was actually terrified of them!

33

Heidi brought the kittens over to Clara, and the two girls giggled with pleasure as they cuddled the baby animals. Clara couldn't have been happier.

Sam, in the meantime, stood in the kitchen holding his stomach, he was laughing so hard. He had heard everything through the door. When he came into the room again, Clara had the kittens on her lap. Heidi knelt beside her.

"Oh, Sam, you must help us." Clara looked up at him. "Find a quiet corner for the kittens, somewhere Miss Meyer won't find them. We want to play with them when she's not around."

"I'll take care of that for you, Miss Clara. Just leave it to me. I'll make a little bed for them, and Miss Meyer won't even know they're in the house." Sam chuckled to himself. He waited until Miss Meyer stuck her head through the door to ask if the "terrible creatures" were gone. Then he snatched up the kittens and brought them to the attic.

Miss Meyer had meant to scold Heidi for being so very naughty, but she found she simply did not have the strength. It had been a day filled with such ups and downs, worry and fright, all she could do was crawl into bed. And Heidi and Clara went happily to sleep, knowing their kittens were safe. It had been quite a day for everyone.

CHAPTER 8
Strange Happenings

The next day Sam showed Mr. Usher into the study, and lessons began calmly enough. Clara wondered if there would be any more excitement, or would her lessons be as boring as usual? A little later in the morning the bell rang so loudly that Sam dashed down the stairs, thinking it was Mr. Sesman himself, coming back from another business trip. When he opened the door, though, he saw a scruffy little boy with a hand organ and a turtle.

"What do you want? Why, I'll teach you to ring bells like that!"

"I want to see Clara," said the boy.

"You little beggar. Don't you even know enough to say 'Miss Clara'? And what would you want with her anyway?"

"She owes me four pennies."

"Nonsense! How do you even know there is a Miss Clara in this house?"

"I showed her the way yesterday for two pennies, and then the way back for another two pennies."

"You're telling lies," Sam said. "Miss Clara never goes out. She can't walk. Now go away before I throw you off these steps myself!"

But the little boy would not budge. He said stubbornly, "I saw her. She's short with black curly hair, black eyes, and she doesn't talk like us."

Sam thought to himself, "Ah, so the little miss has been at it again." He smiled. "All right, come with me." He led the boy upstairs to the study door. Then he turned to the boy and said, "When I let you in, you play a tune. Miss Clara would like that." He tapped on the door. "There's a boy here who wants to speak to Miss Clara."

Clara's eyes lit up. This sort of thing never happened to her. She looked at Mr. Usher, who nodded. "Bring him in," she said. The boy stepped into the room and started turning the crank on the side of his hand organ. Music filled the room. Clara and Heidi clapped their hands, and even Mr. Usher had to smile.

Miss Meyer, however, was in the dining

room. When she heard the music, she could hardly believe her ears. She rushed into the study and took one look around, then yelled, "Stop! Stop that noise at once!" But it was hard for anyone to hear her over the music. She tried to grab the boy, but tripped over a dark thing on the floor. It was the turtle! Miss Meyer jumped in the air, and she hadn't done that for years! Sam, who had been watching from the door, could not keep himself from laughing again.

Miss Meyer fell into a nearby chair. "Get rid of that boy and his animal!" she ordered.

The little organ player grabbed his turtle, and Sam led him away. At the door he gave him a handful of coins, saying, "Here's the money from Miss Clara, and a bit more for playing so nicely."

Miss Meyer decided to stay in the study and make sure nothing else upset the lessons. But no sooner had everyone calmed down when the doorbell rang again. This time Sam brought a huge basket into the study. "A man brought this by for Miss Clara." Clara's eyes grew round.

"Oh please, Mr. Usher, can I open it now?"

Before Mr. Usher could answer, Miss Meyer said, "Certainly not! You finish your lessons first." Clara stared at the basket, wondering what was inside.

She did not have long to wait, since the lid of the basket was not on tight. All of a sudden the room was swarming with kittens! They jumped out one after another and rushed around. One bit Mr. Usher's pants and jumped over his feet. Two others climbed up Miss Meyer's skirt. One climbed onto Clara's lap, mewing and scratching as it came. The whole room was full of kittens, and Clara laughed and laughed.

"Oh, aren't they cute!" she squealed. Heidi chased after the kittens, dashing from one end of the room to the other. Mr. Usher tried to shake the kitten off his leg, while Miss Meyer screamed for Sam and Tina. She didn't dare move, afraid that the horrid little things might jump all over her if she did.

Sam came into the room and quickly grabbed the kittens, stuffing them back into the basket. Then he carried them up to the attic, where he had already made a bed for the two kittens Heidi had brought home the night before.

Once again Clara's lesson time had been far from boring. That evening Miss Meyer sent for Sam and Tina to find out what exactly had happened. Then she sent for the children. "Adelheid, you have been a very bad girl again. I must punish you for such wicked behavior. I have half a mind to send you to the dark cellar. A few hours with the rats and bats might make you learn to be good."

Heidi did not know why Miss Meyer thought it was so bad in a cellar. The only "cellar" she had known was Grandfather's shed, where he had stored cheese and milk. But she had always been glad to go there. Besides, she had never seen any bats or rats.

"Oh, no, Miss Meyer, you can't do that." Clara was horrified. "Wait until Papa comes home. He'll be here soon, and I'll tell him everything. Then he can decide what to do with Heidi." Miss Meyer agreed, and besides, she knew Clara must always have her way.

"Very well, Clara. But I will be sure to speak to your father about this." With that she left the room.

The next few days passed without any more problems, but Miss Meyer was still very nervous. Lessons remained interesting, however, since try as she would, Heidi could not learn her ABC's. And whenever Mr. Usher tried to compare the letters to the shapes of real things, like a beak or horn, Heidi burst out crying. Anything which reminded Heidi of the hawk on the mountain or her goats made her feel terribly homesick.

In the evenings Heidi tried to tell Clara what it was like back home. But more often than not, she ended up crying, "Oh I must go home again. I must go tomorrow!"

Clara begged her to wait, at least until her father came home. Heidi agreed, but only because with each passing day she was able to add one more soft, white roll to the pile which was growing in her closet. She wouldn't eat a single one herself because she knew how much Grannie would enjoy them instead of her hard, black bread.

Heidi had plenty of time during the afternoons when Clara was sleeping to think about home. She would imagine the snow melting and how beautiful it was with the

sun shining on the grass and the little flowers everywhere. Sometimes Heidi felt so homesick, she could hardly stand it. Then suddenly, one afternoon she remembered something very important. Her aunt had told her, after all, that she could go back if she wanted to.

Heidi wrapped all her rolls in a big red scarf, put on her straw hat, and went downstairs. But no sooner was she at the front door when it opened and Miss Meyer walked through it!

"What does this mean, Adelheid? Haven't I told you not to go running around on the streets anymore? Yet here I find you trying it again and looking like a beggar's child."

"I wasn't going to run about," Heidi whispered. "I was going home."

"What's that? You want to go home? What would Mr. Sesman say? And what about Clara? Are you so ungrateful? Now tell me, have you ever had so much to eat and such a nice bed to sleep in before?" Heidi shook her head. "Well, you're just an ungrateful little girl who doesn't even know how lucky she is."

This was too much for Heidi, and she burst out, "I just want to go home because while I'm here Snowflake will be crying and Grannie will be missing me too. And here I can't see the sun saying good night to the mountains. And if the hawk came flying over Frankfurt he'd croak louder than ever because there are such a lot of people here being horrid and mean, instead of climbing high up where everything's so much nicer."

"Heavens!" Miss Meyer cried. "The child's gone completely crazy!" Miss Meyer flew up the stairs, bumping into Sam along the way. "Bring that terrible child up here at once!" she ordered.

"Yes, ma'am." Much to Sam's surprise, little Heidi was so upset, she could do nothing but stand by the front door trembling all over. He patted her shoulder and asked, "What have you done this time?" Heidi didn't move. Her eyes blazed. "Hey, it's all right. Don't take her so seriously. Cheer up and follow me. Afterwards we can go look at the kittens. Would you like to watch them running all over the attic?" Heidi finally nodded. Then Sam slowly led her up the

36

stairs. He brought her to her room, but she still did not say a word. Sam left Heidi, feeling very sorry for the little girl.

At dinner, Miss Meyer said nothing to Heidi. She just glared at her, watching to see if she did any more strange things. And the next day Miss Meyer asked to speak with Mr. Usher alone before lessons began.

"Have you noticed anything strange about Adelheid?" she asked. Then she told him how Heidi had tried to run away and the odd things she had talked about.

"No, Miss Meyer, I don't believe there is anything wrong with Heidi. In some ways she is different than most children, but certainly not crazy. Actually, the only thing I have noticed about her is that she just cannot seem to learn her alphabet."

This made Miss Meyer feel a little better. Later in the day she remembered the old clothes Heidi had been wearing when she tried to leave. She spoke to Clara about giving some of her clothes, which were too small, to Heidi. Clara agreed. So Miss Meyer

went off to Heidi's room to throw away her old clothes. In a few minutes there was a shriek, and Miss Meyer rushed out, calling for Heidi.

"Adelheid! What do I find in your closet? Can I believe my eyes? There, where there should be clothes and shoes, I find a huge pile of stale dry rolls. Tina, go to Miss Adelheid's room at once and throw away the rolls, as well as that awful straw hat."

"Oh no!" Heidi wailed. "I must keep my hat, and the rolls are for Grannie." She tried to run after Tina, but Miss Meyer held her back. "You'll stay right here. That trash is going where it belongs."

Heidi threw herself down beside Clara's chair and began to cry bitterly. "Oh, now Grannie won't get any nice white bread," she sobbed. "The rolls were all for her!" Heidi cried and cried. Clara was very upset by all this and begged Heidi to stop.

"I promise, Heidi. When you go home I promise I'll give you as many white rolls as you want for Grannie. Please, just stop crying."

Finally Heidi calmed down. Clara's promise did make her feel a little better. "Will you really give me as many rolls as I want?"

"Of course I will. Now cheer up."

Heidi came to dinner that night with red eyes, and when she saw the roll by her plate she felt the tears coming again. She swallowed them down, knowing it was forbidden to cry at the dinner table. Sam kept making strange signs at Heidi during the meal, winking and playing with his hair. Heidi did not know what he meant until she went to bed that night.

There, under her covers, she found her old straw hat. She was so glad to see it, she hugged it hard. That was what Sam had been trying to tell her at dinner. When he heard Heidi cry out for her hat that afternoon, he had followed Tina and snatched the hat away from her. "I'll get rid of this," he said. Then he had hidden it in her bed. Heidi stuffed it way in the back of her closet and covered it with her big red handkerchief so no one could find it and take it away from her again.

CHAPTER 9
A Bad Report to Mr. Sesman

A few days later everyone in the house was hustling and bustling. Clara's father was home for a visit! Sam and Tina went up and down the stairs, carrying load after load of suitcases and presents. The first thing he did was go see his daughter. Heidi was with her when Mr. Sesman walked in. He gave Clara a big hug and kiss, stroking her hair fondly. Then he turned to Heidi, who had backed away into the corner, not sure she should stay in the room.

He smiled. "So this is our little Swiss girl. Come and shake hands. That's right. And tell me, are you and Clara good friends? I hope you don't fight with each other."

"No, Clara is always good to me," said Heidi.

"And Heidi never argues with me," added Clara.

"I'm glad to hear that," said Clara's father. "And now I must have something to eat, since I've been traveling all day. I'll be back after that and can show you the presents I brought you."

In the dining room, Mr. Sesman was a little surprised to see Miss Meyer waiting for him with such a grumpy face. "Clara looked well. What can be the problem?" he wondered.

"Yes, Miss Meyer?" he said as he sat down to eat.

"It's that child, Mr. Sesman. Adelheid has caused a great deal of problems since she arrived. She is quite a bit younger than I would have liked. And," Miss Meyer paused to let her words sink in, "I do believe there is something wrong with her mind."

Mr. Sesman looked up. He was used to Miss Meyer going on about things which did not really matter. But if there was indeed something wrong with Heidi, Clara might be in danger. "The child looked fine to me. What do you mean?"

"Well, it's no wonder you don't know what I mean. You should see the sort of people and animals she has been bringing into the house. Ask Mr. Usher. And that's not all.

She just acts in a way which makes me think she's not quite right in her head."

Mr. Sesman looked at Miss Meyer as if she were not quite right in her head. Just then Mr. Usher entered the room. "Ah, just the person I wanted to see," Mr. Sesman said. "Tell me, does the little girl who keeps Clara company seem all right to you? What's all this about her bringing animals into the house? Do you think she's at all odd?"

Mr. Usher hemmed and hawed. He was never one to answer questions short and sweet. And that was exactly what Clara's father wanted to hear. Instead, though, Mr. Usher rambled on, "I should like first of all to say, though she may be slow in some ways because of a late education, and because of her time in the mountains, which of course could be said to be healthy, if not perhaps too long . . ."

"My dear Mr. Usher, can you speed it up a little?"

"I would not like to say anything against the child, for if on one hand she is a bit strange, the change of living in Frankfurt compared with the mountains must be great and . . ."

Mr. Sesman got up. "Excuse me, Mr. Usher. Don't let me disturb you, but I must get back to my daughter."

He hurried out and did not return, but went to the study and sat down beside Clara. Heidi stood up when he came into the room. And since he wanted a few moments alone with Clara, he said, "My dear, will you go and get me a . . . er . . . a glass of water?"

"Fresh water?"

"Yes, fresh cold water." Heidi left the room. Then he pulled his chair closer to his daughter and held her hand. "Clara dear, tell me about these animals our little friend has brought into the house. Why does Miss Meyer think she is not quite right in the head?"

Clara told him just what had happened, about the turtle and the kittens, the rolls and everything. By the time she had finished, her father was laughing hard. "Well then, you don't want me to send her home, Clara? You're not tired of her?"

"Oh no, Papa," she cried. "Since Heidi's been here, wonderful things have happened almost every day. I'm never bored any more."

"That's all right then. And here comes your little friend. Have you brought me nice cold water, my dear?"

"Straight from the fountain," said Heidi, handing it to him.

"But you didn't go all the way to the fountain by yourself, did you?" Clara asked.

"Yes, I did. And I had to go a long way because there were so many people round the first two fountains, I had to go on to the third. And there I met a nice man with white hair who said to say hello to Mr. Sesman for him."

"Who could that be now?" Mr. Sesman asked. "Describe him to us."

"He had a nice smile and wore a fat gold chain with a gold thing hanging on it. And he had a stick with a horse-head handle."

At the same time both Clara and her father cried, "The doctor!" Mr. Sesman laughed at the thought of what his old friend would have to say about this strange way of getting water.

That evening Mr. Sesman told Miss Meyer that Heidi was staying. "You shouldn't think of her funny ways as something wrong with her. And I want you to please make sure that she is treated kindly. If she keeps you too busy, well, you will soon have help since my mother is coming for a visit in a few days. And she can manage anyone, as you know."

"Yes, sir," Miss Meyer said. But she was not very happy about this news. When Mrs. Sesman, Clara's grandmother, came to visit, Miss Meyer was no longer in charge.

Clara's father could only stay another few days, then was off again on a business trip. But he eased the hurt of his going away by telling Clara her grandmother would soon be there. "Oh, Heidi," Clara told her, "Grandmama is the kindest, most wonderful lady in the world." Clara talked so much about her grandmother, that Heidi began to call her "Grandmama" too.

Miss Meyer did not like this, though. "You must always call her 'Honorable Madam.'" Heidi did not quite understand why, and she had never heard such a strange name before. But she could tell by the angry look Miss Meyer gave her that she should not disagree.

CHAPTER 10
Grandmama's Visit

It was easy to see how important Grandmama was. On the day she was due to arrive, Tina put on a new cap. Sam went around putting footstools by chairs. Miss Meyer fussed and complained, trying to show everybody that she was still the boss.

When Grandmama arrived, Tina and Sam rushed down the stairs to greet her, while Miss Meyer followed more slowly. Heidi had been told to stay in her room and wait, so that Clara could have a few moments alone with her grandmother.

She spent the time saying over and over to herself, "Honorable madam, honorable madam." But it sounded so strange, Heidi felt sure Miss Meyer had taught it to her backwards. After a little while, Tina knocked on Heidi's door and said, "Go into the study now."

When Heidi entered the room, Grandmama said in a friendly voice, "Come over here, my dear, and let me have a good look at you."

Heidi went to her and said clearly and carefully, "Good evening, Madam Honorable."

"What was that?" laughed the old lady. "Is that what you call people in the mountains?"

"No. No one's called that at home," Heidi said.

"Well, no one's called that here either. You children should call me 'Grandmama.' Can you say that?"

"Yes, I've used that name before," Heidi said.

"Fine," Grandmama said, patting her cheek. Then she looked closely at Heidi and liked what she saw. The child's eyes were bright and serious.

Heidi saw such a kind and caring look on Grandmama's face that she loved the woman right away. Everything about her was pretty. She had lovely soft white hair, covered with a lace cap that had two ribbons tied at the back. The ribbons fluttered behind Grandmama so that it always looked like a soft breeze blew around her.

In the afternoon, while Clara was taking her nap, Grandmama went to Miss Meyer and asked, "Where is Heidi? What does she usually do during this time of day?"

"She sits in her room and does nothing. If she were a little clever, she would do something useful. But instead she dreams up such crazy plans, you would not believe it if I told you."

"Well, if I was left by myself like that with nothing to do everyday, I would dream up strange things to do too, Meyer. And I doubt if you would believe them if I told you," Grandmama said. She did not like the idea of Heidi's sitting alone in her room every afternoon.

Miss Meyer did not like the way Clara's grandmother called her by her last name, but there was nothing she could do about it. When Mrs. Sesman was in the house, she was in charge.

"Send Heidi to my room. I will show her some books I brought with me."

"Books! The child cannot read. No matter how hard poor Mr. Usher tries, he cannot teach her a thing."

Miss Meyer would have said more, but Grandmama did not let her. "Really? She seems like a clever little girl. Well, send her to me anyway." Grandmama was very puzzled about this.

So when Heidi arrived, she showed her the big picture book she had. They were turning the pages together when suddenly Heidi burst into tears at what she saw. Grandmama looked at the picture and saw animals grazing, watched over by a shepherd. The sun was setting, and the meadow was bathed in golden light.

She patted Heidi's hand and said kindly, "Come, child, don't cry. This must have reminded you of something. But there is a nice story which goes with it." Grandmama waited a few moments for Heidi's tears to stop pouring down her cheeks. Then she said, "That's right. Now we can have a nice little talk. Tell me, what are you learning during lessons?"

"Nothing. But I already knew I wouldn't learn anything."

"But why is that?"

"I already knew from Peter that I

wouldn't learn how to read. He should
know, since he's tried and tried and tried."

"Well, this Peter must be a very odd boy
then. But you shouldn't just accept what he
says. Try for yourself," Grandmama said
hopefully.

"It's no use."

"Now listen to me, Heidi. This Peter must
be very different than other children. I'm
sure you can read, but you have to want to
learn. As soon as you can read, you may
have this book with the picture of the shepherd in the meadow for your very own, and
then you'll be able to read the story for
yourself and find out what happens to him
and his animals. Would you like that?"

"Oh yes!" Heidi's eyes shone.

During the first few days of her visit,

Grandmama watched the children carefully. She was pleased at how well they got along, but she also noticed that little Heidi seemed sad about something.

Ever since Miss Meyer had caught Heidi trying to go home, Heidi had started to change. She now knew Aunt Detie had been wrong when she said Heidi could go home whenever she wanted. Heidi knew she would have to stay in Frankfurt a long, long time. She might never again see Grandfather and Grannie and her beautiful mountains. This made her heart heavy with sadness.

But Heidi did not dare tell anyone how upset she was. She believed that Mr. Sesman would think her very ungrateful if she wanted to go away. Probably Grandmama and Clara would think the same if they knew. Because she had to keep it all locked inside her, Heidi did not feel well. She would not eat.

She had trouble sleeping too. Often for hours she would lay in bed thinking about Grandfather and the goats and her fir trees. Then, when she finally did fall asleep, she dreamt of her mountains in such real ways that she woke up feeling like she'd actually been there. The harsh truth of being in Frankfurt always cut into her like a knife in the mornings. And she often sobbed into her pillow before it was time to get up for breakfast.

Grandmama had noticed Heidi's red eyes in the mornings and waited to see if they would go away. After a few days she took Heidi aside and asked her what was the matter.

Heidi was afraid of making her angry. She said, "I can't tell you."

"Can you tell Clara?"

"No. I can't tell anyone," Heidi said so sadly that the old lady's heart hurt for her.

"Listen to me," Grandmama said, "if we're in trouble and can't tell others about it, we can always talk to God about it."

"Talk to God?" Heidi asked.

"Yes. Every night you should thank Him for all the good things and ask Him to take care of you. And when you are sad and have no one to turn to for help, you can tell God all about it. And God will always help you.

Believe me, He can find some way of making you happy again."

This was very special news for Heidi. Her eyes brightened, and she smiled for the first time in weeks. "May I tell Him everything, really everything?" she asked.

"Yes, everything."

Heidi ran to her own room, sat down on her chair, and folded her hands. Then she poured out her little heart to God and begged Him to help her go home soon.

A little while later Mr. Usher came to Grandmama with a piece of good news. "You will never guess what's happened," he began.

"Ah, but I can," Grandmama said. "Heidi can read."

Mr. Usher's mouth fell open. "How did you know? Yes, you are right. The child is making great progress. Not only has she learned her ABC's, but she can actually read."

That evening when Heidi sat down for dinner, she found the book with the picture of the shepherd by her plate. She looked brightly at Grandmama, who nodded and said, "Yes, it's yours now."

"Forever and ever? Even when I go home?" asked Heidi.

"Yes, of course."

From then on Grandmama often asked Heidi to read stories out loud to her and Clara. Heidi learned to read many books. But her favorite was the book about the shepherd. She now knew it showed him happily taking care of his father's sheep and goats. In the next picture he had left his good home and was taking care of a stranger's pigs. Here the sun was not shining, and the countryside was gray and misty. The last picture showed his old father running with outstretched arms to greet him as he finally came home again.

CHAPTER 11
Homesickness

During Grandmama's visit Heidi learned how to do more than read. She also learned how to sew. While Clara slept in the afternoons, Grandmama showed Heidi how to make little clothes for the dolls she had brought with her. Using scraps of material Grandmama kept in a special bag, Heidi learned how to make dresses, coats, and aprons for the dolls.

But no matter how busy she was with her books and dolls, Heidi never really looked happy. Her eyes had lost their sparkle. And Grandmama had noticed.

One afternoon during the last week of her visit, the old lady called Heidi to her room again and said, "My dear, tell me why you're not happy. Is it still the same trouble?" Heidi nodded, her lip trembling. "Did you tell God about it?" The little girl nodded again. "And do you pray to Him every day to make you happy again?"

"No, not any more. It's no use," Heidi told her. "God didn't hear me, and besides He's too busy trying to take care of all the people in Frankfurt. If we all pray for things at the same time, He can't notice everybody, and I'm sure He didn't hear me."

"Why are you so sure?"

"I prayed the same prayer every day for a long time and nothing happened."

"Oh, Heidi, listen carefully and I will teach you something very important. God is a loving Father who knows what is good for us all. If we ask Him for something that is not right for us to have, He won't give it to us. Instead, in His own good time, if we go on praying and trusting Him, He'll find us something better. You can be sure He heard your prayer. If He didn't answer it right away, it's because there's a better time for it to happen than right away.

"God must have thought, 'I want only the very best for Heidi. If I wait for just the right moment to answer her prayer, then she will really be happy.' He has been watching over you all this time. But when you stopped praying, it showed you did not really believe in Him. If you go on like that, God will let you go your own way. Then if things go

43

wrong and you complain that there's no one to help you, you will really have only yourself to blame, because you will have turned your back on God. Now, do you want that to happen, Heidi?"

The old woman squeezed Heidi's hand. Heidi had been listening carefully and thinking hard. She felt deep down that everything Grandmama had told her was true, and she wanted to remember every word of it.

"Oh no, I won't turn my back on God! May I go and tell Him I'm sorry now?"

"Of course, child." Heidi ran off to her room and asked God to forgive her. Then she thanked Him for taking such good care of her and promised never to forget Him again.

It was a sad day when Grandmama finally left to go back to her own home. The girls did not like the way the house became so quiet. Heidi offered to read a story to Clara, hoping it would cheer them both up. But instead, the story upset Heidi so much she started crying.

The story Heidi read was about a grandmother who died. Heidi thought the grandmother was Peter's Grannie, and she burst into tears. "Grannie is dead!" she sobbed.

Clara had a hard time getting Heidi to stop crying and to see that it was just a story and not Peter's Grannie at all. But even then Heidi was very sad. She knew that while she was so far away from them, Grannie really might die, and her grandfather too. She might arrive to find everything changed and her loved ones gone forever.

Just then Miss Meyer came into the room. "Adelheid, stop howling like that and listen to me. I don't want you to cry like that any more, do you understand? If I ever hear you making such a fuss again while you're reading to Clara, I'll take the book away from you."

This was a terrible thing to say, since Grandmama's book was Heidi's greatest treasure. From then on, though, no matter how sad Heidi felt, or how much something reminded her of home, she gulped back the tears and would not let them fall. It sometimes meant she made funny faces to keep from crying, and sometimes she had a stomach ache.

She also stopped eating, she was so unhappy. Sam was quite upset whenever he saw her sit at dinner and not eat anything. He was always whispering to her, "Have just a little of this, Miss, it's so good. Here, take another spoonful." But no matter what, Heidi just was not hungry.

Time went by, and Heidi's homesickness grew worse every day. Finally, just reading about a mountain or a goat would bring tears to her eyes. But she did not dare let them fall. Autumn and winter passed, but Heidi hardly noticed, she was so miserable. In the spring she thought about how Peter must be bringing the goats up to the pasture every day, of the bright yellow and blue flowers, and how the sun would say good night to the mountains.

When she was in her own room, she would sit with her hands over her eyes to shut out the city sunshine, and would stay like that, forcing back the homesickness which rose up inside her, until Clara wanted her again.

CHAPTER 12
The House Is Haunted!

Before long, strange things began happening in that house in Frankfurt. The servants grew afraid to go into empty rooms alone. Even Miss Meyer was always looking over her shoulder, as if to make sure no one was following her. The reason for this was that every morning, no matter how early someone checked, the front door stood wide open. Sam would lock it with a double lock, and the next morning it would be wide open. Robbers weren't doing it, since nothing was missing. The only answer Miss Meyer and Sam and Tina could think of was . . . a ghost!

Finally Miss Meyer told Sam to stay up one night in the room nearest the front door with a friend of his. She gave them a bottle of wine and a gun, just in case.

That night Sam and John waited and waited. Midnight came and went and nothing happened. About an hour later John went to check, and *whoosh!* a gust of cold air from the open door blew his candle out. As he turned to go back into the living room, he caught sight of a white thing floating up the stairs. He ran back to Sam and slammed the door. "It is a ghost!" he gasped. And the next morning Sam and John told their story to Miss Meyer.

She wrote letters to both Mr. Sesman and his mother, begging them to come and save the household from a ghost. Both wrote her back, calling her silly and saying that as a grown woman she should know better than to be scared by something which does not even exist.

Then Miss Meyer had an idea. Up until then she had not told Clara anything about the strange happenings. But she truly was scared. She would do anything to get Mr. Sesman to come home and protect them from whatever it was that kept unlocking the front door. Miss Meyer went to Clara and told her the whole story.

"Oh, I cannot be left alone after this!" Clara cried. "Miss Meyer, you must move your bed into my room, and Heidi too! Oh,

what if the ghost comes upstairs? This is terrible! I'm so scared!" Clara was very upset at the thought of a ghost coming into her room at night. Heidi had no idea what a ghost was and said she would rather sleep in her own room. She was more afraid of Miss Meyer at night than a ghost.

Miss Meyer's trick had worked. Clara was so upset, Miss Meyer could truthfully write Mr. Sesman, "The ghost continues to bother us, so much so that Clara is becoming much worse."

Her letter succeeded. In two days Mr. Sesman was ringing the bell so loudly, Sam thought the ghost was playing tricks again. The first thing Mr. Sesman did was go see Clara. She was so happy to see him, she almost felt like thanking the ghost.

Then he went to see Miss Meyer. "So how is our 'ghost'?" he asked with a smile.

"This is quite serious. I don't think you will be laughing about it tomorrow."

"Very well . . . Now please send Sam to me." Mr. Sesman had an idea. "Sam," he said once Miss Meyer had showed him in, then left again, "Sam, tell me the truth. Did you pretend to be a ghost to scare Miss Meyer?"

"Oh, sir, please don't think that! I'm just as frightened as she is!" Then Sam told Mr. Sesman the whole story about the night he and John had stayed up and actually seen the ghost.

"Well, Sam, then I think there's nothing left for me to do but show you and John what a ghost looks like by daylight. Now I want you to go to the doctor's. Give him the message that I need him to sit up with me all night. Is that clear?"

"Yes, sir. I'll see to it at once."

Mr. Sesman then went back to Clara to tell her he would catch their "ghost" by the next morning.

That night, after the children and Miss Meyer were asleep in bed, the doorbell rang. Although the doctor's hair was gray, his eyes were bright and kind. He looked rather worried when he came in, but as soon as he saw his friend, he burst out laughing. "I must say you look all right for a man who needs someone to sit up all night with him."

"Not so fast, my friend," Mr. Sesman said. "I'll be needing your help all right. And so will someone else who won't look as well as I do when we've caught him. Why, we're going to catch ourselves a ghost tonight!" Then Mr. Sesman explained to the doctor the whole story. When the doctor laughed, Mr. Sesman said, "Don't let Miss Meyer hear you. She is taking this all very seriously. Now listen, just in case there are robbers trying to scare us into leaving the house empty, I've got two loaded pistols in the room next door here."

The two men disappeared into the same room Sam and John had stayed in a few nights earlier. They settled down to catch up on what was happening in each other's lives and enjoy themselves for the night. Time passed quickly, and they were quite surprised when the clock struck midnight. "The ghost's heard us and isn't coming," said the doctor.

"We must wait and see for about another hour. It isn't supposed to show up until then."

So the two old friends chatted on for another hour. In the street outside everything was quiet, when suddenly the doctor raised his hand. "Did you hear anything, Sesman?" he asked.

They listened carefully and heard the sound of a door being unlocked. Quickly each man snatched up one of the guns and a candle. They went out into the hall and saw a pale streak of moonlight coming through the open door. And in front of the door stood a shining white figure which did not move!

"Who's there?" shouted the doctor so loudly that his voice echoed. Both men moved toward the front door. The figure turned and gave a little cry.

It was Heidi! Barefoot and in her white nightgown, she stared at the weapons and lights. Then she began to shake, and her lips trembled as if she were about to burst into tears. Both men stared at her, then at each other, their mouths open in amazement.

"Why, it's the little girl who went all the way to the fountain for a glass of water!" the doctor cried.

"What are you doing here, child? Why have you come downstairs?" Mr. Sesman asked.

Heidi stood before him, her face as white as her nightgown. "I don't know," she whispered.

"Here, let me take care of this," the doctor said. He put the gun down and took Heidi gently by the hand. "Come, child, don't be afraid. Nothing terrible is going to happen. Let's go back to your bed now."

When they reached her room, he set the light down on the table and lifted Heidi back into bed. He tucked her in, then sat down beside her and waited a few moments. Heidi was now wide awake and no longer looked so terrified. The doctor took her hand again. "Tell me, my dear, where were you going?"

"Nowhere," whispered Heidi. "I didn't know I'd gone downstairs. I just was there."

"I see. Were you by any chance dreaming a dream which seemed very real?"

"Oh yes!" Heidi's eyes met his. "Every night I dream that I'm back with Grandfather and can hear the wind whistling through the fir trees. I know in my dreams all I have to do is get up and open the door of the hut and I will see the stars shining brightly. And I get up and go

outside . . . and it's so beautiful. But when I wake up I'm always still here in Frankfurt."

"Do you ever have any pain anywhere?" the doctor asked.

"Well, sometimes it feels like a big rock is sitting in my throat . . . as if I want to cry."

The doctor squeezed her hand a little. "And do you cry then?"

"No, I'm not allowed to. Miss Meyer has forbidden me to cry."

The doctor was quiet for a few moments. "I see. Tell me about living with your grand-father."

Before Heidi could get more than a few words out, the tears came too quickly to hold back. They rained down her cheeks, and she sobbed bitterly. The doctor got up. "Have a good cry now, it will help you feel better. Then go to sleep, and in the morning everything will be all right." He left the room and went to find Mr. Sesman, who had been pacing the floor in the room below.

"Well, in the first place that little girl is a sleepwalker," the doctor began. "Without knowing it, she has been opening the front door every night. Also, she's terribly home-sick, and she appears to have stopped eat-ing, since she's nothing but skin and bone. Something must be done at once. There's only one cure, and that is to send her back to her mountains . . . and right away. She should leave for home tomorrow. That's my advice."

Mr. Sesman got to his feet, very alarmed. "Sleepwalking, homesick, losing weight! It's a terrible thought that a little girl could suf-fer so much in my home. She was so rosy and strong when she arrived. I don't dare send her back to her grandfather looking so thin. No, you cure her first, and then I'll send her back."

The doctor shook his head. "This cannot be cured with any drugs. I'm warning you, if you don't send her back to the mountains at once, you might have to send her back even worse than she is now. Or not at all."

This upset Mr. Sesman very much. "Yes, of course, Doctor. I'll do as you say," he promised. When the doctor left, the light of dawn was already coming through the front door. It was a new day.

CHAPTER 13
Home Again

Mr. Sesman went straight upstairs and knocked on Miss Meyer's door. "Please get up quickly!" Miss Meyer looked at her clock and gasped. It was 4:30 A.M. She had never been up so early in her life! As Miss Meyer dressed herself, she wondered what on earth could be happening. She was so excited, she kept looking for clothes which she had already put on.

Mr. Sesman then knocked on the doors of Tina and Sam. He ordered Tina to wake up Heidi and get her ready for a trip. Sam was to go get Aunt Detie from the house where she worked.

Everyone thought Mr. Sesman did not look like someone who had just caught a ghost. They wondered what had happened. When Miss Meyer was dressed, she came into the dining room. Her hat was on backwards, but otherwise she seemed to be awake. "Find a trunk and pack Heidi's things at once," he told her. "Put some of Clara's things in as well. Now hurry."

As everyone scurried off to follow Mr. Sesman's orders, he went to Clara's room. She was already awake and full of questions. He sat down on her bed and told her the whole story. "The doctor is afraid Heidi could become very sick. She might even go up on the roof in her sleep. You know how dangerous that would be. So I've made up my mind that she must go home at once. We wouldn't want anything to happen to her, would we?"

Clara was very upset that Heidi was leaving. But she calmed down a little when her father agreed she could help pack Heidi's trunk. That way Clara could put in some nice things which Heidi would like.

By this time Aunt Detie had arrived and wondered what was wrong; why was she sent for at such an early hour? Mr. Sesman told her about Heidi. "I want you to take her home at once, this very day," he said.

Aunt Detie remembered how angry Uncle was when she took Heidi away. She did not dare bring the girl back in worse shape than when she had left. So she said, "Oh, I'm afraid I don't have the time today. In fact, I

don't know when I will ever have the time. We're so busy, you know."

Mr. Sesman saw right through Aunt Detie's excuses and sent her away without saying another word to her. Then he called for Sam. "You're going with Heidi to Switzerland today. When you're about halfway, spend the night at this hotel. Then take her on to Dörfli." He handed Sam a card with an address written on it. "Now listen to me, this is very important. While you are in the hotel, you must make sure all the windows in her room are shut tight. Then, once she's in bed, lock her door from the outside. She walks in her sleep, and in a strange house it might be very dangerous if she wandered downstairs and tried to open the front door. Do you understand?"

Sam looked up in surprise. "So that was it!"

"Yes, that was it. You're a great coward, Sam, scared by a little girl wandering in the night. Now go on and get ready for this trip. I want you to leave as soon as the carriage is here."

Sam left the room shaking his head. Meanwhile, Heidi had been waiting in her bedroom. Tina had not told her anything but that she should wake up and get dressed. When Mr. Sesman sent for her, she came into the dining room. "Good morning," she said.

"Is that all you have to say?" Mr. Sesman asked. But Heidi just looked at him. "I do believe no one has told you," he said with a smile. "You're going home today."

"Home?" she gasped. For a moment she could hardly breathe.

"Yes. Now you must try to eat some breakfast." Heidi did try, but she could not swallow even one mouthful of bread. She thought she might still be dreaming. She felt sure she might wake up to find herself in the middle of the night with the front door open again.

Mr. Sesman told Miss Meyer to be sure and pack plenty of food. "The child hasn't eaten at all, and it's no wonder." He turned to Heidi. "Now go to Clara and stay with her until the carriage arrives." That was just what Heidi wanted to do, and she found Clara with a big trunk open beside her.

"Oh, come and see what I've packed for you, Heidi," Clara said. Together the two girls were so excited about the dresses, aprons, petticoats, and even a basketful of soft white rolls for Grannie that they had no time to feel sad. Before they knew it, Sam was calling to tell Heidi that the carriage was ready.

Heidi dashed off to her own room. She took the book Grandmama had given her from under her pillow. Then she reached way into the back of her closet and brought out her old straw hat and red scarf. Then she ran back to Clara. The two girls quickly hugged each other.

As she passed Miss Meyer on the stairs, though, Miss Meyer cried, "Really, Adelheid, you can't leave this house carrying that old hat and scarf. You won't need them anymore. Good-bye." She snatched the straw hat away.

But Heidi looked so sad that Mr. Sesman said, "Leave the child alone. She can take what she likes with her. Even if she wanted kittens and turtles, there would be no reason to get so excited, Miss Meyer."

Heidi picked up her hat, her eyes shining with thanks and happiness. "Good-bye," Mr. Sesman said as Sam lifted Heidi into the carriage. "Clara and I will often think of you. Have a good trip."

"Thank you for everything," Heidi said. "And please thank the doctor and give him my love." She remembered how the doctor had said the night before that everything would be all right the next day. He had been right.

Soon she and Sam sat on a train headed for Switzerland. Heidi held the basket of soft rolls on her lap. Every now and then she peeked at them and sighed with happiness. She was only just now believing that she really was going home. Suddenly she asked, "Sam, Peter's Grannie won't be dead, will she?"

"Let's hope not," he said. "I expect she's still alive."

Heidi was quiet then, thinking about the rolls she wanted to give her kind old friend. Soon both Heidi and Sam fell asleep. Before long they woke up to the sound of the conductor calling their stop. They spent the night in that town, and Sam did exactly as Mr. Sesman had told him, but Heidi never once got up.

The next day they spent several more hours on a train. When they got out at the stop nearest Dörfli, Sam looked around, wondering how to make the rest of the trip. He did not like the idea of climbing a mountain. Then he saw a man with a cart and horse.

The man said, yes, he was going to Dörfli, and he would carry the child's trunk and take her there too. Sam felt a little guilty not going the rest of the way with Heidi. Before she left, he called her to one side and gave her a thick packet and a letter. "These are for your grandfather. Put them at the bottom of your basket, and be sure not to tell anyone they are there. Don't lose them now, and good-bye."

Heidi did as she was told. As Sam helped her up into the cart, she hugged him good-bye. During the ride, she sat quietly next to the driver, who was the baker at Dörfli. He knew who she was and had known her parents. Finally he asked, "Aren't you the little girl who used to live with your grandfather on the mountain?"

"Yes," Heidi said.

"Did they treat you badly in Frankfurt? Is that why you've come back?"

"Oh no. Everyone was very kind to me. Mr. Sesman said I could come back. I'd much rather be with Grandfather than any-where else in the world," she told him.

"Hmm," the baker said. But he was think-ing it must not be very nice for Heidi to live with her grandfather. Heidi was too busy looking around at the mountain peaks to want to talk. Instead, she shivered with so much excitement she wanted to jump down from the cart and run.

When they reached Dörfli, many people gathered around the cart, asking Heidi ques-tions. But she was in a great hurry to see her old friends. "Thank you," she said to the baker. "Grandfather will come get the trunk later." Then she struggled through the crowd and hurried up the path which led to Peter's hut.

"Look at how pale and scared she looks," the people said. "You can bet she doesn't want to go back to the old man."

But the baker told them she had said she was well taken care of in Frankfurt, but had wanted to come back all the same. These lit-tle bits of news spread through the village in no time at all.

Heidi rushed up the hill as fast as she could go. She had to stop every now and then to catch her breath. The basket was heavy, but she had only one thought. "Will Grannie still be sitting in the corner? Oh, I hope she hasn't died." Then she saw the little house under the trees. Her heart beat faster than ever. She raced up to the door but could hardly open it, she was shaking so much. Then she flew into the little room quite out of breath and not able to talk.

"Goodness me," someone said from the corner of the room. "That was how Heidi used to come in! How I wish she would come back and visit. Who is it?"

"It's Heidi, Grannie!" she cried, and threw herself onto the old woman's lap and hugged her. Heidi was so filled with joy, she could say nothing more.

At first Grannie was so surprised, all she could do was stroke Heidi's head. "Yes, it's Heidi's curly hair and her voice. Praise God, she's come back to us." And a few big tears fell from her old blind eyes.

"Don't cry, Grannie. I promise I'll never leave you again. I'm here to stay now. And you won't have to eat hard bread for a few days, Grannie," she added. Heidi took the rolls out of their basket and laid them on Grannie's lap, one by one.

"Child, what a present to bring me!" the old woman said as her hands moved over the load on her lap. "But you're the best present of all." Grannie's hands fluttered over Heidi's cheek and face, as if to make sure she was real.

After a few moments Heidi stood up and started to take her hat and dress off. "Grannie, I must go on to Grandfather now, but I'll come and see you again tomorrow." Heidi left the dress and hat on the table and gave Grannie a big hug. Then she tied the red scarf around her shoulders and put on the crumpled little straw hat.

Just then Peter's mother, Bridget, came in. "Heidi, you've come back! But why have you taken off these lovely clothes?" she said as she held up the dress and hat.

"I'd rather go to Grandfather like this, otherwise he might not know me. You may have the hat if you want." And before Bridget could say another word, Heidi snatched up her basket and ran out the door.

As she went her way, Heidi saw the evening sun shine rosily on the mountains. She kept turning around and walking backwards so she could look at all the beauty around her. These were her mountains. She saw the pastures, and the valley below, all red and gold. Little pink clouds floated in the sky. It was so lovely! Heidi stood with tears pouring down her cheeks, and thanked God for letting her come home again.

She
waited a
few moments
until the light
began to fade, then ran
on. Soon she could see the
fir trees, then the roof, then the
whole cabin, and last of all she saw
Grandfather sitting on the bench outside
and smoking his pipe, just as he used to do.
Before he had time to see who it was, Heidi
had dropped her basket and flung her arms
around him. "Grandfather, Grandfather!"
She could say no more, and he could not
speak at all. For the first time in years, his
eyes were wet with tears. Then he lifted her
up onto his knee.

"So you've come back, my Heidi," he
said. "And you don't look all that grand
either. Did they send you away?"

"Oh no, Grandfather. Clara and her
father and Grandmama were all very kind
to me. But I was so homesick. I used to get a
lump in my throat and couldn't swallow.
But I didn't say anything, or else they would
have thought I was ungrateful. One night
the doctor told me everything would be all
right, and here I am!"

Then Heidi remembered the letter and
packet. She ran back to the basket and gave
it to Grandfather. He read the letter from
start to finish, then put it in his pocket without saying a word. He stood up and took her
hand. "Do you think you could drink some
milk, Heidi?" he asked. "Bring the packet
with you. There's money in it for you to buy
a bed and any clothes you may need."

When they went into the cabin,
Grandfather had Heidi sit down on her
stool. Then he gave her a mug filled with
goat's milk. She drank it all at once, then
sighed. "There's nothing as good as our milk
anywhere in the world." Grandfather gave
her another mug of milk right away.

Then they both heard a shrill whistle.

Heidi
ran out of
the cabin and saw
Peter bringing the goats
down from the pasture. He
stopped and stared as Heidi came running up to him. Before he could say a word,
Heidi hugged him, then turned to the goats.
Peter's face broke into a wide smile. The
goats pushed and shoved each other, all trying to get close to their friend. Even little
Snowflake gave Big Turk a push, and the old
goat looked very surprised indeed.

Finally Peter found his voice, "So are you
coming up with me tomorrow?"

"Yes, but in the afternoon I'll visit
Grannie." Heidi laughed as Daisy and Dusky
both tried to rub against her at once. Finally
she had to go into the shed and shut the
door before Peter could get the other goats
to follow him down the mountain.

That night, after Grandfather had made
up her bed of sweet-smelling hay again,
Heidi fell fast asleep. Grandfather climbed
the ladder at least ten times to check on
Heidi and see that the little window stayed
covered so the moonlight would not shine
on her face. But she slept soundly and
hardly moved. She had seen the sun say
good night to her mountains. She had heard
the wind rustle through her fir trees. She
was home again.

54

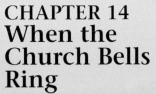

CHAPTER 14
When the Church Bells Ring

The next day Grandfather took Heidi down to Grannie's house. Then he went on to the village to pick up her trunk. As soon as Grannie heard Heidi, she called, "Is that you, child?" She took Heidi's hand and held it tightly as if she were afraid of losing her again.

"How did you like the rolls?" Heidi asked.

"Oh, they were good! I feel better already."

Bridget said, "Grannie wants them to last, so she's only eaten one last night and another this morning. If she were to eat one a day, I'm sure she'd get her strength back."

Heidi listened, then was struck by an idea. "I know," she cried. "I'll write Clara, and she can send more and more rolls every day. That way you'll never run out!"

Bridget said, "Heidi, that is a good idea, but the rolls would be hard by the time they arrived. If only I had a little extra money, I could buy Grannie rolls from the baker in Dörfli." Peter's mother sighed.

"But I have money, lots of it!" Heidi blurted. "Mr. Sesman gave me money. Now Grannie can have a roll every day!" Heidi danced around the tiny room, singing, "Every day, every day, a roll for Grannie every day!" She stopped and hugged Grannie. "Maybe if you get enough of your strength back, you can see again." Grannie just smiled. She would not spoil Heidi's fun.

As she danced around, Heidi remembered something else. "Grannie, I can read now. If you want me to, I'll read to you from your old book."

"Oh, would you? Can you really read?"

Heidi climbed on a stool and took down the songbook. She wiped off the thick layer of dust which had gathered there, then took a stool and sat down near Grannie. "Which shall I read?"

"You choose, child," Grannie said. She pushed her spinning wheel to the side and folded her hands, waiting eagerly for her to begin.

Heidi turned the pages, then said, "Here's one about the sun.

"'The golden sun
His course does run,
And spreads his light,
So warm and bright,
Upon us all.

"'We see God's power
From hour to hour.
His love is sure,
And will endure
For evermore.

"'Sorrow and grief
Are only brief.
True joy we'll find,
And peace of mind,
In God's good time.'"

Grannie sat very still. Heidi had never seen her look so happy, though tears streamed down her cheeks. Finally she said, "Read it again, Heidi. Please read it again." Heidi was only too happy to do so. She liked the words very much herself. "Oh, that's done me so much good," Grannie sighed at last. "It makes my old heart laugh again."

Before long there was a knock on the window, and Heidi saw her grandfather outside. She said good-bye and promised to come back the next afternoon. Heidi had so much to tell Grandfather, she talked the whole way home.

She bounced along next to him, holding his hand. "And I'd like to buy a soft roll for Grannie from the baker in Dörfli every day. I have all that money Mr. Sesman gave me. Grannie doesn't want me to, but I can anyway, can't I?"

"That was for your new bed, though," Grandfather said.

"But I sleep much better on my hay bed than I ever did in that great big bed in Frankfurt. Please, please let me spend the money on rolls."

"Well, the money is yours. Do what you like with it. There will be enough to buy Grannie rolls for many a long year."

"Hurray, hurray! Now she'll never have to eat black bread again. Oh, we are having good times, Grandfather, aren't we?" Heidi skipped along beside him. Then all of a sudden she grew serious.

"If God had let me come back to you right away, none of this would have happened. I could have brought Grannie only the few rolls I had saved. And I wouldn't have known how to read her songbook for her. Grandfather, God knew what was best, just as Grandmama said He did. Look how perfect everything is. We'll pray every day, won't we, Grandfather? That way we'll never forget God again, and He won't forget us."

"And when someone does forget?" he asked softly.

"That's very bad," Heidi said with a serious frown on her little face. "Then God lets him go his own way. And when everything goes wrong, no one will feel sorry for him. They'll only say, 'You didn't bother about God, and now God has left you to yourself.'"

"That's true, Heidi. How did you find out?"

"Grandmama told me."

The old man walked on quietly for a few moments. Then he mumbled, half to himself, "And if God no longer bothers with a man, then it's all over. There's no going back."

"Oh, but there is. Grandmama told me we can always say we're sorry and start over fresh. Then everything is right again, just like it is in the story in my book. You haven't heard it yet, but when we're home I'll read it to you." Heidi hurried the rest of the way to the cabin.

When they were home, Grandfather sat down on the bench outside. He stared at the mountains as if he did not see them. Heidi climbed up next to him. She had her book under her arm and began to read the story.

"'There once was a young man who took care of his father's sheep and goats. One day he asked for all the money his father was going to give him. As soon as he got it, he left home and wasted it all. Then he had no choice but to get a job feeding someone else's pigs. He was so hungry, he wished he could eat the pigs' food. When he felt lonely and miserable and homesick, he remembered how good his father was to his servants. "I will go home and ask to be a servant to my father," the young man thought.'"

Heidi checked to make sure Grandfather was listening. He had not moved. "'When the young man set out, he was still a long way off when his father saw him and came running toward him.'" Heidi broke off and said, "This is the best part, Grandfather. What do you think happens?" She paused, then began reading again. "'When his father saw him, his heart was filled with love and he ran and hugged his son. "Father, I have let you down, and I have failed God. I'm so sorry!"

"'The father called his servants and said, "Bring me the good robe, some shoes and a ring, then put them on him. We will have a great party. This is my son. He was dead to me and now lives. He was lost and now is found!"'"

Heidi looked at Grandfather again. She waited, but he said nothing. After a few moments she put the book on his lap. "You can see how happy he is," and she pointed at the picture.

That night, while Heidi slept, the old man climbed up the ladder to look at her. She lay with her hands folded, as if she had fallen asleep while still praying. He stood watching her for a long time. Then he folded his hands and bowed his head. "Father, I have hurt You, I know. And I have hurt others. I'm not a good man. Please forgive me and help me to start over again." Two large tears rolled down his wrinkled cheeks. Grandfather stayed like that for quite some time, opening himself to God's own healing.

He got up early the next day. It was a beautiful morning . . . a Sunday. The bells in the valley announced the new day as the birds in the fir trees sang along. He called to Heidi, "Time to get up. Put on your best dress, and we'll go to church together."

Heidi had never heard this from Grandfather. She was very excited as she climbed down the ladder. She put on one of her Frankfurt dresses. When she saw Grandfather, she felt even more amazed. "Look at the silver buttons on your jacket. You look so lovely, Grandfather."

The old man smiled at her. "And so do you. Now let's go." Holding hands, they set off down the mountain. Heidi laughed at the sound of all the bells echoing each other.

When they reached the church in Dörfli, most of the people were already inside. Grandfather and Heidi took a seat in the back. The news that Uncle was in church quickly spread as people nudged and whispered to each other. Some even lost their places in the songbooks, they were so busy passing on the news. But when the pastor began to preach, everyone paid close attention. He spoke about love and giving thanks. He spoke so warmly that all the people felt their hearts touched by his words.

After the service, Heidi's grandfather took her hand and walked to the pastor's house. The people who had seen them inside church stood in little groups, pretending not to watch. When the pastor opened the door and invited Grandfather and Heidi inside his house, the villagers turned to each other.

"Did you see that?"

"Yes, and did you see how gently he held on to the little girl's hand?"

"He can't be so bad if the pastor treats him like a friend."

"What did I tell you?" the baker said. "The little girl said she would rather come back and live with him on the mountain than stay in Frankfurt with all she was given there." Slowly but surely they all changed their minds about the lonely old man and began to say nice things about him.

Then some of the women said they had heard from Peter's mother, Bridget, and Grannie how Uncle had come down and fixed their hut so it did not rattle in the wind. As they waited for Grandfather to reappear, they felt more and more like he was an old friend they had not seen for a long time.

The pastor was very happy to welcome Grandfather and Heidi. He shook their hands and smiled. Grandfather could hardly speak, he was so surprised by such kindness. Finally he said, "I've come to say I'm sorry for how I spoke to you that time you visited me. I will do as you say after all and move to Dörfli in the winter. If people here don't trust me, I suppose I deserve no differently. But at least I hope you will trust me."

The pastor's face beamed. "Neighbor, your mountains have been a good church to you. I look forward to our spending many winter evenings together." Then he patted

Heidi's black curls and shook Grandfather's hand again.

As the two came out of the pastor's house all the people crowded around Grandfather and greeted him like some long-lost friend. They were especially happy to hear he would be moving into the village during the winters.

As Grandfather and Heidi headed back home, several of the villagers walked with them part of the way. When they finally said good-bye, they begged him to visit them in their homes soon. Heidi looked up at Grandfather and saw such a kind light in his eyes. She said, "You look different . . . nicer and nicer."

"Heidi, today I am happy in a way I thought I would never be again, much happier than I deserve. It's good to feel at peace with God and man. It was a good day when God sent you to me."

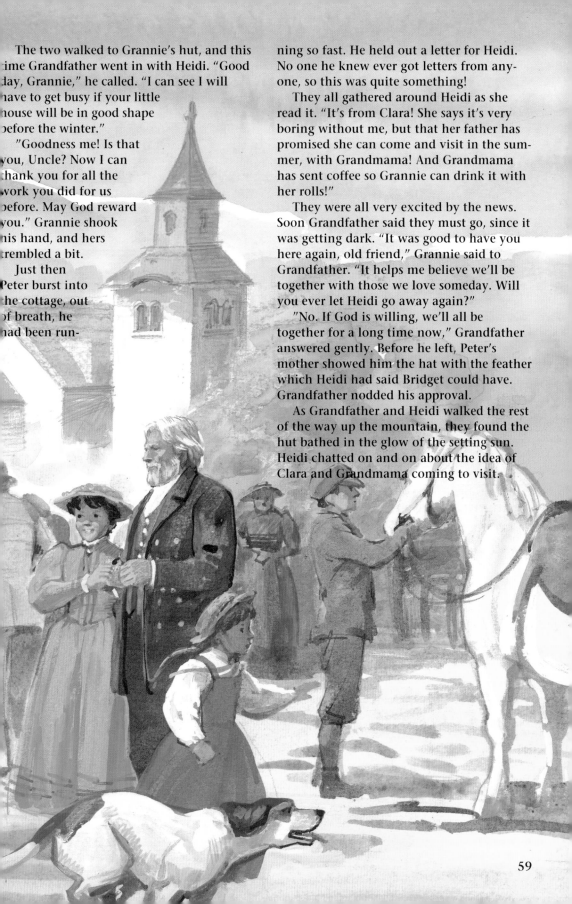

The two walked to Grannie's hut, and this time Grandfather went in with Heidi. "Good day, Grannie," he called. "I can see I will have to get busy if your little house will be in good shape before the winter."

"Goodness me! Is that you, Uncle? Now I can thank you for all the work you did for us before. May God reward you." Grannie shook his hand, and hers trembled a bit.

Just then Peter burst into the cottage, out of breath, he had been run-

ning so fast. He held out a letter for Heidi. No one he knew ever got letters from anyone, so this was quite something!

They all gathered around Heidi as she read it. "It's from Clara! She says it's very boring without me, but that her father has promised she can come and visit in the summer, with Grandmama! And Grandmama has sent coffee so Grannie can drink it with her rolls!"

They were all very excited by the news. Soon Grandfather said they must go, since it was getting dark. "It was good to have you here again, old friend," Grannie said to Grandfather. "It helps me believe we'll be together with those we love someday. Will you ever let Heidi go away again?"

"No. If God is willing, we'll all be together for a long time now," Grandfather answered gently. Before he left, Peter's mother showed him the hat with the feather which Heidi had said Bridget could have. Grandfather nodded his approval.

As Grandfather and Heidi walked the rest of the way up the mountain, they found the hut bathed in the glow of the setting sun. Heidi chatted on and on about the idea of Clara and Grandmama coming to visit.

CHAPTER 15
Getting Ready for a Journey

One sunny autumn morning in Frankfurt, the doctor walked to Mr. Sesman's house. It was the sort of day when everyone should be smiling. But the doctor hardly looked up. He seemed very sad. This was because the doctor's little girl had just died. Like Mr. Sesman, the doctor's wife had died long ago, leaving him with a daughter. She had been his greatest joy since his wife's death, and now she was gone too.

Sam opened the door. He was always glad to see the kind doctor. When Sam showed the doctor into the study, Mr. Sesman got up right away and gave his old friend a warm handshake. "Won't you please change your mind?" Mr. Sesman asked.

"Sesman, I've never known anyone so stubborn!" the doctor said. "This is the third time I've had to come here and tell you the same answer. No, Clara has been much too sick this summer. She could not possibly go all the way to Switzerland. We must wait until next spring."

Mr. Sesman knew the doctor was right, but he hated saying no to Clara, especially after he had promised her she could visit Heidi. Then he had what he felt sure was a very good idea. "Doctor, I've just thought of something! I can't bear to see you looking so unhappy. You need a change. How would it be if you were to go to Switzerland and visit Heidi for us?"

The doctor was very surprised by this, but before he could say anything, Mr. Sesman had him climbing the stairs to Clara's room. The two men sat down on her bed, and her father started talking.

"You see, Clara, there is just no way you would be strong enough for such a trip, and the nights will be cold in the mountains now. Let's wait until next spring, then you can stay longer." He dreaded upsetting her, so he quickly went on to his plan for the doctor to go instead of them.

It was very hard for Clara to give up the visit to Heidi. She had counted the weeks and months during the long and lonely hours of being so sick. She knew, though, that her father only wanted what was best for her. And she also hated to see the doctor looking so sad. So she turned to the doctor.

"Oh please," she begged softly, "please go and see Heidi for me. When you come back, you can tell me what it looks like there. And when you go, you can take all the presents I've been thinking of sending them. And I promise I'll take as much medicine as I'm supposed to!"

Despite himself, the doctor had to smile.

Then of course I must go. When would you like me to start?"

"Tomorrow," Clara answered right away.

"She's right," Mr. Sesman said. "You shouldn't miss one day of this lovely weather in the mountains." So it was all decided. While the doctor went home to pack, Mr. Sesman asked Miss Meyer to help Clara.

Clara had already sent Tina out to buy a box of little cakes. These were for Grannie to eat with her coffee, as a change from the soft rolls. It was quite a job to pack everything, there were so many different gifts. First there was a thick coat with a hood so Heidi could visit Grannie during the winter whenever she wanted to, without having to wait until Grandfather could wrap her in the old sack. Next came a thick, warm shawl for Grannie. There was a huge sausage which Clara wanted Peter to share with Grannie and Bridget, so Peter would not eat it all by himself. There was a pouch of tobacco for Grandfather, who liked to smoke when he sat outside his cabin in the evenings. And finally, there were a lot of little surprise gifts for Heidi which Clara had been collecting for quite some time. When the packing was finally done, Sam brought the bundle over to the doctor's house.

CHAPTER 16
A Visitor for Heidi

The sun had just peeked over the mountains when Heidi woke up to the sound of the breeze blowing in the old fir trees. Heidi loved that rustling sound and jumped out of bed, getting dressed as fast as she could. She ran outside to find Grandfather already looking around, as he did every morning, to see what kind of day it was going to be. Rosy clouds floated by in the clear blue morning sky, and the sun washed the rocky peaks and pastures in pure golden light.

"Good morning, Grandfather!" Heidi dashed over to her trees and waved her arms as she danced with the branches. She gave an extra little jump with each gust of wind which blew through them. Before long Peter whistled and the goats pushed and shoved their way to greet Heidi.

Peter asked Heidi, "Will you be coming up with me today?"

"I can't, Peter. My nice people from Frankfurt might come any minute now, and I must be here when they do."

"You've said that every day for a while now," he grumbled.

"And I'll keep saying it until they arrive," she answered. Peter marched off with his army of goats and did not say a word.

Heidi went back inside, where she and Grandfather sat down to have breakfast together. Then Heidi started the housework. She had brought back home some new ideas from Frankfurt. Every morning she made her bed, then tidied up the cabin, putting everything in its proper place. Then she dusted the chairs and polished the table until it shone. When Grandfather came in, he looked around and thought to himself, "Our home used to look this way only on Sundays, when I gave it a good cleaning. Now every day looks like Sunday!"

The only problem was, no sooner would Heidi begin one job when she would think she should do something else. She started polishing the table, and a sunbeam shone straight through the open window. It seemed to be calling her to come outside. So out she ran, and found everything so beautiful and the ground so warm and dry that she just had to sit down for a while. She stared at the meadows and trees and mountains. Then she remembered her polishing, so up she jumped and ran back in. But before long the rustling fir trees seemed to sing her song, and she just had to run out again and dance to the tune.

Just at that moment she saw someone coming up the path toward her little home. "Grandfather! Come quickly!" He hurried out of the shed, afraid that she was hurt, but Heidi was already running down the slope. "They're here! They're here!" Heidi called over her shoulder. "And look, the doctor is in front!"

The little girl ran to the doctor and gave him the biggest hug she could. "Oh, Doctor! Thank you again, thank you a thousand times."

The doctor, who was surprised by such a warm welcome, said, "Goodness, child, why are you thanking me?"

"Because you sent me home to Grandfather."

The doctor's face brightened. He had not expected a welcome like this. He thought Heidi would be so sad about Clara's not coming that she would not want to see him instead. But she was overjoyed. She held his arm tightly and lovingly.

Heidi looked down the mountain path. "But where are Clara and Grandmama?" she asked.

"I'm afraid they could not come. Clara has been very sick, so Grandmama stayed with her. But they'll come in the spring, I'm sure."

Heidi found this very hard to believe. After all the months of waiting, there was nothing left to do but wait some more. It hurt. But when she looked up at the doctor's face and saw the lonely look in his eyes, she

62

thought he hurt for the same reason. She tried to cheer him up. "It's all right, Doctor. Time goes by so quickly up here, it'll be springtime in no time at all."

They walked towards the cabin hand in hand. Heidi wanted to chase the shadow from his eyes so badly, she told him again and again how soon summer would come. By the time they reached Grandfather, she believed it herself. "They haven't come yet, but they will quite soon," she called out.

Grandfather welcomed the doctor warmly. They hardly seemed like strangers, since Heidi had told each of them so much about the other. They sat down on the seat outside. Sitting in the sunshine, the doctor told them how Mr. Sesman had said the doctor should visit since he hadn't been feeling well lately. Then he whispered to Heidi that there was something coming up the mountain for her which would give her much more pleasure than he could.

"I hope you spend as many of these sunny days with us as you can," Grandfather said. "You can stay in the inn at Dörfli and visit us every day. I will gladly show you around any part of the mountains you want to see." Grandfather explained they would like the doctor to stay with them, but there just was not enough room in the cabin.

The doctor smiled and said he would be very pleased to visit them in this way. Then Grandfather went inside and brought out the table. "Heidi, run and bring out the food for lunch. Our food is simple," he told the doctor, "but the dining room is fine."

"It certainly is," the doctor sighed as he looked out over the valley, which gleamed in the sunlight. Heidi was proud to help, and soon they feasted on thick slices of bread covered with toasted cheese. There were slices of the delicious meat Grandfather had dried during the summer and steaming milk to drink. The doctor said it was the best meal he had eaten that year.

"Clara must come visit you," he said. "She would soon become a different person, breathing this fresh air and eating like I have."

The little group soon saw a man carrying a large bundle up the path. "Ah, Heidi, here are your presents from Frankfurt," the doctor said. It did not take the little girl long to unwrap her gifts and spread them out on the grass. She was so surprised, she could hardly talk. She thought the little cakes for Grannie were the best of all. When she gave Grandfather his pouch of tobacco, he filled his pipe at once and sat on the bench next to the doctor, smoking and talking.

Finally Heidi ran over to the doctor. "What you said wasn't right. All these nice things put together aren't as nice as seeing you!" Both men laughed at this, and the doctor was very surprised.

As the sun started setting, the doctor said he must get back to the village and see about finding a room. He took Heidi's hand, and her grandfather carried the box with the cakes, the shawl, and the sausage. Together they walked to Peter's home. There Heidi asked the doctor, "Would you like to come up to the pastures tomorrow?" This was the best treat she could offer him. The

doctor said he would like nothing more. Then he walked off with Grandfather toward Dörfli. Grandfather, meanwhile, had set the gifts down on the doorstep and said a quick hello to Grannie before going on with the doctor.

Heidi opened the door and struggled to carry the heavy box of cakes. "Look, Grannie, Clara sent you presents!" One by one she put them on Grannie's lap so she could run her hands over them. "They've come all the way from Frankfurt, from Clara and Grandmama," she said.

Heidi was surprised that Grannie seemed to like the gray shawl even better than the cakes. But Bridget stood staring at the sausage. She had never seen such a big sausage before. When Peter burst through the door, he too was unable to talk when he saw the huge piece of meat.

Heidi smiled all over, then gave them all hugs since she knew Grandfather would be waiting for her. Outside, Grandfather took Heidi's hand, and they went up the path under the starry sky to their peaceful little home.

CHAPTER 17
Happy Days

Early the next morning the doctor walked up the mountain with Peter and his goats. Heidi was waiting for them. Grandfather came out of the cabin carrying a sack of food for lunches. Peter grinned when he felt how heavy it was.

As the doctor climbed to the pastures, Heidi skipped at his side, chatting away. She told him all about the goats and their funny ways and the names of the mountains they saw.

Peter said very little. He was angry that Heidi paid so much attention to the doctor. After all, it was the first time she had come to the pastures with him in weeks. And that was another reason why Peter did not like the doctor. Heidi had spent way too many days at the cabin, waiting for the people from Frankfurt. All that time she could have been with him.

Soon the group reached the pastures. Heidi led the way to her favorite spot. From there she looked down on the faraway valley, so green below them, and up to the great mountains where snow sparkled even in the summer. Heidi and the doctor sat on the grass and watched the goats move about to graze. The goats' bells tinkled. The hawk soared overhead, making no sound. It was very still, and Heidi looked around at the summer flowers and everything else which she loved so well. She turned to the doctor.

But he sat as if he did not see any of it. The sadness had not left his eyes. "Yes, Heidi, it's lovely, but can a heart forget its sadness and feel happy, even here?"

"No one is sad here," she told him, "only in Frankfurt."

A smile flitted across the doctor's face. "But what if the sadness could not be left behind in Frankfurt, but followed me up here too? What then?"

"When you've done everything you can, tell God." Heidi spoke in a sure voice.

"Those are good words, my dear." The doctor took a deep breath. "But what if God is the One who sent the sadness?"

Heidi sat still for a few moments. She was sure God could always help, but she wanted to think about what she herself had learned and knew to be true. "I think you have to wait and keep on thinking that God has something good which He's going to give you out of the sad thing. But you have to be patient. You see, when something's awfully bad, you think it will last forever, and you don't know about it getting better."

The doctor said, "I hope you will always feel like that, Heidi. But this sadness I have in me will never go away. It touches everything I see and feel. Do you know what I mean?"

Heidi thought about the sadness she felt whenever she thought about Grannie's blindness. "Yes, I know," she said. "Maybe it would help to hear one of Grannie's songs. She says they bring the light back to her."

"Yes, Heidi, please do let me hear the words to Grannie's song."

Heidi nodded. "It goes like this:

"'Tell God your cares,
On Him your burden cast,
He hears all your prayers
And sends relief at last.

"'His never-failing love,
His wisdom sure and true,
Bring comfort from above
And all your hopes renew.'"

Heidi stopped because she was not sure the doctor was listening. He sat so still, with his hand covering his eyes. But he was not asleep, but only thinking hard and remembering when he was a child. His mother had sung that very song for him when he was Heidi's age. And now he was lost in the memories of how safe and sure he had felt then. Now that his lit-tle girl was dead, nothing seemed sure any more.

A few moments later, the doctor seemed to wake up from all his remembering. He took Heidi's hand and said, "Thank you, my child, that was very nice. We'll come up here again and you can tell me some more."

Meanwhile, Peter had been watching Heidi and the doctor, acting as if he did not care. But he minded very much that Heidi spent so much time with the doctor. So when it was time to eat, he yelled in a nasty way, "Lunchtime!"

The doctor told Heidi all he wanted was some milk. She agreed she would have the same. Then afterwards they set off on another walk. Peter was left with the big bag of food, including a chunk of Grandfather's delicious meat. When he realized all that food was his now, he stopped feeling badly toward the doctor. After all, thanks to the doctor Peter would have a fine lunch.

The doctor and Heidi explored the pas-tures higher up. She showed him where Finch had almost fallen into the ravine. They watched the hawk circle above them. Finally the doctor said he wanted to go back down to the cabin. He had hardly said any-thing all afternoon. It was as if the peace in those mountains and Heidi's happy chatter could not touch his heart. The sadness which hung over him was too great. When he left Heidi and went the rest of the way back to Grandfather's house by himself, she stood waving after him. And he thought to himself that was just what his own dear daughter used to do.

All that month the weather was lovely and warm. The doctor came up to the cabin every morning. He and Grandfather often went on long walks. Together they climbed high up, even to where the hawk nested. Grandfather knew all the names of the tiny plants and flowers. He could also tell many good stories about the animals which lived in caves or holes in the ground or even in the branches of the trees. One afternoon the doctor said, "My friend, I learn something new every time I am with you."

Several times, when the sun was especially warm, the doctor went up to the pasture with Heidi. There they always rested on the grass while she talked away or said the words to songs she had learned from reading to Grannie. Peter never joined them, but he no longer felt angry at the doctor.

Finally the last day of the doctor's visit came. It was a sad day for everybody. Grandfather said good-bye to his friend. The doctor took Heidi's hand and started down the path. "Heidi," he sighed, "I wish I could take you back with me to Frankfurt." He stroked her black curls.

Heidi saw in her mind the tall buildings and stony streets of that place. A shiver ran up her back. "It would be much nicer if you came here again," she whispered.

"Yes, you are right, quite right. Good-bye, my dear."

As she gave him a hug, she thought there were tears in his kind eyes. Then he turned quickly and hurried away. Heidi stood watching him, feeling very sad. After a few moments, she ran after him as fast as she could. "Doctor! Doctor!" He turned as he heard her, and when she reached him she sobbed, "I will come with you to Frankfurt and stay with you as long as you like. Just let me go tell Grandfather first."

The doctor held her tight. "No, no, you must stay here with your fir trees or you might get sick again. But do you promise that if I am ever sick and lonely you will come take care of me? It would be a great comfort to know that someone who loves me would look after me then."

"Oh yes, I'll come at once, the moment you send for me," Heidi promised. "And I love you almost as much as Grandfather."

He thanked her and went on his way again, while she stood and continued to wave long after he was out of sight.

CHAPTER 18
Winter in Dörfli

That winter was very cold and the snow deeper than anyone ever remembered it being before. Peter's hut was more than half buried. Every morning he squeezed out through the window since the door was jammed shut. Then his mother handed him a broom so he could sweep a little path through the snow.

On the mornings after the snow had frozen into a hard crust, Peter had great fun. He took his sled and almost flew down to Dörfli, where he was supposed to go to school every day.

Grandfather would have had the same trouble with the snow, except that he had kept his promise to the pastor. After the first snowfall he and Heidi moved down to the village. Grandfather had found a huge old house which needed lots of work. There were great holes and cracks in the roof and walls, and icy winds blew right through the windows. Grandfather was able to fix the house up enough so that he and Heidi could use two rooms and the kitchen, all snug and warm.

When Heidi saw her room, she clapped her hands. It had wooden walls and in one corner stood a huge white-tiled fireplace with a seat built around it. "Your bed is here, where it's nice and warm." Grandfather showed her a narrow place between the wall and the fireplace. It was just Heidi's size.

"Oh, Grandfather, my room! Isn't it lovely! Where are you going to sleep?"

Grandfather led her into the next room, where he had set up his bed. Next to that there was a huge kitchen. And beyond that was a room where he had built a stall for Daisy and Dusky. Heidi liked their new home very much. She explored it from corner to corner, and when Peter came to visit the next day she showed him every inch of it.

During her first night there she slept well, but when she woke up she wondered why the fir trees were so quiet. Then she remembered, and heard Grandfather's voice as he talked to the goats in the other room. Heidi knew that this place was just as much home as their little cabin on the mountain.

On the fourth morning there she said, "Today I must go and see Grannie. She'll be missing me." But Grandfather would not hear of it. "The snow is much too deep on the mountain. Peter can hardly struggle through it. No, Heidi, you must wait until it freezes, then you can walk on top of it."

Heidi did not like having to wait. But now that they lived in Dörfli, there were plenty of things to keep her busy. And so the time flew by. Heidi went to school every day and worked hard to learn all she could. Peter often missed school, but the teacher, who was very patient and kind, said, "I suppose the snow is too deep for him to make it to school." Still, Peter did manage to visit Heidi every evening.

One night the moon shone in a sky full of stars. There were no clouds. And the next morning the snow had frozen into a sparkling crust. Then Peter, thinking he would sink into soft snow as usual, jumped out of his window and found himself slipping and spinning over the slick surface.

Peter took his sled and shot off like a streak of lightning all the way to Dörfli. But because the mountain was so slick, he could not stop and skimmed clear to the next village. He decided happily that it was too late for school. It would take him a good hour to climb up to Dörfli, and school would have already started. He finally reached Dörfli by the time Heidi was sitting down to eat lunch with Grandfather. "There's frost," he said as he came into their kitchen.

"Oh, now I can go and see Grannie," cried Heidi. "Why weren't you at school then, Peter? You could easily have come down on your sled." It did not seem right to Heidi that Peter stayed away from school so often.

"I went too far, and then it was too late."

"But you're the general, remember?" Grandfather said. "Now what would you do to your goats if they were to run away and not follow your orders?"

"Spank them."

"And what would you say if a boy who behaved like a naughty goat got spanked for it?"

"Served him right."

"Then listen to me, General. If you ever again let your sled carry you off when you should be at school, you can come to me later and get what you deserve."

The light dawned as Peter looked carefully around the room for a stick which Grandfather might use to spank him.

Grandfather smiled at him. "Now come and have something to eat, and then Heidi can go home with you and visit Grannie. Bring her back tonight and you can stay with us and have dinner."

Peter grinned at this and sat down. Heidi was so excited at the idea of finally seeing Grannie again that she could not eat any more and passed him the rest of her potatoes and cheese. She went to the cupboard and put on the coat which Clara had sent her. She pulled the hood over her head and stood beside Peter. She hopped on one foot, then the other, waiting for him to finish.

When he was ready, they left and she ran along next to him, chattering away about how miserable Daisy and Dusky had been on the first day in their new stall. "They didn't eat, but just stood so still, drooping their heads. Grandfather said they were feeling like I did in Frankfurt," she told him. "It was their first time away from home."

Peter was not really listening. All he could think about was what Grandfather had said about punishing him for missing school. Just as they reached his house he said, "I'd rather go to school than have Uncle do what he said." Heidi thought this was quite right, and said so.

When the children walked into the hut, Heidi looked all around for Grannie. She was not in her corner! Bridget told Heidi, "Grannie's in bed. She's sick and feels cold all the time."

This was something new to Heidi. Heidi had never seen Grannie anywhere but sitting at her spinning wheel. She ran quickly into the next room, where the old woman lay on her skinny bed. Only one thin blanket covered her, but she had wrapped the warm gray shawl around her shoulders.

"Thank God," said Grannie as she heard Heidi's step. All during these last cold weeks she had worried about the doctor's visit, which Peter had told her about. She had been afraid the visitor from Frankfurt might take Heidi away again.

"Are you very sick, Grannie?" asked Heidi, standing next to the bed.

"No, no," said the old woman, patting her little hand. "It's only the cold which has got into my old bones."

"Will you be better when it turns warm again?"

"Oh, I'll be back at my spinning wheel long before that, God willing," Grannie said. "I'm sure I'll be up and around by tomorrow, in fact."

Heidi relaxed. But she saw something else which did not seem quite right. "Grannie, your bed is slanted the wrong way. Your head is lower than your feet. That's not right."

"I know, child," said Grannie. "It's not very comfortable," and she tried to find a soft place for her head on the pillow, which was not much better than a piece of wood.

"I wish I'd asked Clara if I could bring my bed from Frankfurt with me. It had three fat pillows, and I kept slipping down the bed, away from them. Would you have liked sleeping in a bed like that?"

"Oh yes. It would be very cozy. It's easier to breathe, sleeping on pillows like that." Grannie sighed. "But we won't talk about that. I have so much to be thankful for—fresh rolls every day, this fine warm shawl, and now you to visit me. Will you read to me today?"

Heidi ran and got the old book of church songs. She read all of Grannie's favorites. Grannie lay with her hands folded, a happy look on her thin face. When Heidi had finished, Grannie asked her to repeat over and over again the last lines of a favorite song.

"'My heart is sad, my eyes grow dim,
Yet do I put my trust in Him,
And in due time, all sorrow past,
In safety home I'll come at last.'"

Heidi liked the words just as much as Grannie did. They made her think about the sunny day when she came back to the mountains. "I know what it feels like to come home," she said.

Grannie took the little girl's hand. "Yes, I am happier now. You don't know what it means to lie for days on end in darkness, and most of the time in silence. Sometimes I'm ready to give up, knowing I shall never see the sunshine again. But when you come and read these words, God gives me back my hope. My heart looks up again and I feel much better."

Heidi said good night then and went outside with Peter. The moon shining on the snow made it as light as day. Peter climbed on his sled, with Heidi hugging him from behind. Together they skimmed down the hill like a couple of birds.

That night as Heidi lay snug in her little bed behind the fireplace, she thought about Grannie having to stay in bed like that day after day. "If only I could read to her every day," she thought to herself. "Grannie might get better." But she knew it might be a week or more before she could visit again. Suddenly she had an idea which made her sit straight up in bed. She was so excited she clapped her hands, although there was no one to hear her.

Then she said her prayers. Now she never finished a day without them. She prayed for Grannie and Grandfather, as well as for herself. Then she lay back down and fell asleep, a big smile on her little face.

CHAPTER 19
Peter Surprises Everyone

The next day Peter arrived at school on time. In the afternoon, when most of the children went home for lunch, Peter visited Grandfather and Heidi. She had been waiting for him and ran up to Peter as soon as he came in the door.

"I've had such a good idea, Peter! And you must help me. You have to learn how to read."

"But I know how to read," Peter said with a frown on his face.

"No, I mean you have to learn how to read well." Heidi told him her plan. "That way you can read a song for Grannie every day whenever the snow keeps me from going to your house."

Peter shook his head. "Can't be done. I've tried."

"That's silly. You haven't tried," Heidi said. "Grandmama in Frankfurt said anyone can learn how to read, and that means you." Heidi looked very angry. Peter was surprised that the people in Frankfurt knew about him. He already knew they were never wrong. "I'll teach you," Heidi said.

"Not me," Peter growled.

Heidi would not allow to him spoil her plan. Her black eyes flashed, and she said in an angry voice, "If you won't let me teach you, then you'll have to go away to Frankfurt to learn. And there the teachers aren't half as nice as the one here. In Frankfurt the teachers wear black clothes and tall, black hats like this." Heidi stretched her hand high above her head. "There if you don't know how to answer, they make fun of you."

Peter had heard enough. A shiver ran down his back. "Oh, all right, I'll do what you want," he mumbled.

Right away Heidi was all smiles again. "That's good. We'll start right away. Now come here." She pulled Peter over to the table and had him sit down. Heidi took down a book Clara had sent her which showed all the letters of the alphabet, and they got started.

From then on Peter visited Heidi every day. She drilled him over and over again on each letter until he had finally learned them by heart. Often Grandfather came into the room to watch. He sat quietly in the corner, smoking his pipe and trying not to laugh at what he saw. Sometimes he invited Peter to stay for dinner. Peter thought the dinners made his hard work worth it.

A few days later it began to snow very hard again. Heidi was not able to visit Grannie for three weeks. She worked and worked with Peter. Finally the day came when he went home and said to his mother, "I can do it."

"Do what?" she asked.

"I can read," Peter said.

"Can you really?" Bridget said. "Grannie, did you hear that?"

"I did indeed, and I wonder how such a miracle could have happened?"

Peter ignored their surprise and said simply, "Heidi said I have to read you one song every day." His mother ran to get the book. Grannie put aside her spinning and folded her hands.

Peter began to read. At the end of every line his mother said, "Well, would you ever believe it!" Grannie just sat still and listened, quietly smiling.

At school in the village the next day, the teacher held his usual reading lesson. When it was Peter's turn to read, the teacher said with a sigh, "I suppose we'll have to skip Peter again. Or will you try to at least pick out a few words you might know?"

Peter stood up and held the book in front of him. Then he began to read. The teacher was so surprised, it was not until Peter had finished three lines that he found his voice again.

"Peter, you can read! How did this happen when I have tried all these hours, weeks and years to teach you? How is it that you can suddenly stand up and read so well?"

"It was Heidi," Peter said.

The teacher looked over at Heidi. But she sat very still in her seat, grinning away. "And, Peter, you've been doing well in other ways too," the teacher continued. "You haven't been late for school in months. And I can't remember the last time you missed a day of school. Why is this?"

"Uncle," Peter answered simply.

The teacher looked at Heidi again. He knew Peter meant her grandfather, but Heidi just smiled sweetly back at him. After school the teacher went straight over to the pastor and told him how much good Heidi and her grandfather were doing in their little village. Both men agreed it was a happy day for them all when Uncle had decided to live near them for the winter.

From then on, no matter how bad the weather was, Grannie was able to hear the words to one of her favorite church songs every day. After reading just one, though, Peter would say, "No more. Heidi said I only have to read one."

Grannie was glad that Peter had finally learned how to read. But she also looked forward to when the snow would melt and Heidi could visit her again. Somehow it just was not the same whenever Peter read from the songbook. Grannie knew Peter skipped any words he did not know how to say. This meant that sometimes what he read hardly made any sense at all.

"I keep trying to fill in the holes," she told Bridget. "But then I miss what comes next. The songs just don't do me as much good as when Heidi reads them," she said with a sigh.

CHAPTER 20
More Visitors

The winter passed, and soon it was May again. The last snows had melted, and little streams of ice water ran through the new grass. Clear sunlight made everything feel warm. High in the sky the golden hawk circled his mountain, while Heidi ran from one favorite place to another.

She stood looking up at her mountains and listened as the wind blew its way through the fir trees. She lay on the ground and watched all the insects around her. To Heidi, it seemed like the little animals sang, "We're on the mountain! We're on the mountain!" in tune with her own heart. She thought spring had never been so beautiful.

The sounds of a hammer and saw came from Grandfather's shed. Heidi ran there to see why he was so busy. Inside, she saw one new chair standing by the door and Grandfather working on another.

"Oh, I know why you're making those!" she cried. "They're for Clara and Grandmama! They could come any day now! Oh, Grandfather, I can hardly wait!" Heidi danced around the shed and gave Grandfather a big hug.

Just then there was a shrill whistle outside. Heidi ran to meet Peter and the goats. Soon she was surrounded by all her old friends. The animals pushed against her, each wanting to be the closest. Peter handed her a letter. "Here you are," he said.

"Did the postman give this to you?" she asked him. When he shook his head no, she asked, "Where did you find it then?"

Peter said, "In my bag." The truth was, the postman had given it to him the day before, but he had put his bread and cheese on top and forgotten all about it until lunchtime, when he saw it underneath the crumbs.

Heidi took the letter and ran to Grandfather. "Look! I have a letter from Clara! Do you want to hear what she's written?" Grandfather sat down, and Peter stood in the doorway. Heidi was very excited to hear what the people from Frankfurt had to say.

"'Dear Heidi,

"'We are all packed and ready to leave in two or three days. Father has had to go to Paris, so it will just be Grandmama and myself. The doctor comes every day and keeps telling us to hurry up and go. He came to see me often during the winter and used to say no one could help getting better in your wonderful mountains.

"'I cannot wait to see you. Once we leave it will still be another six weeks before we see you since I must go to another place in Switzerland for some special treatment. Sam will come that far with us, but Miss Meyer says she is scared of the mountains.

"'I can hardly wait to see you!

"'Grandmama sends you her love.

"'See you soon, Clara.'"

When Heidi finished the letter, Peter walked back to his goats without saying a word. He was so upset by what he had heard, he swished his stick through the air as hard as he could. The goats saw his stick and ran all the way down the mountain. The news of more visitors from Frankfurt was not good news to him.

Heidi, though, could not wait to tell Grannie all about it. Now that the snow had melted, she could go down the mountain by herself.

Early the next morning she ran down the slope. The wind sang against her back, and soon she was there. When she entered the little hut, she saw Grannie in her usual corner, spinning. But Grannie was not happy. Peter had come home the evening before looking angry and upset. He had told them about Clara's letter, and all night Grannie had worried that the people from Frankfurt would come and take Heidi away again.

Heidi sat down on her little stool and began to chatter away about the letter. She became more and more excited. Then all of a sudden she stopped right in the middle of a word. "Grannie, what's the matter? Aren't you happy about them coming?"

"Yes, yes," Grannie said, trying to smile. "I'm glad for your sake, because it makes you so happy."

"But there's still something wrong. What is it, Grannie?"

Grannie felt sure the people from Frankfurt wanted to have Heidi back, now that she was all better. That was what bothered her, but she wished she had not let Heidi see it. On the other hand, the child was so tenderhearted, she might say no to going away, and that might not be right. Grannie was very confused. To stop Heidi from finding out why she was upset, Grannie said, "I know what would make me happy again. Please read me the song about the storm clouds in the sky."

By now Heidi knew the old songbook very well. She soon found the one Grannie wanted and began to read in a clear voice:

"'Though the storm clouds gather,
God, your heavenly Father,
Gives you peace inside.
Nothing shall bother you,
If God keeps and blesses you,
Lasting joy lives by your side.'"

"I needed to hear that again," Grannie said. The worried look had left her face.

It was almost evening when Heidi went home. The stars came twinkling out one by one as she climbed up to the hut. Each one seemed to shout "Hello!" with its bright white light. She stopped a few times to say a little prayer of thanks. When she reached the hut, she found Grandfather also looking at the stars. Together they went into the cabin.

For the next six weeks the sun shone down every day. Morning after morning Grandfather looked outside and was amazed. "This is our warmest spring ever. There will be more grass and flowers than usual, and Peter will have to watch out that the goats don't get too fat."

Now that it was summer, the days grew longer and the sunshine that much warmer. Just as Grandfather had predicted, thousands of flowers covered the mountain. They filled the air with sweetness.

One morning Heidi came out of the cabin after doing her housework. She wanted to peek again at some blue flowers under the fir trees. The sunlight seemed to dance in front of her feet. No sooner had she reached the corner of the hut, though, when she gave a shout which brought Grandfather running out of the shed. "Grandfather, come and look! Come and look!" She bounced up and down, clapping her hands with excitement.

Grandfather looked down the slope and saw an amazing sight. There was a little parade winding its way up the mountain! Two men carried a chair on long poles between them. In the chair sat a girl, very carefully wrapped in blankets. Behind them walked a man leading a horse. And on the horse sat a lady. At the end of the parade walked two more men, one pushing an empty wheelchair and the other carrying a huge basket of blankets.

"They've come! They've come!" Heidi shouted, jumping up and down with delight. And sure enough, it was the long-expected group from Frankfurt. As they came near the cabin, the chair-carriers set Clara down on the ground. Heidi ran as fast as she could to Clara, throwing her arms around her. When Grandmama was helped off the horse, Heidi hugged her too.

Grandmama turned to Heidi's grandfather, who walked toward her with a smile of welcome on his face. They had heard so much about each other. They were more like old friends than people who had never seen each other.

75

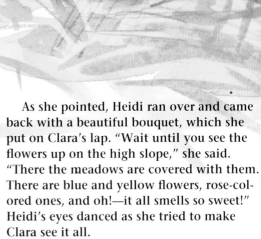

"My dear Uncle!" Grandmama said. "What a beautiful place to live! I cannot think of anything more lovely. This place is fit for a king! And my little friend Heidi looks so well, like a June rose." Grandmama stroked Heidi's fresh pink cheeks lovingly. "It's all so wonderful, I don't know where to look first. What do you think of it, Clara?"

Clara had never seen or dreamed of anything like it. "It's heavenly," she sighed. "Oh, Grandmama, I wish I could stay here forever!"

Grandfather crossed over to Clara. "Would it be all right if I carried you to your usual chair? You'd feel better there, I'm sure. This one must be quite hard." Without another word, he lifted her up in his strong arms and set her gently in the wheelchair. He had covered it with some of the blankets from the basket. Then he covered her with more blankets.

Grandmama watched him with astonishment. "My dear Uncle," she said, "if I knew where you learned how to take care of the sick like that, I would send all the nurses I know to the same place. How have you learned to be so gentle?"

"From experience, not in any school," he said as a shadow crossed his face. Although he said nothing, Grandfather's thoughts traveled back to the time when he had been a soldier and had brought his captain off the battlefield. The captain had been so badly wounded, he spent the rest of his days in bed, hardly able to move. No one but Grandfather was allowed near him, and he had taken care of him until he died.

When Grandfather picked Clara up, he had quite naturally held her in the same gentle way he had held his captain. He knew without having to be told all the little things you can do for sick people which help them feel better.

Clara could not drag her eyes from the scene stretched before her: the fir trees, the mountains, all of it shining in the sun. "Oh, Heidi!" she cried. "If only I could run with you and look more closely at it all. Just look at the pretty red flowers over there."

As she pointed, Heidi ran over and came back with a beautiful bouquet, which she put on Clara's lap. "Wait until you see the flowers up on the high slope," she said. "There the meadows are covered with them. There are blue and yellow flowers, rose-colored ones, and oh!—it all smells so sweet!" Heidi's eyes danced as she tried to make Clara see it all.

"Do you think I could ever get up as high as that, Grandmama?" she asked. "Oh, if only I could walk."

Grandmama patted the little girl's hand and tried to comfort her. As they talked, Grandfather brought out the new chairs, along with plates of bread with roasted cheese on them. The little group sat down to lunch, and everyone said how hungry they were. Grandmama liked the unusual dining room. The view stretched right down the valley and away over the peaks to the blue sky beyond. A gentle breeze rustled in the old fir trees above them.

"I have never enjoyed any meal as much as this one," Grandmama said. "What's this I see? Clara is taking a second piece of toasted cheese?"

"Oh, it's so good. Better than anything I've eaten before," Clara said with a big smile.

76

"Just you keep eating like that. The mountain air makes everything taste good," Grandfather said.

After lunch Grandfather carried Clara into the cabin so she could see the inside of the cabin too. Grandmama was especially pleased to see how cleverly everything had its own place and how clean it all was.

"Is your bed up here, Heidi?" Grandmama asked, as she started up the little ladder. "Oh, how sweet it smells. Why this is a fine, healthy place to sleep." Then Grandfather followed, carrying Clara in his arms and setting her carefully onto Heidi's bed.

"Oh, Heidi, it's even nicer than what I thought. Look, you can sleep and see the stars through the window, can't you?" Clara was so excited, she hardly knew which way to turn.

Grandfather looked at Grandmama. "I've been thinking," he began, "and I hope you won't think I'm being too pushy. But what would you say to leaving your little girl here for a time? I'm sure it wouldn't take her long to grow strong again. You brought so many blankets, we could easily make her a good bed up here. I promise to take good care of her. You'd have no reason to worry."

Grandmama beamed at him. "Oh, you are the kindest man. Yes, of course—that is a fine idea. It had crossed my mind, but I didn't want to ask, knowing how hard it can be to take care of the sick. I can't thank you enough."

Heidi and Clara shouted and clapped their hands. The little group made their way down the ladder, while Heidi danced at the bottom. As Grandmama and Grandfather brought the blankets up to the loft and made up Clara's bed, the two girls chattered away about all they would do in the days to come.

Finally Clara asked Grandmama, "How long can I stay?"

"Well, let's ask Uncle that."

Grandfather said in a serious way, "I would think if she stays four weeks, we'd know whether or not the mountain air is doing Clara any good." The children clapped their hands since this was even longer than what they had hoped for.

77

Later in the afternoon, Grandmama climbed back on the horse, and the men were sent down below with Clara's pole-chair. Grandfather insisted that he lead the horse safely back to the village. Grandmama told Clara she would go back to the city, but would come up and visit several times, bringing whatever Clara might need. She hugged her little granddaughter, adding, "So this isn't good-bye."

Clara's nicest moment of that exciting day came when she and Heidi were in bed in the hayloft. She looked up through the window, straight into the starry sky. "Oh, Heidi," she cried, "it feels like we're riding in a coach right through heaven."

"Do you know why the stars twinkle so brightly at us?" Heidi asked.

"I don't know. Tell me."

"Because they're up in heaven and they know God is taking care of all the people on Earth. They want us to know we shouldn't be afraid since everything is bound to be all right in the end. Now let's say our prayers, Clara."

So the two little girls sat in their hay bed underneath the winking stars and asked God to take care of them and all their friends and family. Then Heidi laid her head on her arm and was asleep in no time.

But Clara lay awake, looking out at the sky, hardly able to close her eyes and shut out the sight of the wonderful stars. At home in Frankfurt she had hardly ever seen them, since the curtains were always shut at night and she never went outside then. Even when her eyes grew heavy, she kept opening them to peek at the two brightest stars which still shone into the room. And when she could not stay awake any longer, the stars seemed to stay with her, even in her dreams.

CHAPTER 21
Clara Begins to Enjoy Life

As the sun rose next morning, Grandfather was outside as usual, quietly watching the mists disappear and the light clouds glow pink. Then he went indoors and climbed up the ladder to the loft. Clara had just opened her eyes and was watching the sunbeams dance on her bed. It had taken her a few moments to remember where she was. Grandfather asked, "Did you sleep well? Do you feel rested this morning?"

"Oh yes," Clara said. "I didn't wake up once during the night."

Grandfather nodded and lifted her in the same gentle way he had the night before. By the time Heidi woke up, Clara was dressed and already downstairs. Heidi jumped out of bed, threw on her clothes, and was down the ladder in a flash.

Grandfather had already brought the wheelchair from the shed and placed it under the fir trees. He carried Clara outside and put her in the chair, then wheeled her into the sunshine. He left the two girls alone for a few minutes to go get some milk from Daisy.

Clara turned this way and that. She had never been outside so early before. And it was all too beautiful for her to believe. She still thought she might be dreaming about heaven. She felt the warm sunshine on her face and hands, and she took deep breaths of the fresh air. "I wish I could stay here forever," she told Heidi.

"Now do you see why I had to come back to Grandfather?" Heidi asked.

At that moment Grandfather returned with two mugs filled with steaming milk. Clara sniffed at hers, not sure if she would like goat's milk. But when she saw how quickly Heidi drank the milk, she did the same. She was surprised that it tasted sweet, but almost like it had cinnamon in it too.

Just then Peter showed up with the goats. He did not look very happy to see Heidi sitting with Clara. Before he could do or say anything, though, Grandfather called him to one side. "Peter, I want you to let Daisy

eat wherever she chooses. Let her go up to the very high pastures to eat the sweet herbs there. She knows what is good for her. Her milk needs to be especially healthy now."

Peter nodded, but as he took the goats up the slope he walked backwards, shaking his stick in the direction of Clara's wheelchair. Then he turned and ran the rest of the way, afraid Grandfather might have seen him.

All that morning the girls sat in the sunshine, chatting away and making plans. They decided they would write Grandmama every day, since she wasn't there with them. Then she would not worry and could feel close to them. Writing their letters took quite some time, though, since Clara kept stopping to take just one more good look around her. She still did not believe how wonderful it all was. A gentle breeze whispered through the trees. The mountain was very still.

The morning passed quickly, and soon Grandfather appeared from the cabin with two steaming bowls of warm milk. He said Clara should sit outside as long as it was light. So they had another lovely picnic. And afterwards the girls picked right up where they had left off in the morning, talking away about all that had happened in the long months since they had last seen each other. The birds in the branches of the fir trees above them twittered and sang, adding their chatter to the sound of the little girls' voices.

Soon the light changed and Peter came down the mountain with the goats. He was still in a bad mood. When Heidi saw he did not mean to stop, she called after him, but Peter just went on, not even waving.

Clara saw Grandfather take Daisy to her stall, and found herself looking forward to the milk she knew he would bring her. "It's strange," she told Heidi. "I've never wanted to eat before. It was always something I had to do. But today I can hardly wait for Grandfather to bring the milk."

"I know what you mean," Heidi said. She remembered the way the good food in Frankfurt used to stick in her throat.

Clara was surprised at herself. This was the first time in her life she had ever spent a whole day outside. She wondered why the high mountain air made her feel so much stronger. When Grandfather brought her milk over, she drank it faster than Heidi and asked for a second cup.

Grandfather smiled and brought them more milk, together with thick slices of bread with butter smeared on top. This was a special treat! That afternoon he had gone to another hut, where they made delicious butter, and brought back a fine big ball of it.

The next few days passed quickly. Then there was a great surprise for the children. Two strong men arrived, each carrying a bed and mattress. Grandmama had sent the girls their own beds! She wanted Heidi to have one in Dörfli during the winter, and the other was to stay at the cabin.

Clara wrote in her letters to Grandmama that she was happy and having fun everyday. Grandfather was so kind, and Heidi was a much happier best friend than she had been in Frankfurt. Every morning Clara woke up and thought to herself again, "Oh, how lovely!"

Grandfather tried every way he knew to help Clara grow stronger. In the afternoons he climbed up to the very highest pasture and picked special sweet herbs. These he gave to Daisy when she came home each night. They made her milk even healthier than it already was. These days Daisy's eyes shone very bright.

After about two weeks Grandfather asked Clara to try standing each morning. "Won't the little one get up for just a minute?" he asked gently. To please him, she did try, but soon gave up because it hurt her. Each day, though, she managed to stand just a little longer than the day before.

There had not been such a beautiful summer on the mountain for many, many years. No one could remember when the sun had shone so much and the flowers bloomed so colorfully. In the evenings the snowfields and rocky peaks were a blaze of purple, pink and gold. But the most beautiful sights of all could only be seen in the high pastures.

Heidi told Clara all about it. One evening in particular, all she could think about was how much she wanted to show Clara the mountain. She ran to Grandfather and cried, "Oh, will you take us up to the pasture tomorrow? Please?"

"All right," Grandfather said. "But first the little one must try her best to stand alone this evening." Heidi ran back to tell Clara the good news, and Clara promised to try hard for Grandfather.

Clara and Heidi went to bed so full of plans for the next day that they agreed to stay awake all night long. But their heads had hardly touched the pillows of their new beds, which were scooted together so they could both look out the window, when they fell asleep. Clara dreamed of meadows brimming over with wildflowers. Heidi saw the hawk croaking away, as if he were calling, "Come, come, come!"

CHAPTER 22
The Unexpected Happens

Grandfather was up with the sun the next morning to see what kind of day it would be. The sun rose in a pink glow, and he knew it would be warm again. He brought the wheelchair to the door of the cabin and went inside to wake up the girls.

Just then Peter arrived with the goats. He had been angry for weeks that Heidi had spent every single day with Clara instead of with him. Grandfather had told him the evening before that both girls would go up with him to the pasture. But he did not like that idea either, since he knew Heidi would still only be spending time with Clara.

When Peter saw the empty wheelchair standing outside the cabin, he glared at it as if it were his worst enemy, the cause of all his troubles. He looked around, saw no one was watching, and heard nothing from inside the cabin. Suddenly he lunged at the chair and shoved it over the cliff. It rolled down, down, down, going faster and faster, until he could not see it any more!

In a flash he ran up the slope with the goats. They could hardly keep up. From the high pasture he could see the chair far, far down below, and it did not look the same as when he had pushed it. He jumped up and down and laughed out loud. "Now that other girl will go away and Heidi can come up here with me again," he thought to himself. He did not know yet just how bad he had been. And he had no idea what this might mean to Clara.

Heidi came out of the cabin. She ran around the shed and came back just as Grandfather carried Clara out. "Heidi, what have you done with the chair?" he asked.

"You said it was in front of the door, but I can't see it anywhere," she said.

Just then a strong gust of wind sent the shed door slamming back against the wall.

"Perhaps the wind has blown it away," Heidi cried. "If it has gone all the way down to Dörfli, we'll never get it back in time to go for our walk."

"If it's gone that far, we'll never get it back at all," Grandfather said. "It will be broken into a thousand pieces." Grandfather set Clara down on a blanket in the sun. Then he went to the edge of the cliff and saw the chair. "That's strange," he thought to himself. "Where the chair has fallen, it would have had to turn a corner around the shed first."

"Oh, this is terrible!" Clara wailed. She was very upset. "Now we can't go up to the pasture. We can't go today, and we'll never get to go! I can't go anywhere without my chair! Oh what shall I do?"

"We're going all right," Grandfather said kindly. "After that, we'll see."

Then he went inside and brought them breakfast. Afterwards, he tucked some blankets around Clara and picked her up. Then off they went, up to the high pasture.

Daisy and Dusky walked on both sides of Heidi. Peter had forgotten to take them with him. But the animals were so happy to be with Heidi, they hardly missed their goat friends. When the little group reached the meadow, they saw the other goats grazing peacefully in little groups, and Peter looked like he was asleep on the ground.

"You there!" Grandfather called. "Why didn't you take my goats with you this morning?"

Peter stood up like a shot. "No one was awake."

"Did you see what happened to Clara's chair?" Grandfather asked.

"What chair?" Peter mumbled. But he would not look Grandfather in the eye.

Grandfather said no more. He found a sunny place and set Clara down, covering her with blankets and making sure she was comfortable. "Now have a good day. I have to go down below to find out about the chair. Don't forget to eat your lunch, and ask Peter to get your milk for you. But make sure he only takes it from Daisy."

Clara looked up. The deep blue sky was empty of clouds. The snowfield on the high cliff across from them sparkled. The two girls sat side by side, as happy as could be. Every now and then one of the goats came to nuzzle them. Snowflake came the most often, wanting to be near Heidi, until one of the others pushed her away. Soon Clara knew all their names. Some came right up to her and rubbed against her shoulders, a sure sign that they trusted her.

Heidi thought about the meadow farther up, where flowers covered the grass by the thousands. She wanted to see if they were as beautiful as last year, but Clara could not go until Grandfather could carry her in the evening. By then the flowers would have closed their petals for the night. She wanted to go so badly, she said, "Would it be all right if I left you alone for a few minutes? Then I could go and look at the flowers farther up. Wait a minute." Heidi picked a handful of grass and set it on Clara's lap. Then she brought Snowflake over. The little goat lay down on the ground and Clara fed her the grass blade by blade.

"Go and look at the flowers for as long as you want," Clara said. "I like sitting here with Snowflake." So Heidi ran off. Clara looked around again. It was all so still. To be here, all by herself, outside, this was something very new for Clara. It gave her a little taste of what it must be like for girls who could walk. She wished more than anything else that she could run around and play like them, instead of always having to sit still and wait for others to help her.

When Heidi reached the flowery meadow, she turned full circle, unable to believe the beauty of it all. Hundreds and thousands of flowers of every color in the rainbow seemed to stretch as far as she could see. And they smelled as sweet as any perfume.

Suddenly she raced back to Clara. "Oh,

you must come too!" she said. "Don't you think I could carry you?"

"No, Heidi." Clara shook her head sadly. "You're smaller than I am. Oh, if only I could walk!"

Heidi looked around. She saw Peter sitting higher up on the slope. He had been sitting there trying to figure out how it had happened that Clara was still there, even after he had ruined her chair. His plan had not worked at all!

"Come down here, Peter," called Heidi.

"Don't want to," he mumbled.

"Oh, but you must. I want you. Quick!"

"Don't want to."

Heidi put her hands on her hips. "If you don't come at once, I'll do something you won't like. I mean it!"

This scared Peter. He didn't think anyone knew what he had done to the chair, but it sounded like Heidi might. To be on the safe side, he did as she said.

Heidi showed him how to stand on one side of Clara while she stood on the other. They held Clara up between them and each gave her an arm to lean on.

This did not work very well, though, since Heidi was much shorter than Peter. Clara stood lopsided, one shoulder higher than the other. She tried moving one foot forward, but pulled it back quickly. "Try putting your foot down and pressing hard," Heidi said. "That might not hurt so much."

"Do you think so?" Clara asked. She tried it and cried, "You're right! That didn't hurt nearly as much!"

"Try again," Heidi said. Clara took a few

more steps, still leaning on the other two children.

"Oh, Heidi! Look at me! I'm walking! I'm walking!"

"Yes—you are, you are! All by yourself! Oh, I wish Grandfather could see this!"

Clara still had to lean on Heidi and Peter. Slowly but surely, though, she made her way toward the meadow. With each step she could feel herself getting steadier on her feet. Heidi was wild with joy.

Soon Clara sat down on the warm grass, surrounded by all the beautiful flowers. She was so deeply touched by all that had happened, and by the lovely colors around her, that she sat silently, just soaking it in. But Heidi could not keep still. She kept running back and forth, dumping loads of flowers on Clara's lap and making her laugh. Peter lay down and fell asleep.

Some time later the goats wandered over to the little group, and Heidi realized it was

time for lunch. She ran back to the first pasture and brought up the bag of food. Peter took some milk from Daisy and gave it to the girls in the two cups Grandfather had packed. Heidi and Clara had plenty of food left over, which they gave to Peter. But although he ate it all, he did not like it as he usually did. He felt like something was eating him up inside, and the food felt heavy.

They had eaten so late that soon after they finished, Grandfather came looking for them. Heidi saw him and raced down to the pasture to be the first to tell him the great news. But he had already guessed what had happened when he saw the children up in the high meadow. He came toward Heidi with a big smile on his face.

Heidi was so excited, she could hardly get the words out, but he knew what she meant, and his face lit up even more. He went over to Clara and said, "Something tried, something won."

He helped her up and put one arm
around her and the other in front so she
could hold onto it. Clara took several sure
steps. Heidi skipped around them, and the
old man looked as though a great happiness
had come to him. After a little while he
scooped Clara up into his arms. "We don't
want to overdo things," he said. "Let's go
home now so you can rest." He could see the
child was tired.

When Peter went down to Dörfli that
night, he noticed a little crowd staring at
something. He wormed his way through
them . . . and saw what was left of Clara's
chair.

"I saw them bring it up when the people
from Frankfurt arrived," said the baker. "It
must have cost a lot of money. How could
such a terrible thing have happened?"

"Uncle said the wind might have blown it
down," a woman said.

"Let's hope he's right," the baker said.
"Or someone will be in big trouble. The man
from Frankfurt is sure to be angry when he
finds out."

Peter had heard enough. He slunk toward
home, looking over his shoulder every now
and then. Any minute he expected to see a
policeman from Frankfurt coming to take
him away to prison. At home, he could not
talk or eat, but went straight to bed and
groaned under the blankets. His mother
thought he must have eaten something bad.

As Clara and Heidi lay in bed that night,

looking at the stars, Heidi said, "I've been
thinking. It's good that God doesn't always
give us just what we're asking for, even
though we think we need something badly.
He always knows what is best for us."

"Why do you say that?" Clara asked.

"When I was in Frankfurt I prayed so
hard to go home right away, but God didn't
let me. I thought He had forgotten me. But
if I had gone home when I wanted to, you
would never have come here and learned
how to walk."

"But that means there's no need to pray,
since God already knows what's best for us,"
Clara said.

"I don't think so," Heidi said. "We should
pray to Him every day to show how we trust
Him and that we know everything comes
from God. If we forget Him, then He might
let us go our own way, and then things go
very wrong. Grandmama taught me that,
and she was right. So now we should thank
Him for making you walk."

"Oh, yes!" Clara cried. "I almost forgot."

The next morning Grandfather suggested
they write Grandmama and ask her to visit
in a week. The children wanted to surprise
her, so they said nothing in their letters
about Clara walking.

The next days were the happiest Clara
had known. Each morning she was able to
walk farther and farther. And all day long
there seemed to be a little song going
through her head: "I am better! I can walk!"

CHAPTER 23
Good-bye for Now!

On the day when Grandmama was due to visit, the girls got up early and sat outside, waiting. Grandfather had a smile on his lips as the girls chattered and laughed.

When Peter came up to get Daisy and Dusky, he hardly said a word to them, but hurried up the mountain. "Grandfather," Heidi asked, "why does Peter have the same look on his face as one of the goats whenever they think they should be spanked?"

"Maybe he thinks he needs a spanking," Grandfather said. Peter ran until he knew Grandfather could not see him any more. Then he stopped and looked behind him again. He was growing more and more worried.

Heidi spent the morning dashing back and forth between Clara and the cabin. She cleaned and polished. She wanted everything to shine for Grandmama. Grandfather went up the mountain and picked some especially pretty blue flowers, then lay them between the fir trees.

At last the children caught sight of the little parade coming up the slope below them. The same man led Grandmama's horse, and another man followed her, carrying a basket on his shoulder. Heidi quickly sat down next to Clara.

When Grandmama came close to the hut, she looked worried. "Clara! Where is your chair? Why are you sitting on the ground where you might catch cold?"

Then Heidi got up, and so did Clara! Both girls walked toward Grandmama. Clara stood straight and tall and, except for a hand on Heidi's shoulder, walked with no problem at all. Grandmama's mouth fell open. She saw the two rosy faces glowing with happiness. Half laughing, almost crying, Grandmama asked one of the men to help her off the horse, then hugged the two girls. But she still could find no words to say.

Then she saw Grandfather, who had happily watched the little scene. She took Clara's arm and together they walked to the old man. "My dear Uncle, how can we ever thank you! Your kind care has done this."

"And God's good sun and His mountain air," he said.

"And don't forget Daisy's milk," Clara laughed. "Grandmama, you would not believe how much of it I drank."

"Your rosy cheeks tell me that. I hardly knew you. You're not thin any more, and I think you've even grown taller! Why, it's a miracle! I must telegram your father at once in Paris and have him come right away. But don't worry, I won't tell him why. You can surprise him like you did me. Uncle, how can I send a telegram from here?"

In answer, Grandfather brought two fingers to his lips and whistled so loud, the sound bounced off the cliffs. Peter knew what that meant and came running to see what Grandfather wanted. He felt sure the policeman from Frankfurt had finally arrived.

When Grandmama gave him a piece of paper and told him to take it to the post office in Dörfli, he breathed a sigh of relief. There was no policeman in sight. He ran down to the village.

Grandfather set the table outside, and the little group sat down to eat another picnic. Grandmama kept saying, "I can hardly believe it!" The girls told her the story from start to finish. Then Grandmama sighed, "It's too good to be true." This kept Clara and Heidi bubbling over with smiles.

over heels, just like the wheelchair, down, down, down! Luckily he was not hurt, but the piece of paper he had been holding blew away and was lost.

Mr. Sesman watched him and shook his head. "I do hope he wasn't hurt," he thought to himself. "But what was he so scared about, I wonder?" A little farther along he saw Peter's hut and knew from Clara's letter that the hut was halfway up the path which led to Heidi's home. So he kept on climbing.

Before long he saw the fir trees, and then the little cabin nestled beneath them. He chuckled to himself about the surprise and wondered what the children's faces would look like when they saw him.

This would not happen, though, since the group at the cabin had already seen him while he was still a long way off. They had hurried to get their own surprise ready. As Clara's father finally reached the cabin, he saw two people walking towards him: a tall blonde girl leaning a little bit on a smaller, dark girl.

He stood still and stared. Then suddenly his eyes filled with tears. The tall girl looked so much like his long-ago dead wife, he thought he might be dreaming.

"Don't you know me, Papa?" Clara cried. "Am I so different?"

Her father ran over to her and held her tightly. "Different!" he cried. "I can't believe this. Is it possible?"

His mother came to his side. "Well, my son, you thought you would surprise us, but it turned out the other way around." She kissed him. "Now let's both go over and show our thanks to the good Uncle who has made all our dreams come true."

Mr. Sesman said, "Oh yes. And to our own little Heidi too." He took her hand in his. "I'm glad to see you looking so much better, my dear, and so happy. It looks like there are roses blooming in your cheeks."

Heidi smiled up at him. She was so glad that it was here, on her mountain, that her friends had found so much happiness. Mr. Sesman walked over to Grandfather and shook his hand over and over, thanking him for helping Clara learn how to walk.

While the two men talked, Grandmama

As it happened, though, Clara's father had been planning a surprise of his own. He had finished his business in Paris early and, without telling anyone, had gone straight over to Switzerland. He wanted to see Clara and had hired a coach to bring him to Dörfli as fast as possible.

From the village, he climbed and climbed. But he was not used to walking so far. He was just beginning to wonder if he had taken the wrong path when he saw a boy running down the mountain toward him. He called out, "You there! Boy!" He was very hot and tired. "Can you tell me if this path leads to the cabin where the old man lives with a child called Heidi, where some people from Frankfurt are staying?"

Peter saw the stranger and thought, "The policeman! Oh no! The policeman from Frankfurt has found me!" He was so scared, he did not watch where he was going, and he tripped. He fell head over heels, head happened to walk over to the fir trees. There she saw her favorite blue flowers nestled between the trees. "Who did this?" she asked out loud.

Just then Peter arrived after climbing back up from where he had fallen. He was hiding around the corner of the shed, afraid to let Grandfather see him since he had lost the paper. When he heard Grandmama, he thought she was talking to him. "I did it. And I'm sorry it got all broken and can't be fixed."

Grandmama stared at Peter. She saw how scared he looked and shook her head.

"There's no reason to be afraid. Come here, please, come sit down." Then she went over to Grandfather and asked, "Is there something wrong with that boy? He is acting very strangely."

Grandfather said, "Oh, there's nothing wrong with him. But he's the 'wind' which blew your granddaughter's chair away, and now he knows he's in trouble."

Grandmama did not think Peter looked like a bad boy. Then Grandfather told her how Peter had not liked it when Clara took up so much of Heidi's time. But he also said Peter had been quite scared during the past week, afraid someone would come from Frankfurt to take him away for being so bad.

"Poor boy, he's punished himself enough already. Of course it was hard for him to see Heidi spending so much time with someone else while he was left all alone. We are all foolish when we are angry."

She crossed over to the trees and sat down

near Peter. "Come here, boy," she said in a friendly voice. "You sent Miss Clara's wheelchair over the cliff so that it smashed into bits, didn't you? And you knew all the time it was wrong, and were waiting to get into trouble, isn't that right?"

Peter could not speak, he felt such a huge lump in his throat. He only nodded. "Well, if you think you can do wrong and no one will know about it, you are making a big mistake," Grandmama continued. "God sees and hears everything. When He sees someone trying to hide what they have done, He stirs up the little watchman we all have living inside us. This little man sleeps until we do something wrong. Then he wakes up and pokes us so we feel bad. Isn't that what has been happening to you lately?" Peter nodded.

"And nothing has turned out as you thought it would, has it? Instead of hurting Clara, you've actually done her good. Without her chair Clara had to learn how to walk. And that's how God brings good out of bad. You who did wrong were the one to suffer. Do you understand, Peter?"

"Yes." Peter finally found his voice. "I won't be bad again." But he was still scared of Clara's father since he thought he was the policeman from Frankfurt.

"Then we won't say any more about it," Grandmama said. "And I would like to give you a present so you can have nice thoughts about the people from Frankfurt. What would you like?"

This was too much for Peter. Here he had thought he would be sent to jail and now he would get a present instead! Peter slowly let a smile creep over his face. Then he remembered something else he had done wrong, and the smile disappeared. "The paper . . . I lost the paper," he said, thinking about how

he had fallen when he saw Clara's father for the first time.

"The paper? Oh, yes. You're a good boy for telling me. Now, what would you like for your present?"

Peter thought and thought. So he wasn't going to get in trouble for losing the paper either! What did he want? There were so many things . . . Then he had an idea. If he asked for money, he could buy whatever he wanted. "A penny!"

Grandmama laughed. "That's hardly anything. But come here." She opened her purse and gave him a handful of coins. "Look, here are as many pennies as weeks in the year. You can have one penny every Sunday."

"Every Sunday forever?" Peter asked, his eyes wide open.

Just then Clara's father came over and laughed. "Yes, Peter, I'll make sure you get a penny a week forever and ever." Then everyone laughed, and Peter was so excited, he

thanked the Sesmans and ran down the mountain to the village.

Then Clara's father turned to Grandfather. He put out his hand and held Grandfather's. "Dear friend, for many years I have not even dared to hope that Clara would walk, and now I have seen the miracle for myself today. Please, is there anything at all I can do to show our thanks?"

Grandfather stood quietly smiling at the happiness he saw in the other man's face. Then he said gently, "I have a share in your joy as well. But I have only one worry. I am an old man, and someday Heidi may be left alone. I only ask that you could see she never has to go and work for strangers to make her living."

Mr. Sesman nodded. "Of course. Why, Heidi is already like a daughter to me. We will make sure she always has enough money to live off of. And I know another man who would like to help take care of her, and that is our good doctor. He is already in Frankfurt, getting ready to move here. He was so happy with you and Heidi last year. So you see, with you and him, Heidi will have two good friends, and I hope you both live for many, many years."

"Amen to that," Grandmama said, shaking Grandfather's hand. Then she put her arm around Heidi and kissed her. "And now, my dear, what about you? What wish would you like to have come true?"

"Oh, I do have a wish," Heidi said softly. "I wish the bed I had in Frankfurt, with its three pillows and the warm blankets, could be given to Grannie so that she won't have to lie with her head down low or wear her beautiful shawl in bed."

"What a good child you are!" Grandmama said. "It's too easy, when we are happy, to forget those who are not so well off. Yes, of course. I will telegraph Miss Meyer in Frankfurt. She will pack up the bed and send it off. Grannie should have it in a day or two."

After that, there was no stopping Heidi, who wanted to run straight down the mountain and tell Grannie the good news. So everyone decided it would be nice to walk together to the village. Then Grandmama could send her telegram right away from the post office.

As they walked, Clara's father said he would like to spend a little more time in Switzerland and then continue his trip since he had more business to do. Now that Clara

90

could walk, he could take her with him, something he had always wanted to do. It was hard for Clara, because she did not want to leave the mountains, but when her father promised they would come and visit every summer, that made her and Heidi feel a little better.

Once they reached Grannie's hut, Heidi ran in and told Grannie all about the bed. But Grannie did not look very happy. "Grannie, don't you want the bed?" Heidi asked softly.

"Of course, child. And Mrs. Sesman is very kind. I should be glad you're going with her, but I think I shall die without you." Grannie still thought the people from Frankfurt had come to take Heidi away.

"What's this I hear?" Grandmama walked over to Grannie and said kindly, "No, that won't happen again. Heidi stays here with you. When we want to see Heidi, we will come here. And we'll come every summer to give thanks for our Clara's wonderful miracle."

Grannie's face lit up, and she held onto Grandmama's hand, hardly able to speak. Then she hugged Heidi again.

"Oh, hasn't everything turned out fine?" Heidi cried.

"Yes, child. I didn't know there were such good people in the world. It makes me trust in God to know they would bother with a poor old thing like me."

"We are all poor in God's sight," Grandmama said. "We all need His care. And now we must say good-bye for now. But as I said, we shall be back next year, and you should be getting the bed in a few days." Grandmama shook hands warmly with Grannie, while Grannie thanked her again and again.

The girls cried when they finally had to say good-bye to each other in Dörfli. Clara's father kept telling them, "It's only a year . . . We'll come back every summer." Then they were gone, and Grandfather and Heidi walked up the mountain alone. They had both seen such wonderful things happen that day, there were no words to describe how good they felt inside.

A few days later the bed arrived, and when it was put up, Grannie slipped into it and slept soundly all night. Kind Grandmama had also sent a box full of warm clothes for Grannie.

But there was more. A few weeks later the good doctor came back to Dörfli. He and Grandfather bought the old house where Grandfather and Heidi had stayed during the winter. Then together they fixed up all the rooms, so the doctor could live in one half and Grandfather and Heidi in the other. During the summers, though, they would still stay in the cabin on the mountain.

One day the two men stood watching the workmen make repairs on their house, and the doctor took Grandfather's arm. "I think we both love dear little Heidi the same way. I wonder, would you please let me help take care of her too? It would warm my heart to know she would be with me in my old age. You know, she's like my own dear daughter was, and I shall leave everything I have to her when I die."

Grandfather said nothing, but took the doctor's hand, and they both understood how the other felt.

Just about the same time, Heidi sat on her stool in Grannie's hut. She was reading to Grannie when Bridget came running in to tell them she had only just heard that Peter would get a penny a week for the rest of his life. Heidi grinned. Grannie asked Heidi to read another song from her book. Then Grannie said, "If I spend every moment for the rest of my days thanking God for all His goodness to us, that still would not be enough." And everyone agreed.

THE NEW HANDBOOK
OF HANDGUNNING

ABOUT THE AUTHOR:

Paul B. Weston is Professor of Criminal Justice at California State University at Sacramento. He is a retired Deputy Chief Inspector for the New York City Police Department. Professor Weston served as gunnery specialist with the United States Navy during World War II and is a former shooting member of the New York National Guard and New York City Police Department pistol teams. He has published widely in the areas of police science and shooting.

THE NEW HANDBOOK
OF HANDGUNNING

By

PAUL B. WESTON

Deputy Chief Inspector (Ret.)
New York City Police Department
Professor
Department of Criminal Justice
California State University
Sacramento, California

Drawings by

Edith Schmidt

Photographs by

Donald Klopp

CHARLES C THOMAS • PUBLISHER
Springfield • Illinois • U.S.A.

Published and Distributed Throughout the World by

CHARLES C THOMAS ● PUBLISHER

Bannerstone House

301-327 East Lawrence Avenue, Springfield, Illinois, U.S.A.

© *1980, by* CHARLES C THOMAS ● PUBLISHER

ISBN 0-398-04092-3

Library of Congress Catalog Card Number: 80-13745

With THOMAS BOOKS *careful attention is given to all details of
manufacturing and design. It is the Publisher's desire to present books that
are satisfactory as to their physical qualities and artistic possibilities and
appropriate for their particular use.* THOMAS BOOKS *will be true to those
laws of quality that assure a good name and good will.*

Printed in the United States of America
V-R-1

799.3
W 56h
1980

Library of Congress Cataloging in Publication Data

Weston, Paul B
  The new handbook of handgunning.

  Edition for 1968 published under title: The handbook
of handgunning.
  Bibliography: p.
  Includes index.
  1. Pistol shooting. I. Title.
GV1175.W49   1980   799.3'1   80-13745
ISBN 0-398-04092-3

PREFACE

I WRITE from the study and experience of a half century of handgunning. My first coach was John A. Dietz, former Olympic shooter and world record holder. James E. Amos, a firearms unit instructor of the Federal Bureau of Investigation, developed my interest in combat shooting. Adolph Schuber, captain of the New York City Police Department's pistol team encouraged my interest in competitive shooting. More recently, students at California State University at Sacramento have contributed to my continued interest in handgunning.

I do no more than detail what I have learned in these years. Things that have happened and the friends I have made have all contributed to this body of knowledge. I have enjoyed shooting over the years: instruction, coaching, and competition. I hope and trust that the contents of this book (practices, theories, and concepts) will lead to the equal enjoyment of every reader.

P.B.W.

v

CONTENTS

Other Shooting Books by the Author
    TARGET SHOOTING TODAY (1950)
    COMBAT SHOOTING FOR POLICE (1st Edition, 1967, 2nd
    Edition, 1978)
    THE HANDBOOK OF HANDGUNNING (1968)

THE NEW HANDBOOK
OF HANDGUNNING

Chapter 1

NOMENCLATURE AND FUNCTIONING

THE handgun is a weapon for personal defense. It can be the last resource in a life-threatening situation. Handguns are designed for use in one hand and for quick work at close quarters: never more than fifty to sixty yards and sometimes at arm's length.

Handguns are purchased to defend self, home, and family; for target shooting; and for hunting. They may be purchased by police officers and other law enforcement agents to cope with the hazards of this profession, or they may be issued to them as "safety equipment" necessary to their duties. Military personnel, depending on their rank and assignment, are issued handguns. The type of handgun that is purchased or assigned because of police or military duty varies with the reason for its possession. No one handgun can meet the demands of personal defense, target shooting, hunting, and official duty.

Handguns are either revolvers or pistols. In a revolver, the chambers are separate from the barrel. The cylinder turns as each shot is fired, placing a new chamber in line with the barrel. In a pistol, the single chamber is part of the barrel, and cartridges are placed in the chamber by hand or fed from a magazine containing cartridges.

There are four types of revolvers and pistols:

1. single-action revolvers — must be cocked by hand before each firing
2. double-action revolvers — can be fired single action or as a self-cocking revolver; pulling the trigger cocks and fires this gun
3. auto-loading (automatic) pistols — a shot is fired each time the trigger is pulled fully to the rear, with some of the energy of each fired shot actuating the pistol's mechanism to place a fresh cartridge in firing position. The so-called double-action feature of some automatic pistols does not place a fresh cartridge in firing position, as does the double-

3

action mechanism of a revolver, but does offer a second chance to ignite the primer of a cartridge that misfired.

4. single-shot pistols — only one shot can be fired prior to reloading. The hammer or other firing mechanism is cocked by hand and the trigger pull is quite light, with no perceptible motion. The use of single-shot pistols is primarily (1) in the "free" pistol field of super-accurate competitive shooting; (2) in the field as a hunting weapon, and (3) in metallic silhouette competition. They are termed *pistols* because the chamber is part of the barrel. Two-shot Derringers are really single shot pistols in which the barrels are placed one above the other and the firing mechanism fires one cartridge and then the other.

Handiness is the primary characteristic of handguns. They can be carried within easy reach, and they can be quickly drawn and fired. This first-shot capability is the ultimate in handiness. While modern handguns offer a multifiring capability of from six to eighteen shots, the bottom line of personal defense may be this handiness and the accuracy of the first shot fired.

Nomenclature consists of the names used to describe the various parts of handguns, and the components of cartridges. Functioning describes these parts and components in action. Knowing the various parts of a handgun and the components of cartridges are a prerequisite to understanding the operation of these guns.

Nomenclature

The names of the major parts of a revolver are shown in Figure 1-1A. There is a slight difference between the names used to describe the major parts of a revolver and those of an auto-loading pistol (automatic or auto). The major parts of an automatic pistol are shown in Figure 1-1B.

Barrels are crowned at their muzzle (front end), i.e. rounded to allow bullets to properly exit from the barrel. The *bore* is the inside of the barrel and it contains *lands* and *grooves*. The lands are the portion of the barrel between the grooves. Lands and grooves are cut in a spiral design (left or right) to spin the bullet on its own axis and achieve in-flight stability. It is this

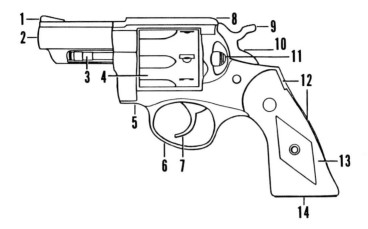

Figure 1-1A. Parts of a revolver.
1. Front sight
2. Barrel (the muzzle is the front end of the barrel)
3. Ejector rod (extractor is at rear end of rod)
4. Cylinder (contains chambers for cartridges)
5. Frame
6. Trigger guard
7. Trigger
8. Rear sight
9. Hammer spur (projecting rear portion of hammer)
10. Hammer (firing pin is located at the front of most hammers; it is sometimes encased in the frame of a gun in front of the hammer)
11. Cylinder latch (opens/locks cylinder)
12. Backstrap (rear portion of grip)
13. Grip (stocks are fastened to each side of this portion of revolver's frame)
14. Butt.

stability that gives rifles greater accuracy than ancient smooth-bore muskets. *Caliber* is the diameter of the barrel measured from land to land. (See Fig. 1-2.)

Barrels in revolvers have a throat to accept the bullet as it is propelled from the chamber of this weapon. Automatic pistols also have a throat, but of lesser dimensions because the rear end of the barrel is the chamber and there is no jump of the bullet from chamber to barrel.

Cartridges used in revolvers have a projecting rim at their base. This rim insures the proper placement of cartridges for

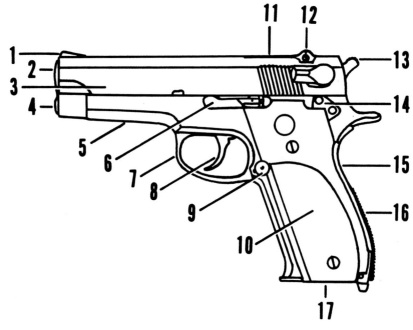

Figure 1-1B. Parts of an automatic pistol.
1. Front sight
2. Barrel
3. Slide (extractor is attached to slide and firing pin is part of the slide assembly)
4. Barrel bushing
5. Receiver (frame)
6. Slide stop
7. Trigger guard
8. Trigger
9. Magazine release
10. Grip (stocks are on each side of grip; grip serves as housing for magazine)
11. Ejection port (ejector is attached to receiver near this opening)
12. Rear sight
13. Hammer (and hammer spur)
14. Safety lever
15. Grip safety
16. Main spring housing
17. Butt — and opening for insertion of magazine

firing in the chamber of a revolver and facilitates their extraction after firing. Rimless cartridges were designed for use in automatic weapons. They stack neatly in magazines and feed

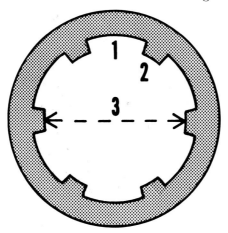

Figure 1-2. The barrel and its rifling: (1) grooves, (2) lands, and (3) caliber.

from magazine to chamber smoothly. A cannelure (groove) just above the base of the cartridge allows the extractor of automatic pistols to draw the cartridge out of the chamber of the pistol. (See Fig. 1-3.)

To allow for the use of a popular cartridge, innovative gunsmiths and designers have adapted automatic pistols to shoot rimmed cartridges by changing the design of magazines and the mechanism for feeding and extracting cartridges. For the same reason, revolvers can be converted to shoot rimless cartridges. Metal or plastic clips hold two, three, or five cartridges, and space is allowed at the rear of the revolver's cylinder for the clip to serve in lieu of a rim to position cartridges and facilitate their extraction.

A rimfire cartridge has its ignition compound inside the outer edge of its folded-over base. A sharp blow (as a firing pin) causes ignition. Small caliber (.22) cartridges are still available in rimfire. The manufacturing process is simple and economical, and these cartridges function well in this caliber.

Centerfire cartridges have a primer set in the middle of the base of the cartridge case. The development of centerfire cartridges resulted from the faulty ignition common in large caliber rimfire cartridges as well as the fact that centerfire primers are not as likely to be struck in handling and cause an accidental ignition. The centerfire primer is sunk below the level of

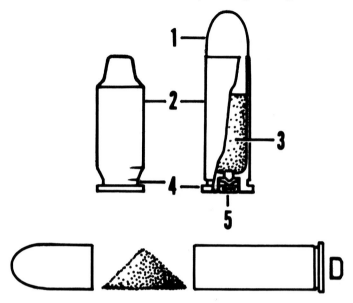

Figure 1-3. Cartridge components. (1) bullet, (2) case, (3) powder, or charge, (4) cannelure of rimless case (left) and rim of standard revolver cartridge (right), and (5) primer, which contains anvil and priming/ignition compound. Bottom: bullet, powder, case, and primer (left to right).

the cartridge base. This position offers the priming compound much better protection than around the rim of the case.

Functioning

Cartridges are loaded in the chambers of a revolver and the cylinder closed and locked in place prior to firing. The front and rear sight, when aligned properly with each other, are guides for pointing (aiming and sighting) the weapon.

To shoot a revolver in single-action fire after it is loaded, the shooter cocks the hammer by thumb pressure all the way to the rear until it comes to rest in the full-cock position. In this loaded-and-cocked position the revolver is fired by pressure on the trigger. In single-action shooting, a pressure of only a few pounds and no perceptible motion will fire the revolver because the cocking of the hammer compresses the main spring, turns the cylinder to place a chamber in firing position, and poises the hammer at the top of its swing.

To shoot a revolver double-action, the shooter puts pressure on the trigger to both cock and release the hammer. The trigger pressure hauls the hammer back through its cocking motion to compress the main spring and releases it in the final stage of this pressure when the hammer has reached the top of its swing backward. This requires a very heavy pressure as the trigger motion is not only opposed to the spring-loaded hammer but also must turn the cylinder to place a chamber in firing position. There is also considerable perceptible motion in the double-action trigger pressure.

When the trigger of a revolver releases the hammer, the hammer swings forward. At the end of its forward motion the firing pin strikes the primer of the cartridge a sharp blow, which compresses the priming compound and ignites it. The resulting spark ignites the powder charge. As the powder burns, gas pressures are generated within the cartridge case. The walls of the revolver's chamber and the breachblock (in the frame of the gun at the rear of the chamber in firing position) contain these pressures until they can only expand by thrusting the bullet forward into the barrel and on its way toward the target.

After a shot is fired, the trigger is released forward and the revolver is ready to fire the next shot. When the weapon is empty, the cylinder is unlocked and swung outward. In this position, finger pressure to the rear on the ejector rod will extract the fired cases.

To shoot an automatic pistol, after it is loaded, the safety is released (moved to fire position) and the trigger pressed to the rear. This is a short motion with little weight — very similar to the single-action trigger pressure of revolvers. At its rearmost position, the trigger mechanism releases the hammer, and the hammer swings forward and drives the firing pin into the primer of the cartridge in firing position.

Once the bullet is on its way to the target, the residual effects of the combustion of the gunpowder activates the slide assembly rearward. This motion extracts and ejects the fired cartridge case, compresses the main and slide (recoil) springs, and cocks the hammer. The slide (recoil) spring returns the slide to battery, and returns the trigger to firing position as it picks up a new cartridge from the magazine and pushes it into firing position. This auto-loading motion does *not* reset the safety: the weapon is ready to fire at the conclusion of this micro second rearward-and-forward motion of the slide assembly.

Revolvers do not have a safety lever built into their functioning mechanism. No device mechanically blocks the hammer from swinging into firing position when sufficient pressure is placed upon the trigger. Modern handguns of responsible manufacturers do have a safety block that prevents the firing pin from contacting a cartridge in firing position when there is no pressure on the trigger — such as when the hammer is falling and the finger is off the trigger or when the hammer is struck a sharp blow, as when the revolver is dropped. However, this is not a true safety that can be moved to safe or fire position.

Maintenance

Handguns can be fired for years and years without requiring more than ordinary care. Care should be taken not to drop any handgun, and no one should use one as a striking weapon.

Open and close a revolver's cylinder with care. Do not release the cylinder latch and then flip the cylinder open with a hand motion; do not slam it inward with a similar motion to close and lock it. Cylinders and their turning motion are a core area of revolver functioning; any abuse will displace it and cause it to shave lead or fail to lock properly. Be certain that the hammer of a revolver is always forward in its position of rest. When the hammer of a revolver is cocked, the main spring of the gun is compressed. If this spring is compressed over a long period of time, it will lose its tension and its functioning will be impaired.

The slide of an automatic pistol is at rest in the forward position. Do not keep this slide locked back for any considerable length of time as the main and recoil springs will be compressed and are likely to lose strength. A magazine for an automatic pistol can be stored in a pistol, but it should be emptied. Magazine springs lose their strength when cartridges are in the magazine (compressing the spring) for any considerable length of time. In any handling of magazines, from feeding cartridges when loading or upon insertion into the pistol, protect the lips (open end) as any deformation causes jams that must be cleared before the weapon can be fired.

In cleaning any handgun, concentration should be in the areas around the chamber and barrel. The residue left by fired cartridges and traces of lead from the bullet must be removed. A secondary concern is to prevent rust. For this type of cleaning, it is not necessary to strip a revolver. These guns were not designed for the field-stripping designed into automatic pistols. The major assemblies of some revolvers can be easily dismantled without tools, but it is a practice that is not necessary as a general rule. Almost all automatic pistols require field-stripping for proper cleaning, but the major assemblies of these guns are easily disassembled for cleaning — and as easily reassembled.

The barrel of a revolver can only be cleaned from the muzzle. For this reason, care must be exercised to keep the cleaning rod from scraping against the barrel's rifling at the muzzle. The barrels of automatic pistols can and should be cleaned from the rear. A few drops of solvent (as Hoppe's No. 9) should be placed on a bristle or brass brush (brass if lead bullets have been fired), the brush attached to a cleaning rod, and the rod pushed through the bore. This is followed by placing a patch (sized to the caliber of the weapon) on the patch-tip of the cleaning rod and running it back and forth through the bore. Successive patches are pushed through the barrel until one of them comes out clean. Then a *lightly* oiled patch is run down the barrel.

The exterior of a revolver or pistol requires no more cleaning than wiping it with a patch soaked in solvent, wiping clean and dry with a dry cloth, and then oiling it with a *lightly* oiled patch.

As the cleaning of a handgun is concluded, care is taken to handle it only by the wooden grips, and to wipe away any trace of finger prints left when closing the cylinder of a revolver or snapping a slide into the forward position. Fingers leave a moisture-laden or promoting residue that leads to rusting.

Handguns should not be stored in a holster or wrapped in

cloth; the leather and cloth tends to retain moisture and leads to rusting.

Police and other law enforcement officers who must carry their handgun in the course of their official duties should make certain that the weapon is properly loaded between the time cleaning is completed and the time of official duties. A very disagreeable surprise is to find out that a service weapon has been unloaded for cleaning, cleaned, but not reloaded for duty. Some officers have carried a gun in this condition for weeks.

Common Faults

Failing to care for a handgun is not usually a common fault, but it does happen. A hasty cleaning of a pistol or revolver is much more common. Either fault can seriously interfere with the functioning of a handgun, particularly when such carelessness causes the cylinder of a revolver or the feeding mechanism (cartridges) of an automatic pistol to malfunction.

Summary

A shooter must learn the names of the major parts of handguns in order to understand their operation, safety precautions, and instructions in which the nomenclature of these guns is used. Revolvers function similarly to automatic pistols, with the trigger and hammer being the primary functional mechanism. Cartridges have a primer, gunpowder charge, and a bullet and are fired by a sharp blow from the handgun's firing pin upon the primer. Handguns require no more than low-level maintenance highlighted by a thorough cleaning after each firing.

Chapter 2

SAFETY

SAFETY rules must dominate all other factors when handling any firearm because of the injury potential of these weapons. It is of extreme importance in handling pistols and revolvers because of the short barrel of these firearms.

Safety rules are established practices that serve as a guide to usage in order to prevent accidents. They are authoritative regulations that have the impact of a command and require a responsive obedience at all times.

Basic Rules for Handgun Safety

1. The only safe weapon is an empty gun, and a weapon is not to be considered as empty until it has been examined carefully and unloaded or found to be empty, and the magazine removed and the chamber checked if an automatic pistol.
2. Never hand a revolver to another person unless it is unloaded and the cylinder open. An automatic pistol must have its magazine out and slide locked in rearward or open position before transfer to another individual. (See Figs. 2-1 and 2-2.)
3. Never lay a loaded handgun down where someone else may pick it up. Always unload a handgun if it is left where someone else may handle it. Keep ammunition in a separate location to safeguard weapon and ammunition from children. Any place of storage should have an adequate lock to prevent intrusion by children or others.
4. Never point a weapon, loaded or empty, in a direction where an accidental discharge may do harm.
5. When a weapon is in use, never place a finger within the trigger guard until ready to fire.
6. Upon arrival at any firing range unload weapon and place it on firing line bench in "safe" (unloaded) condition: cyl-

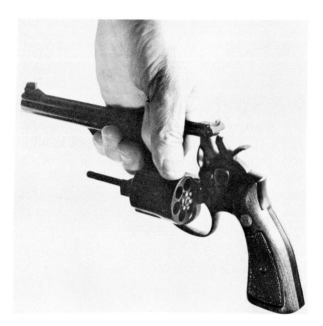

Figure 2-1. The revolver in open or safe position.

Figure 2-2. Automatic pistol in open or safe position.

inder open and swung out (revolvers) or slide locked back and magazine removed from weapon (automatics).

7. Before shooting at any practice session, check to see that the bore is free from dirt or any other obstruction.

8. On a firing range, the muzzle of a handgun is always pointed downrange: toward the targets. In any target practice, be sure the backstop is adequate to stop the bullet; never shoot at a flat or rounded hard surface (or the surface of water).

9. On a firing range (under range officer supervision) *do not:* (a) move up to the firing line until the range officer commands "On the Firing Line." (This command may be prefaced by the names of the shooters or some designation such as "First Relay," "Second Relay"); (b) load until command to load is given by the range officer; (c) cock revolvers or release the safety on automatic pistols until the command "Ready on the Firing Line" is given; (d) fire until the command is given to "Commence Fire."

10. Assume the position of "Raise Pistol" when a handgun has been loaded on the firing range. (See Fig. 2-3.)

11. When firing empties a handgun, shooters should return to

Figure 2-3. "Raise Pistol" position.

the "Raise Pistol" position and await the command "Unload, Make Your Guns Safe."

12. Freeze (gun in aiming position) for at least fifteen seconds if a cartridge fails to fire (misfire). Assume the position of "Raise Pistol" and call for the range officer if a fired shot sounds weak and lacks recoil (bullet may still be in barrel, primer ignition alone is sufficient to move bullet slightly). This malfunction is not common with "factory" ammunition but may happen when "reloads" are used.

13. Do not advance beyond the firing line until the line is "clear" (all guns are unloaded and safe, placed on the bench, and all shooters have stepped back from the firing line) and range officer commands "Advance and Score." While any shooter is downrange, shooters remain in the rear of the firing line, out of reach of the weapons on the firing line bench.

14. Do not shoot alone on a firing range. A companion or other shooters are not only a resource if an accident does occur, but they can also act as a range officer — delivering commands and enforcing reasonable safety rules: range discipline.

15. When back of the firing line (off the line, not temporarily while targets are being scored), all unholstered guns must be unloaded and carried in an apparently unloaded position: (1) revolvers — cylinder held in open position; (2) automatic pistols — slide locked back and magazine removed. Guns carried in this position indicate to range officers and others that they are safe. Snapping guns or dry shooting in back of a firing line violates this rule of safety. When shooting boxes are used, guns may be placed therein with the cylinder closed or the slide forward, but only after they have been unloaded and checked on the firing line. (These shooting boxes are an excellent means of transporting handguns and the necessary equipment for shooting. See Fig. 2-4.)

16. Develop safe habits for handling holstered handguns. A general rule is *not* to remove the weapon from the holster except for good cause. For instance, a holstered weapon can be swung aside when the wearer is using a toilet (as op-

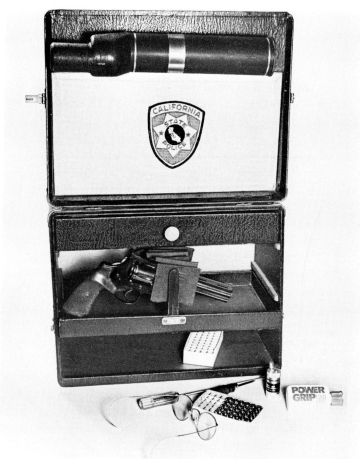

Figure 2-4. The author's shooting box. These boxes hold from three to five handguns in their tray, while a drawer holds shooting equipment (cleaning rod, screwdriver, carbide lamp for blacking sights, cartridges, and a rosin compound to aid in grip retention). A shooting scope to spot shots is mounted on the lid of this box. When lid is opened, it locks in place and serves as a scope mount. Safety shooting (sun) glasses are standard equipment with most shooters. Tempered glass protects the eyes from injury and sun shield lenses reduces the glare of sunlight.

posed to separating the gun from its holster).

17. Remember that handguns have short barrels; keep fingers away from the muzzle of these guns.

18. Remember quick-draw practice is hazardous. It should not

be attempted until a new shooter has learned the how-to of shooting and safe gun handling, and — even then — initial practice should be under the close supervision of a knowledgeable shooter/instructor.

19. Do not holster a cocked revolver.
20. Do not holster an automatic pistol with the safety in "fire" position.
21. Only police duty or similar situations justify holstering a cocked automatic pistol on "safe" with a cartridge in the chamber. Otherwise, these weapons should be holstered with the chamber empty and the magazine loaded. Check carefully with manufacturer's instructions and local handgun experts before holstering an automatic pistol with a double-action feature with the hammer down (forward) and a cartridge in firing position. It can be unsafe.
22. Learn how to "uncock" a revolver for a situation in which the revolver is cocked but the shooter decides not to fire and wishes to return the hammer to its "uncocked" position. To accomplish this, place the thumb on the hammer spur as in cocking, holding the hammer firmly to the rear; press on the trigger until the hammer is released and, relaxing the rearward pressure of the thumb, allow the hammer to move forward about halfway; now release the trigger and take the trigger finger out of the trigger guard; finally, lower the hammer slowly the remainder of the way until it arrives in its forward position.
23. Learn how to clear an automatic pistol malfunction ("jam") safely: (1) keep muzzle down range, (2) remove magazine, (3) activate slide to rear to "clear" malfunction, and (4) when cleared, place gun on bench or reload.
24. Learn about ammunition that can be used safely in the handgun (s). Do not use "P" (indicates above average pressure) cartridges unless the handgun's manufacturer has certified that the use of such extra pressure cartridges is safe in a specific handgun. Do not attempt to use any caliber of cartridge other than the caliber for which a handgun has been designed, and do not — as a general rule — use "reloads" made by others unless certain they were assembled

with care and are safe.

25. Do not place a loaded handgun under a pillow or close to a bed prior to going to sleep. When fear of a nighttime intruder warrants keeping a loaded handgun available, it should be stored in a safe place (protected from others) far enough away from a bed to make certain the sleeper is fully awake by the time this place of storage is reached. [One of the "war stories" told by members of the faculty of the police academy in New York City concerns a police recruit who habitually slept with his loaded service revolver under his pillow. He was awakened (?) one night by a feeling that an intruder was in his bedroom, and in a moment he made out a shadowy shape hunched at the foot of his bed with both hands on the rail of the bed. The officer slid his revolver out from under his pillow, pointed it at the nebulous shape of the intruder, and warned: "Put your hands up." When the intruder failed to heed this warning, the officer repeated it, adding, "Put them up, or I shoot." When the intruder failed to move, the officer fired — and shot off the big toe of his right foot!]

Safe Handling

Many police and military organizations have developed an in-house "Manual of the Pistol" for the safe handling of service pistols or revolvers. This is not a prescribed drill in the handling of weapons (as the military's manual of arms for the rifle) but rather a standard method of handling pistols and revolvers to promote safety. Firing range discipline, enforced by range officers throughout the country, also calls for certain standard movements in response to the commands of the range officer.

The procedures and commands from which a "Manual of the Pistol" can be developed for the safe handling of handguns follow.

1. PRESENT PISTOL. At this command the handgun is drawn from the holster or picked up from a firing line bench, *unloaded* or visually checked to make certain it is unloaded,

and then presented for inspection (range or inspecting officer). Revolvers are presented with butt up and toward the inspector, and with cylinder open. The gun is grasped firmly
in one hand, the index finger is inserted in the cylinder
opening, the thumb is placed against the swung-out cylinder
to hold it in the open position, and the three remaining
fingers are wrapped around the barrel. (See Fig. 2-1.) Automatic pistols are presented with the slide up and locked
back, the muzzle pointed above the head of the inspector.
The trigger finger is outside the trigger guard, and the remaining fingers grasp the grip of the gun. The empty magazine is grasped loosely in the other hand, and presented with
its open end up and toward the inspector — somewhere
between waist level and the level at which the pistol is presented. (See Fig. 2-2.)

2. LOAD OR ON THE FIRING LINE, LOAD. At this command, the
handgun is loaded. Throughout the loading, the muzzle of
the weapon is pointed downrange. Revolvers are loaded by
holding the gun in the palm of the nonshooting hand,
thumb and two middle fingers of this hand holding the

Figure 2-5. Load position for revolvers.

Figure 2-6. Revolver speedloader. These devices, when loaded with six cartridges, speed the loading of revolvers. They are sized to the frame of a revolver and cartridge. The Six Second® reloader shown drops all six cartridges into the chambers of a revolver at the turn of the top knob. In operation, the shooter opens a revolver, holds it in the loading position, lines up one or two cartridges with cylinder holes, then turns the knob to drop all of them into place.

cylinder in swung-out position. Cartridges are inserted one by one with the other hand, the cylinder being rotated as each chamber is loaded. (See Fig. 2-5.) Special loading devices containing six cartridges can be used to speed-load. (See Fig. 2-6.) When fully loaded, the fingers grasping the cylinder push it closed into locked position (when only five cartridges are loaded, the cylinder is closed with the empty chamber under the hammer — aligned with the barrel). The nonshooting hand is used to fit the loaded gun into the shooting hand.

Automatic pistols are loaded by grasping the gun firmly in the shooting hand, with the thumb just under the slide stop and the trigger finger outside the trigger guard. (See Fig. 2-7.) The nonshooting hand then slides the magazine into place with a firm push that makes certain it is properly in place. After this insertion of the magazine, the shooter pushes downward on the slide stop, causing the slide to slap forward and pick up a cartridge from the magazine and place it in the chamber ready to fire. The thumb then moves to the rear to slide the safety lever on safe (or this can be accomplished with the thumb of the nonshooting hand). The nonshooting hand helps in fitting the gun to the shooting hand while the safety is on safe and the trigger finger is outside the trigger guard — and the gun muzzle points downrange.

3. RAISE PISTOL. This is the immediate prefiring position, a

Figure 2-7. Load position for automatic pistols.

position of rest. The revolver or pistol is grasped firmly in the shooting hand, muzzle is up and downrange, elbow is bent (resting comfortably on the hip), trigger finger is outside the trigger guard. (See Fig. 2-3.) It is the position taken subsequent to loading and just prior to the firing command.

4. READY ON THE FIRING LINE. This is a query command. Any shooters not ready should so indicate by raising the non-shooting hand. This command is usually prefaced by: READY ON THE RIGHT; READY ON THE LEFT. When used, this command is the query as to readiness and must be responded to promptly if a shooter is not ready. When these two commands are used, the "Ready on the Firing Line" command is used to indicate that the "Commence Firing" order is to be expected (usually in three seconds). Either "ready" command is the range officer's signal that shooters may now cock their revolvers or take the safety off of automatic pis-

tols, and extend their arm to the shooting position.

5. COMMENCE FIRING. At this command shooters aim at their targets and apply trigger pressure, until they have fired all the cartridges that have been loaded. When the gun is empty, the shooter comes back to the "Raised Pistol" position to indicate all shots have been fired.

6. UNLOAD, MAKE YOUR GUNS SAFE. The unloading procedure reverses the loading process, with the muzzle downrange throughout the unloading. Sometimes an additional command is given to enhance safety: CYLINDERS OUT, MAGAZINES OUT, BENCH YOUR GUNS. Shooters place their unloaded weapons on the firing line bench (muzzle downrange) and step backward a few feet — off the firing line.

7. ADVANCE AND SCORE. When range officers are certain all guns are safe, this command is given to move shooters ahead of the firing line and up to the targets. When finished scoring, shooters return to their positions just behind the firing line, ready to move up into position when they receive the load command, or pick up their weapon and move off the line if firing has been completed.

Common Faults

Faulty obedience to safety rules and unsafe gun handling do not have to be common and should not be, as they can lead to an accident. The disobedience that is most likely to lead to a serious accident may be summed up as follows:

1. not knowing if a handgun is unloaded or loaded
2. pointing a handgun's muzzle in a direction in which accidental discharge could result in injury or death
3. not keeping the trigger finger away from the trigger, except as necessary when intentionally firing the gun (on a firing range, for legal cause, etc.)

Summary

All handgunners should know the basics of safety. Accidents are caused by some human failure. Safety rules are the *com-*

mandments of safety with handguns. The evolution of the "Manual of the Pistol" offers instructions for what to do and when to do it, and range discipline provides for procedures likely to make firing ranges safe places.

Chapter 3

POSITION

$\mathbf{A}$ STABLE shooting position provides the necessary base or foundation for aiming and firing a handgun with accuracy. In combat shooting, or hunting with a handgun, increased stability may be obtained by resting the gun hand on a barricade, the knees, or some other support. The basic position for target practice requires the handgunner to stand without support of any kind.

Muscular strength must be sufficient to stand and hold a pistol at arm's length without apparent effort. It is difficult to relax muscles when they are strained by the weight of the handgun. Exercise may be necessary to condition the body's muscular system to accept this slight strain. The legs, back, shoulders, and arms frequently need strengthening so that a handgun can be held effortlessly in the basic or combat position.

Any muscular tension, other than the normal effort of sighting and aiming at arm's length, will cause movement in the shooter's extended arm or cause a handgun to pull away from its place of aim at the moment of firing. The key to a correct shooting position is controlled muscular relaxation.

The Basic Shooting Position

The basic shooting position is a comfortable standing position adapted to the general physical structure of individual shooters. In this basic position the body is unsupported. The body's weight rests evenly on both feet, the handgun is gripped in one hand at the end of a fully extended arm, and the free (nonshooting) hand is placed at the shooter's side or in a side trousers pocket. (See Fig. 3-1.)

A basic three-step footwork is helpful in securing a comfortable position. (See Fig. 3-2.) The shooter faces the target squarely, with feet together; turns left (right-handed shooters)

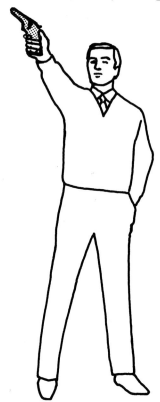

Figure 3-1. Basic shooting position.

about a quarter face or 45 degrees: and then spreads his or her feet about sixteen to eighteen inches apart. Practice this movement several times. It is helpful for shot-to-shot accuracy to drop into the same position every time the handgun is fired, and this three-step method provides a routine for putting the feet in the same place each time the position is assumed.

Some shooters face the target more squarely, others face away from the target more than 45 degrees. When a shooter's feet are placed too close together, some body sway may occur; a spread-eagle position with the feet wide apart may develop massive body tension — unless special exercises have prepared a shooter for this position.

TARGET AREA

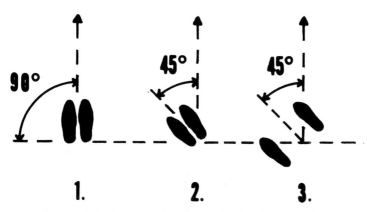

Figure 3-2. Footwork for the basic shooting position.

The shooting arm's shoulder should not be hunched up into a knot of muscular tension. The extension of the shooting arm toward the target is a natural flexing of the arm up and forward. The elbow is neither bent nor locked — the arm is simply extended to its full length without strain. Most shooters can easily observe a bent or locked elbow, but a great many of them cannot tell when they are raising the shoulder unnaturally as the arm is extended into the aiming position. Practice extending the arm up and forward *without raising the shoulder.* (See Fig. 3-3.)

Face and neck tension must be avoided. It may be linked to hunched shoulder or a tendency to bend the head downward as the weapon is extended and aimed. In any event, it tends to tighten arm and shoulder muscles and prevents any real relaxation of the upper body.

Tension in the chest area also puts a stress on the muscles of the upper body. Many shooters, as they assume the position, take several deep breaths or slowly exhale as much air as possible until the diaphragm feels relaxed.

Leaning back from the waist is common and ruins an otherwise good position. It starts with beginners who have difficulty

A

in holding a heavy handgun in the aiming position. A small amount of leaning does not matter, but some shooters lean back a little more as each shot is fired, with increasing body tension building up until the last shot is fired from a bowed position. Others appear to lean back to a greater degree with each range session until the tension created reminds them to straighten up. The best safeguard against becoming a "leaner" is to displace the weight of the body *slightly forward,* toward the balls of the feet, every time the three-step footwork is performed in taking the basic position. It is a case of facing the target, turning left, spreading the legs, and leaning *slightly forward* on the balls of the feet.

When the free arm of a shooter is rested on the hip or the free hand placed in a hip pocket, the tendency to lean backward is aggravated. For this reason, the free arm of a shooter should be placed in a side pants pocket or rested without movement at the side of the shooter. Any movement of this free arm when aiming and firing will cause the body to sway and threaten the

Figure 3-3. Arm extension to shooting position. *A*. "Raise Pistol" position with line of sight to target established. *B*. Arm is extended up into the line of sight without any other movement of the body. Note lack of tension in the face and neck area.

stability of the entire body position.

Tightness in the knee area will tense the entire lower body and must be avoided. An effective procedure for discovering and lessening tension in the knee area is to flex the knees slowly several times just before extending the arm into the aiming position. This is no more than a slight movement, a loosening-up exercise.

Both feet of the shooter are solidly in ground contact, with the weight of the body *slightly* toward the front — on the balls of the feet. Since this is the foundation area of the basic shooting position, any unequal displacement of weight can cause tension in the legs and body.

Once this basic shooting position has been learned, it is safeguarded by repeating a standard procedure of moving into position (footwork). A shooter must "groove" a shooting position. Then it must be taken naturally time after time.

Two-Hand Position

In the two-hand combat position, the left foot is brought forward, and the gun is moved over toward the center of the shooter's body. The triangular support of both arms cuts down on the swing-and-sway motion and permits better control in getting the gun back on target for following shots in rapid fire. (See Fig. 3-4.)

A basic three-step footwork to secure a comfortable position: (1) the shooter faces the target squarely with feet together, (2) spreads feet about sixteen to twenty inches apart, and (3) slides left foot (right-handed shooters) slightly to the rear. (See Fig. 3-5.) Some shooters do not draw this foot back from the square-

Figure 3-4. Two-hand standing position.

on position; others have found it helpful in reducing body sway and promoting the dominance of the shooting arm.

TARGET AREA

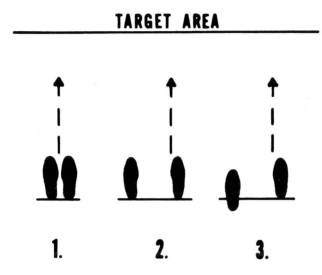

Figure 3-5. Footwork for the two-hand standing position.

Combat Positions

Combat positions are (1) two-hand standing, (2) crouch or hip-shooting, (3) sitting, and (4) prone. In the standing position the gun can be rested against a "barricade" or other support. Each position offers, respectively, greater target reduction. (See Fig. 3-6.) There is a kneeling position, but it is not too supportive or comfortable. It is an alternative, however, between the standing and sitting positions, and offers greater target reduction than the standing position but less stability than the sitting position.

Directed fire (as opposed to aimed fire) is possible from any combat position, but the crouch or hip-shooting position facilitates this type of combat shooting.

In shooting from the hip level, the shooter looks at the target and "throws" the weapon toward it. At very short range, hip-shooting can be fast and accurate within the demands of short-range combat (seven yards).

Figure 3-6. Combat shooting positions. Note target reduction from standing to prone positions.

Directed fire can also be delivered from a modified standing position. This is point-shoulder shooting. The weapon is brought up to shoulder level, just below the eye-to-target line, and pointed at the target without any attempt to use the sights to aim. It is slower in getting off the first shot than hip-shooting, equally fast on following shots, and more accurate than hip-shooting. It is suitable for combat shooting up to fifteen yards.

The Weaver position (after combat champion Jack Weaver) is an ideal all-purpose combat position. It is a two-hand position in which a right-handed shooter advances his or her left side toward the target several inches ahead of the square-on position, and bends both elbows — the left elbow a good deal more than the right. It is a left-foot forward position in which one or both knees can be bent, and it can be used in place of the crouch (hip shooting) or point-shoulder positions. Jack Weaver and other combat shooters have demonstrated that this is a position that facilitates both a quick-draw and a rapid pointing of the gun. Drawing and firing at chest level from this position is only slightly slower than shooting at the hip level from the crouch position; firing at shoulder level is on a par with the standard point-shoulder position; and the handgun's sights can be picked up at eye level for aimed fire (two-hand standing).

Up until the introduction of the Weaver position, most combat shooters extended their arms fully in the belief that bending the elbow created muscular tension and brought the sights too close to the shooter's eyes for effective sight alignment. Now, shooters can test the arm position best suited to their body structure and use whatever they find is a position in which they are comfortable, have support, and can shoot from effectively.

Common Faults

Assuming the same position time and again requires extensive practice and eternal vigilance. Shooters must check their shooting positions time and time again and make certain they have not drifted into some of the more common faults. A minor fault may be difficult to determine solely on the basis of comfort, but the condition that should alert a shooter to body tension is an increase in the shiver-and-shake area when aiming, or the flipping of shots away from where they are carefully aimed. The shooting position must provide a stable platform to aim and fire the handgun.

The areas of the body concerned with the most common faults in the basic shooting position are shown in Figure 3-7.

Combat positions should also be checked in these common fault areas. Despite the fact that many combat positions provide greater support than is possible in any standing position, tension in one or more of the above areas is always possible.

Summary

The shooting position must serve as a stable platform for delivering aimed or directed fire from a handgun. Holding a gun at arm's length, with one or two hands, does require some muscular strength and shooters may need exercise equipment to strengthen body muscles in the arm, shoulder, back, and legs. The basic shooting position is one-hand standing without any body support. Combat positions make use of both hands and, for purposes of target reduction and support, allow shooters to stand (with and without support such as a barricade), crouch, kneel, sit, or stretch out in the prone position.

Tightness or tension in the body's muscular system makes

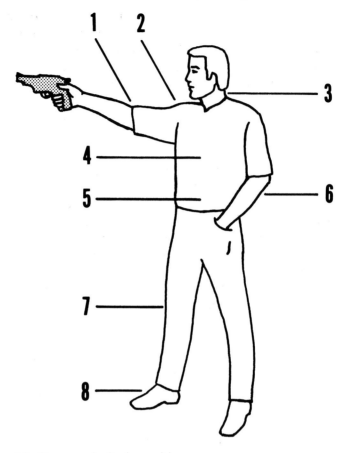

Figure 3-7. Common faults in position.
1. Shooting-arm elbow
2. Shoulder of shooting arm
3. Head (neck and face)
4. Chest (thoracic area)
5. Waist
6. Free (non-shooting) arm
7. Legs and knees
8. Feet

any shooting position less stable: the shooter's arm when extended to aim will move about more than is normal (as when
the body is tensed no more than necessary to grip, aim, and fire
the gun), and erratic and sudden movements away from where

the handgun was aimed at the moment of firing may occur. Body areas in which muscular tension is common are the shooting arm and shoulder, head (neck and face), chest, waist, and legs. Each time a shooting position is taken it should be checked: Is it the *same* position — the stance I think best suited to my body structure? Is it free of muscular tension?

Chapter 4

GRIP

LEARNING to shoot a handgun should start with the first contact with the weapon — picking it up. The best way to grip a handgun is just to shake hands with it. Handguns should be gripped firmly, like a friendly handshake. Do not use a wet fish or bone-crusher pressure, but the firm handshake normal to American adults.

The key to the most desirable grip for an individual is in developing a way of grasping the weapon that can be used again and again, in exactly the same manner. Not only should the gun be grasped with the fingers in the same relationship every time it is fired, but it must also be gripped with a uniform and constant pressure.

First, make certain your handgun is unloaded and that you can point its muzzle in a safe direction.

Second, knowing your handgun is unloaded, pick the gun up, point the muzzle in a safe direction, and shake hands with it. The gun should be so positioned by this hand-shaking procedure that the rear portion of the grip is covered by the palm of your hand and the fleshy base of your thumb. The index (trigger) finger is free, resting outside of the trigger guard; the remaining fingers of the hand are wrapped snugly about the grip of the gun; and the thumb is placed along the side of the weapon at about the same level as the index finger.

Third, examine Figures 4-1 and 4-2. Note how the weapon is fitted into the center of the V of the hand midway in the web between thumb and index finger, the thumb positioned high, the first joint of the index finger resting on the lower portion of the trigger, and the three remaining fingers wrapped firmly around the stock. (Thumb position varies in shooting revolvers: (1) in single action it is high, (2) in double-action it is low.)

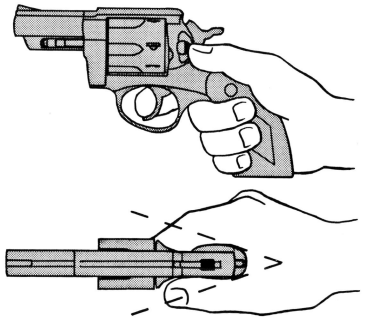

Figure 4-1. Grip: revolver. Top: side view, thumb in high (single action) position. Bottom: top view, gun is placed in the *V* shown.

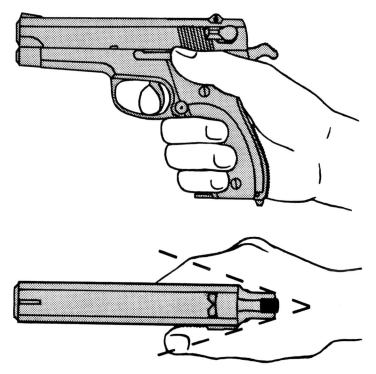

Figure 4-2. Grip: automatic pistol. Centering gun in hand insures a wraparound grip.

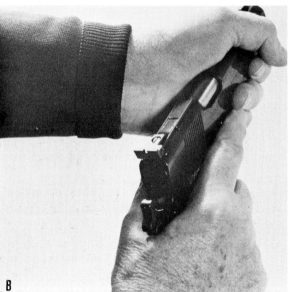

Figure 4-3. Fitting the grip. *A*. In single-action shooting, experienced shooters will cock the hammer before fitting the hand to the grip. For safety, the thumb of the free hand is placed in front of the hammer to guard against any accidental finger contact with the trigger. *B*. In shooting the automatic pistol, slightly more pressure is used in fitting the gun to the hand, but the safety is kept on safe and not moved to fire until the grip has been taken and the shooter is ready to fire.

Fourth, practice taking this grip using the free hand to aid in fitting the gun to your shooting hand, and find a comfortable position for your thumb. (See Fig. 4-3.)

Fifth, practice taking the basic shooting position, fitting the gun to the shooting hand, and extending it to the aiming position. Return to the "Raise Pistol" position and adjust the grip as necessary until the grip feels comfortable in the aiming position.

Lastly, turn your gun hand over slightly and look at your grip from the side. Is it unusually high or low on the grip? If the weapon is an automatic pistol, the grip should be crowding the top rear portion of the pistol's frame where it fits into the base of the *V* of thumb-index finger. If a revolver, the grip should be crowding the space between the rear of the trigger guard and the front of the grip (usually filled in with a grip adaptor or special stocks). The crowding keeps the grip from climbing after each shot as a result of recoil.

The Single-Action Grip

In firing a revolver single-action, the thumb must be taken from its resting place and utilized in cocking the hammer. The high-riding thumb is almost alongside the hammer, developed from the need to cock the hammer with the thumb for each shot when shooting single action. It saves a great deal of time to move the thumb only about a quarter of an inch, from its high position, than to move it an inch or more from the low position.

This motion of cocking a revolver often degenerates into a juggling session in which the basic grip is relaxed and frequently lost entirely. The middle and ring fingers of the hand retain grip pressure, the fleshy ball of the thumb is placed upon the hammer spur with a downward and rearward pressure, a bending of the thumb, until the hammer is cocked, and then the thumb is promptly returned to its resting place. This must be developed, through practice, into a smooth motion in which the hammer is cocked by thumb movement without bending the elbow or twisting the muzzle of the weapon a great deal otf target, and this cocking motion should become an

Figure 4-4. Maintaining grip while cocking hammer. *A.* Three lower fingers of the hand hold the gun as close to aiming position as possible while the thumb moves to cock the hammer. *B.* At full cock, the three lower fingers still grasp the gun firmly.

automatic reflex after firing a shot. (See Fig. 4-4.)

A grip high on a revolver cramps the thumb when cocking the hammer in single-action firing. The vertical grip adjustment can be tested by taking a grip and reaching for the uncocked hammer to make certain the thumb is positioned so that it can be bent without difficulty.

The correct position for the back of a shooter's hand can be *indexed* with the hammer spur. Grip the gun naturally, reach for the hammer (to cock it) with the thumb. The hammer spur should contact the center of the fleshy pad of the first joint of shooter's thumb. (See Fig. 4-5.)

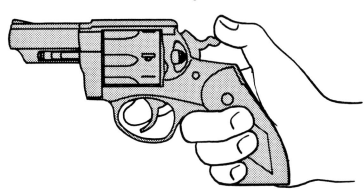

Figure 4-5. Indexing the single-action grip. Shooter tests for "height" of grip by reaching for hammer with thumb. The fleshy portion of the thumb's first joint should be centered on the hammer spur for a smooth cocking motion. Grip can be moved up or down to place thumb in proper position.

The Double-Action Grip

Most shooters, but particularly those with small hands, will find that the hand must be moved slightly to the right of the grip when shooting double action. Most shooters find it helpful to get a good portion of the index finger on the trigger as it is helpful in manipulating the trigger through its cocking-and-firing cycle.

It is highly desirable that a shooter reach down with his or her trigger finger to the lowest possible point on the revolver's trigger. The weight of a double-action trigger pull is about three times that of a single-action trigger pull, and the lower the finger on the trigger, the greater the leverage that can be exerted.

The thumb of the shooting hand is down in a locked position as it is not necessary to cock the hammer with the thumb for each shot. The thumb is locked down on the frame of the gun and held there. The double-action grip is a locked, thumbs-down grip, in which the only thing that moves is the trigger finger of the shooter. (See Fig. 4-6.) This is an excellent grip for pointability in directed fire (combat) shooting and to hold a heavy-caliber handgun on target when fired rapidly.

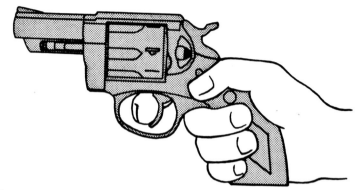

Figure 4-6. Double-action grip. Thumb is in a locked-down position.

The Automatic Pistol Grip

Placing the automatic pistol in the *V* between thumb and index finger of the shooting hand aligns the barrel (central axis of automatic pistols) with the shooting arm: the pistol becomes a natural extension of the shooting arm when extended in the aiming position. In this position, the arm and shoulder of the shooter absorbs the recoil of large-caliber pistols; when the pistol is not centered in the thumb-index finger *V*, the thumb is punished as it takes most of the recoil punch after each shot fired. A collateral and important factor is that this *V*-centered placement establishes a wraparound grip with the thumb and the fingers grasping the gun. The thumb rests firmly along the receiver just above the grip (or at the top of the grip), and the fingers grasping the grip are fully extended and wrapped around it.

The Two-Hand Grip

The two-hand grip was developed for combat shooting as part of the practical training of police officers. The support of the nonshooting hand improves the accuracy of aimed or directed fire, and allows the shooter better control in recovering from the recoil after each shot. The two-hand grip, therefore, not only improves the accuracy of all shots fired, but also improves the rate of fire (time between shots).

In assuming the two-hand grip, the handgun is gripped by the shooting hand in a standard grip, and then — usually as the gun is extended toward the aiming position — the non-shooting hand grasps the base and lower fingers of the shooting hand with sufficient firmness to join the two hands in supporting the gun. (See Fig. 4-7.) Some shooters position the nonshooting hand in a high position, often clamping the thumb into a position over the thumb of the shooting grip. Others position the second hand well forward.

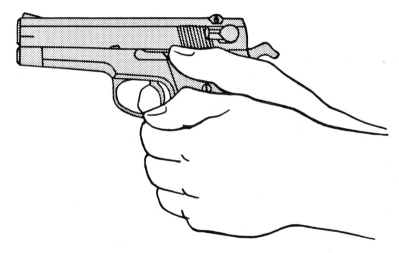

Figure 4-7. Two-hand grip. The grip is generally the same with revolvers and automatic pistols: the free hand supports the shooting hand and strengthens the shooting hand's grip. Shooters can vary the position of the free hand, but when a comfortable and supportive grip is developed, it should not be changed without just cause.

Some handguns have spurs or extensions from the forward portion of their trigger guards to position the nonshooting hand in this forward position.

The exact position of the nonshooting hand in the two-hand grip is at the option of the shooter. Whatever appears to be comfortable and supportive can be developed into an effective grip.

One of the problems of the two-hand grip is that the pressure and support of the one hand leads to a loosening of the basic grip on the weapon by the other hand. The shooting hand grips the gun, and the supporting hand reinforces this one-hand grip — no more.

Uniformity

Novices cannot grip a handgun very tightly; the tension sets up tremors in the hand and arm that ruin any attempt to hold within a suitable aiming area on a target. However, practice will increase the firmness with which a gun can be grasped without setting up tension tremors. The important thing to remember is that the pressure of the grip must be uniform.

Thumb pressure is not a digging-in but a resting of the thumb upon the gun; little finger pressure is subordinated to pressure with the middle and ring fingers. The pressure with which a shooter's thumb rests upon a handgun, or the little finger rests upon the bottom of the grip, depends upon the firmness of the grip. A very firm grip is accompanied by very firm thumb or little finger pressure; a less firm grip by less pressure. There must be a balancing in this relationship of thumb and little finger to basic grip pressure. Unbalanced pressure will flip a handgun away from its aiming area at the moment a shot is fired.

Every opportunity should be taken to fit the gun into the hand with a uniform grip until a "feel" is developed. Uniformity, sought after and achieved, should not be discarded lightly. Gross changes should not be made. Stay with a uniform grip. If there is a need for change, confine it to a minor change, and work at the new grip until it can be taken again and again, in the same manner.

Constancy

Constancy is uniformity in grip pressure, or firmness. The firmness with which the handgun is grasped must be constant as it is aimed and fired.

There is a certain insidiousness about increasing grip pressure as a pistol or revolver is aimed and pressure is put upon the trigger. Possibly it is an attempt to hold the sights in better alignment or just to reduce the shiver-and-shake of the gun or to help in putting pressure on the trigger. It must be guarded against with continual watchfulness, for it ruins the skill potential of any shooter.

As a gun is aimed and fired, many shooters actually increase grip pressure to the point of muscle freezing. As a result, they are unable to put any pressure upon the trigger, squeezing the grip rather than the trigger. Often they force a spasmodic, jerking motion — pretty close to a convulsive muscle spasm — to actuate the trigger.

Another factor requiring a constant grip in handgunning is that the sights cannot be held in careful alignment with each other when a gradually increasing pressure on the grip of a gun sets up tension tremors in the arm of a shooter. This muscular tension often doubles and triples the normal shiver-and-shake area in which a handgun is aimed.

Top accuracy with any handgun demands a constant *vise-*

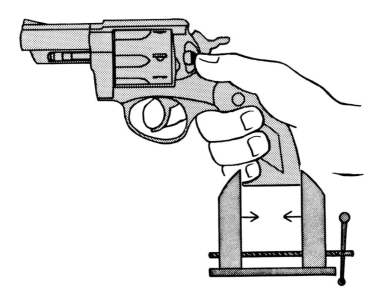

Figure 4-8. Viselike grip. The palm of the hand presses forward while the pressure of the lower three fingers is to the rear — compressing the grip in between. There is no side pressure; the palm of the hand and the fingers serve as the jaws of a vise. As in a vise, the grip pressure is uniform and constant (no change).

like grip. The hand functions in a manner similar to the jaws of a vise: there is a fore-and-aft pressure on the grip that is tightened within the shooter's muscular limits and held firmly at that level — without increasing or decreasing grip pressure. (See Fig. 4-8.)

Custom Grips

Custom grips are popular because they are cut to size to fit a shooter's hand. They make it much easier to hold a revolver for shot-to-shot accuracy as the filler behind the trigger guard prevents the grip from climbing in response to the recoil of fired shots. They also facilitate cocking the hammer, without losing the grip, in single-action fire and tend to guide the fingers to the same place each time the gun is fitted into the shooting hand. Some custom grips have memory grooves for the fingers and palm swells to enhance the uniformity of the grip. (See Fig. 4-9.)

Custom grips can also enlarge the size of the grip, front to

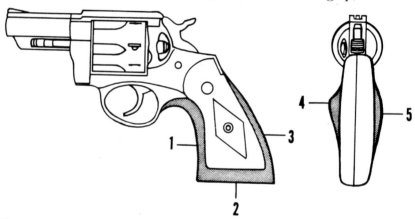

Figure 4-9. Custom grips: (1) filler block behind trigger guard keeps grip from climbing upon recoil, (2) material added at butt helps to control the recoil of large-caliber handguns, (3) covering backstrap adds to overall dimensions of grip — generally restricted to large caliber handguns, (4) thumb rest (low for double-action combat guns, high for single-action weapons), and (5) palm swell that helps to index hand in proper position — sometimes used in place of memory grooves cut for fingers in the forward segment of the grip.

rear and at the bottom of the grip (butt). Thumb rests are suitable for either revolvers or automatic pistols, but the shelf area will be less for combat weapons as it cannot interfere with either holstering the gun or ejecting shells from revolvers. (See Fig. 4-10.)

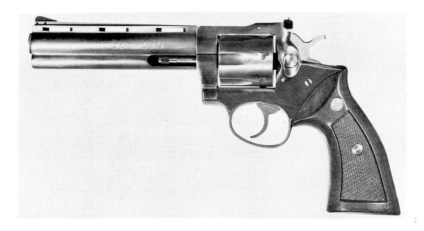

Figure 4-10. Combat custom grips by Ruger. They add to the overall dimensions of the factory grip and offer a modified thumb rest for the down-thumb position in double-action combat shooting. They offer excellent clearance for the use of speedloaders (no wood to interfere with the ejection of empty shells or the insertion of fresh cartridges in a speedloader). The gun shown is a "hybrid" by Bill David (Cake-Davis, West Sacramento, California): a Colt Python barrel is mated to a .357 Ruger Security Six.

Automatic pistols, as a general rule, do not require custom grips. The grip safety or top-rear portion of the grip and the position of the trigger guard usually keeps even heavy-caliber automatic pistols from climbing in the hand due to recoil, but memory grooves, a palm swell, and some thickening of the grip does lead to a more uniform and constant grip with these pistols.

Common Faults

There are a half-dozen common faults that must be guarded against every time a handgun is fired. As a shooter fits a gun into his or her hand, and aims and fires it, there is a subliminal checking of these grip hazards. Actually, it is only a rapid mental review of some of the pitfalls associated with gripping a handgun. It is impossible to say which of the common faults is most likely to be encountered. Some shooters seem to favor certain poor habits; others believe in variety. See Figure 4-11 for these grip hazards.

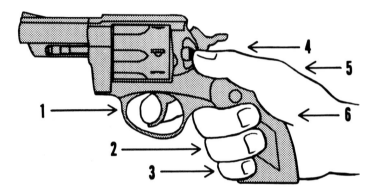

Figure 4-11. The six most common grip hazards

1. Faulty *trigger finger* placement — index finger incorrectly placed on trigger, or finger moved to different positions on the trigger from shot to shot
2. *Fingertips* digging into the stock — a tension builder. Watch for the telltale white half-moons under the fingernails
3. *Pinkie* muscle — too much pressure at the bottom of the grip
4. *Thumb* problems — the thumb not placed in the same position of rest for each shot, or digging in with excessive pressure
5. *Gun not centered in V of grip* — there is some variation possible in centering the gun, and it is often impossible for individuals with small hands to center a gun accurately, but a grip too far to one side or the other is undesirable
6. *Movement of gun* — grip not tight against weapon to prevent upward movement upon recoil.

Summary

The basic characteristics of a good grip are uniformity and an unchanging pressure. Beginning shooters must practice taking a uniform grip, extending the arm up and forward to its full length, to the aiming position, and holding the handgun with a grip pressure that neither diminishes or increases: a constant grip.

The manner of grasping a revolver differs slightly from single-action to double-action, with the position of the thumb moving from a high to a low position, and the trigger finger contact point with the trigger moving from the tip of the trigger finger to the end of its first joint. Custom grips are more likely to be necessary when shooting heavy caliber handguns, particularly revolvers. Faulty placement of fingers and variance in grip pressure sum up the common faults likely to be associated with gripping a handgun correctly.

Chapter 5

SIGHTING

SIGHTING is pointing. The front and rear sights of a handgun, when properly aligned, are the guides for pointing accurately. These sights are in proper alignment when the front sight is centered in the notch of the rear sight, and the top of both sights are level.

The normal movement (shiver-and-shake) of the entire arm will not hurt accuracy because it is controllable, but movement *within* the sight alignment is ruinous. The gun points where it is apparently aimed only when the sights are carefully aligned with each other.

The importance of sight alignment, the two sights in relationship to each other, is easy to demonstrate. Take a short pencil, hold one end and move the other end slightly. Note the distance laterally. Take a longer pencil and do the same thing, notice how the same later movement is increased when a longer pencil is moved. Do the same thing with two fingers. Make a *V* at the base; the fingers are still close together, but they are far apart at their tips. Now, when an error is made in sight alignment when aiming a handgun with a six-inch sight radius (distance between front and rear sights), what is the error when extended to seventy-five feet? Work it out along the lines indicated by the *V* of the fingers. The error in sight alignment is going to be magnified in relationship to the distance to the target by a large amount. Sight alignment errors form an angle of error that increases in mathematical progression along the path of the bullet.

There are five reference points in the sight alignment in handgunning:

1. the rear sight notch
2. the body of the front sight
3. the top of the front sight
4. the top of either side of the rear sight immediately adjacent to the rear sight notch

5. the line of white on either side of the front sight when it is centered in the rear sight.

The fifth relationship above is inherent in the first two. The *line of white* on either side of the front sight when it is placed in the rear sight notch during the aiming-and-firing stage is the means for the effective alignment of the two sights horizontially. Items three and four above are the means for gauging the vertical alignment of the two sights.

Correct sight alignment is summed up as follows: line up the two sights with each other by placing the body of the front sight squarely in the middle of the rear sight notch with the top of the front sight on a level with the top of the rear sight. The line of white on either side of the body of the front sight is exactly the same on both sides when the front sight is aligned correctly. It is continual watchfulness and supervision over the line-of-white dimensions on either side of the front sight that aids a shooter in holding the front sight squarely in the middle of the rear sight notch and serves to guide the top of the front sight to a level with either side of the rear sight notch.

The dimensions of these reference points are important. Generally, it is easier to align a wide (about 1/8 inch) front sight in a generous notch in a rear sight, and it can be done more rapidly. The fat lines of white on either side act as a ready reference. On the other hand, thin lines of white or a narrow front sight, or both, are difficult to hold in focus and often blur into a fuzzy sight picture in which it is difficult or impossible to align the two sights.

The depth of the notch in the rear sight is of some importance — within reasonable limits. A fairly deep notch makes the lines of white in the sight picture somewhat easier to line up, but when it is cut too deep it draws the eyes away from the tops of the two sights and makes it more difficult to hold the vertical alignment.

The Line of Sight

The line of sight is a simple but important concept in handgunning. It is simply a matter of looking at the target and bringing the gun up into this line of sight as the arm is extended to its full length.

The best stance from which to establish a line of sight is the "Raise Pistol" position. This puts the muzzle of the gun down range, about six to eight inches ahead of the shoulder and *below* the line of sight. In this position, the visual concentration is directed toward the target, and the pistol or revolver is moved up and forward until the sights settle in front of the eyes directly on the line of sight. When this up-and-forward movement is executed properly (without any unnecessary movement of the gun) the shooter learns to move into position simply by pointing the gun where he or she is looking. (See Fig. 5-1.)

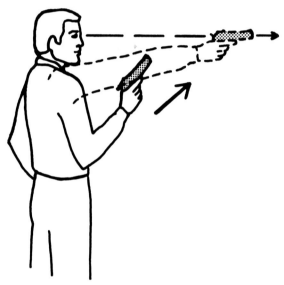

Figure 5-1. Line of sight.

Practice picking up a line of sight and bringing the handgun up to intercept the line. Fit the handgun into the shooting hand and take the correct grip. Take the "Raise Pistol" position. Remember, it is a position of rest; relax. Pick a target area; look at it. Bring the gun up and forward until the shooting arm is fully extended without forcing the elbow to lock and the sights settle into the established line of sight. Be careful not to move the head to meet the gun. Try it from the sitting position, or the standing position. It is the same procedure from any position. It would be the same movement if the weapon was drawn from a holster.

Focusing Eyes in Sight Alignment

The eyes of the shooter should be focused directly upon the handgun sights. The normal shooting distance for pistols and revolvers is never so great that any need exists for a shuttling back and forth of visual concentration between the sights and the target. In handgunning, the sights are the object of visual concentration, and the shooter sees the target in his or her secondary vision — definitely out of focus. This is the reason shooters around the world are told by pistol instructors: "You must see the sights clearly, but it is *not* necessary that your aiming area upon the target be equally clear."

No one can actually focus the eyes on an object at arm's length and an object fifteen to fifty yards distant at the same time. What is usually misconstrued as this double focusing is in reality a rapid shuttling of the eyes back and forth. Some experienced shooters do this, many of them without being aware of it: it does not ruin accuracy; it does not end up by changing the focus of the eyes to either the target alone or the target and the front sight.

Shooters using glasses for reading may need glasses for this distance: eye to end of arm. Prescription shooting glasses can be secured, which will correct any loss of visual acuity.

It is this almost normal, and therefore quite common, tendency to look *through* the sights at the target, or *through* the rear sight notch at the front sight and the target, that created the instructional theme: "Look *at* the sights, not *through* them."

When a shooter looks through the sights, the front sight is outlined clearly against the target, but the rear sight and its notch are blurred and out of focus — and since the basic reference points in sight alignment are the *two* sights, little accuracy is possible. A warning that the viewing is not being concentrated on the two sights occurs when a shooter notices that the sight picture (sights and the lines of white) is indistinct and fuzzy. This is termed "losing the rear sight." (See Fig. 5-2.)

The target acts as an attractive nuisance and draws the eyes of

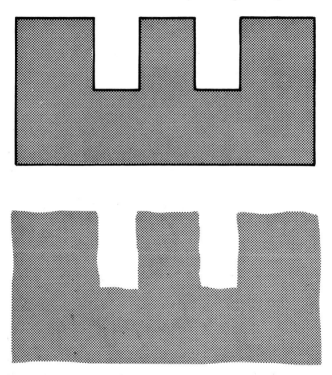

Figure 5-2. Sight alignment. Top: aligned sights in focus. Bottom: aligned sights out of focus — wavy, "hairy."

a shooter. The shooter must look at the target, point the gun, then transfer the primary focus of the eyes to the two sights.

The Master Eye

The stronger of a person's eyes is termed the master eye. It is the eye that should be placed directly behind the gun when aiming. A simple test will identify the master eye. Hold a pencil at arm's length and cover some object with it, using both eyes. Now close one eye. If the pencil does not "move" away from the covered object, then the master eye is open. If it moves away, try closing the other eye.

The recommended basic shooting position stresses the importance of keeping the head erect and steady, and the neck not twisted in any way. The basic position will require slight adjustments for right-handed shooters whose left eye is their master eye or vice versa. The adjustment is to move toward a square-on position to the target so that the aimed handgun can be shifted over slightly in front of the master eye. Similar adjustments are necessary for two-hand shooting.

Binocular Vision

Two-eyes-open sighting is best for combat shooting and less tiring when shooting over a long period. It is not difficult to develop the ability to shoot with both eyes open. This binocular vision aids in aligning the sights as everything is less flat and has dimensions in depth. Shoot if desired with one eye closed, making certain it is not the master eye, but every now and then — after lining up the sights with each other — slowly open the closed eye. If the sights move or get out of focus, close the eye quickly, realign the sights, and repeat the process. Do this exercise an increasing number of times when sighting the gun, and in a short time binocular vision will be achieved — and enjoy shooting with both eyes open.

In case binocular vision cannot be achieved conveniently, shoot with the master eye open. However, the facial and neck muscles should not be twisted into a knot just to keep one eye closed. An otherwise stable and tension-free position can be ruined by unnecessary tension in holding an eyelid shut.

The Grip as a Factor in Sighting

A constant, viselike grip helps to hold the sights in alignment. When the muscles of the hand hold the handgun in a constant grip, the unchanging pressure on the grip aids in holding the sights in alignment with each other. The set of this type of grip keeps the wrist tightened up the necessary amount for a firmness in this area that will also prevent the sights from shaking about in relation to each other.

All shooters must understand why a differing pressure on the handgun's grip from shot to shot, or an increasing pressure as the trigger is pressed, will interfere with holding the sights in alignment with each other. This is also true of the need of a constant (and firm) grip to hold the wrist as an unmoving joint between the hand and arm. Try it; it is self-instructing. Pick up the empty gun (check it), point it in a safe direction (check that, too), and line up the sights with each other. Get a good sight picture. Now squeeze harder on the grip — and watch the sights move out of alignment. Do it again. This time tighten the grip pressure somewhere — possibly dig in with the thumb or little finger — and again sight the gun. Now, note the sights moving about in their alignment. Loosen up the grip so the wrist of the shooting arm feels loose, and *try* to hold the two sights in alignment — it is difficult.

Common Faults

The most common faults in sighting are concerned with sight alignment:

1. top of front sight above top of rear sight (shot goes high)
2. top of front sight below top of rear sight (shot goes low)
3. front sight not in center of rear sight notch; line of white on left is much narrower than on right (shot goes left)

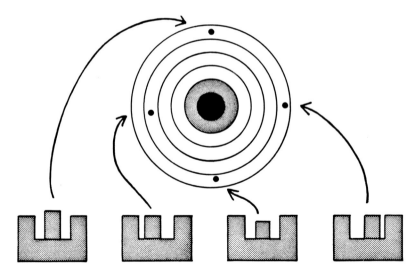

Figure 5-3. Common faults in sighting. Various sights errors cause shots to strike target away from where shooter believed he or she was aiming.

4. front sight not centered in rear sight; line of white on right is much narrower than on left (shot goes right). (See Fig. 5-3.)

Canting, also a common sighting fault, is a twisting of the entire gun to right or left off the horizontal level. It is sometimes linked to poor sight alignment, but otherwise perfectly aligned sights can be twisted sideways. This canting will cause some inaccuracy, but not as much as the inaccuracy resulting from poorly aligned sights. Canting is easily detected by the shooter, a companion on the firing line, a coach, or range officer: it is readily apparent the gun is not level, that it is twisted sideways.

Summary

To sight a handgun is to point it, using the front and rear sights as reference points. For bullets to strike where the gun is pointed these sights must be in perfect alignment with each other; any error in this sighting is multiplied in the distance of gun-to-target. The handgun is brought up into the shooter's line of sight, gun-to-target, prior to aligning the sights. As it enters the line of sight, the shooter focuses on the sights to properly align them and keep them in alignment.

The master eye must be dominant in sighting, and binocular vision can be readily mastered. In this shooting with both eyes open, the master eye will dominate vision. The grip, if too loose or changing in pressure, can make it difficult or impossible to hold sights in alignment.

Common faults range through all possible misalignment of the sights and their "canting" to one side or the other.

Chapter 6

AIMING

AIMING is the movement of the aligned sights to the aiming point. The shooter extends his or her handgun up into the line of sight (eye-to-target), picks up and aligns the sights properly, and — in aiming — moves the gun and its aligned sights to point at the selected point on the target. However, because of the movement of the aligned sights around this aiming point, shooting instructors have long termed it an aiming area.

It is difficult to hold a handgun steady; instructing shooters to hold on an aiming point leads to an attempt to make the gun go off when the aligned sights are hanging precisely on this aiming point. The resultant awareness that the handgun is about to fire leads to poor habits such as jerking (sudden trigger pressure), or flinching and heeling (lunging forward to meet the pushing-back of recoil).

Area aiming recognizes and accepts the fact that any marksman naturally wavers (shivers and shakes, in fact) in aiming a pistol or revolver, and that this wavering motion itself does not cause poor scores, but poor scores will occur when *sudden* trigger finger motion habits develop from attempts to aim the handgun at a point on the target despite this wavering. (See Fig. 6-1.)

Area Aiming

Area aiming is based on the idea that sudden trigger pressure or flinching moves the bullet's point of impact away from where it had been aimed. This away theory has been proved. Any sudden trigger pressure or lunging forward will move the gun *away* from wherever it had been aimed, and this sudden trigger pressure and possible flinching, or both, move the gun much further away from this aiming point than any natural sway.

58

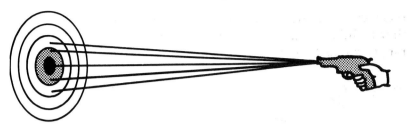

Figure 6-1. Area aiming. The normal waver (shiver and shake) of any shooter holding a handgun at arm's length moves the aimed gun around on a target. This is a normal movement: all shooters move to and fro on the target. The concept of area aiming accepts this movement and calls for concentration of sight alignment and trigger finger control to make certain that shots strike in this normal waver area, and do not strike outside it because of poor sight alignment or trigger motion.

As a shooter gains experience, he or she can be really precise in holding and can fire six to eight shots out of each string of ten with remarkable accuracy by making the gun go off just when it is hanging on an aiming point. Sudden trigger pressures can be put on smoothly most of the time. The lunging forward characteristic of flinching can be controlled most of the time. Most-of-the-time accuracy, however, is not good enough for target shooting, hunting, or self-defense. Shot-after-shot accuracy is essential at all times.

Failure to accept normal gun movement in handgunnery probably resulted from the work of nonshooting artists in illustrating older gun books, military publications, and the charts put out by various gun companies on sighting and aiming. The artists depicted the ideal when they illustrated a set of sights aimed under a bull's-eye without motion of any kind. Most shooters mistakenly assumed the illustrated sight picture was attainable. Actually, to shoot a possible score of 100 on a bull's-eye target only requires the shooter to hold his aligned sights within a three- to five-inch circle (depending on the target), and this does not require the motionless sight picture used in some books and charts.

The beginning shooter cannot hold in a small area because he is not yet accustomed to the weight of the gun at the end of his arm. With normal practice, most shooters will find that their area of aiming becomes less the more they practice, until they stabilize in an area about equal to any demands of firing range, combat, or hunting.

The Hold in Area Aiming

The hold in area aiming is the area of your normal shivering-and-shaking. The area is increased or decreased by the "holding" ability of individual shooters.

Once the shooting arm is extended and the sights are lined up with each other, the gun and arm both settle down into a tight movement. This is the aiming area of your hold. A good hold is *anywhere* in this area. There cannot be any attempt to fire shots only when the gun swings in the center of this area, or the shooter regresses to precision-point aiming (framing shots). Shots fired when the aligned sights are in this area will group within it.

Most handguns can be sighted in to shoot in any area desired. Normal factory procedure is to sight a handgun in to shoot several inches above where it is aimed at twenty-five yards. If the sights can be moved, a good adjustment for area aiming is the *rough center* of the aiming area: bullet's point of impact at twenty-five yards is where the gun is aimed.

In shooting at silhouette targets at longer ranges (50 to 60 yards), the aiming area is raised (neck hold) to compensate for the drop of most revolver bullets at this range. This center hold adjustment of a handgun's sights permit a shooter to use the center of the silhouette target as an aiming area at twenty-five yards or less — and is excellent preparation for combat shooting in life-threatening situations.

Directed Fire

Pointing is aiming and is akin to throwing and punching. In directed fire there is no time to sight and aim, the gun is pointed at the target and fired. Directed fire requires a response to visual cues: the shooter looks at the target and points the gun at this point of visual concentration. The visual concentration makes it possible to point the gun instinctively, so that the point of aim coincides on the target with the line of sight. The weapon is not within the shooter's primary vision — that is reserved for the target. In shooting from the hip (crouch position), the gun can be seen just at the edge of the field of secondary vision. In point-shoulder (standing position) shooting, the gun is just below the line of sight. The shooter does not look at the gun to see where it is pointing. To do so would ruin visual concentration. It is this looking *hard* at the target that makes it possible to point, punch, or throw the muzzle of the gun toward the target so that the bullets strike in the area of visual concentration.

Some shooters find it advantageous to think of this pointing motion as a throwing or punching motion, similar to throwing a ball or a punch at an object. Ideally, if the target was in reach of the outstretched hand, the gun's muzzle would punch a hole in the target in the center of the selected aiming area — the area of visual concentration.

The pointability skill necessary to first-shot accuracy can be learned. Initial directed fire practice should be at short ranges to enable shooters to note the point of impact of each shot fired and to make corrections from shot to shot, until his or her body responds to the visual cues of looking intently at the center of the target. Shooters develop a feel for the pointing position of their gun hands, when a gun is pointed where they are looking. This is a necessity when shooting a handgun without using the sights for aiming.

Common Faults

Worrying about poor shooting (or the desire to do very well) is the major fault in aiming. It leads to framing the shot.

Framing is the attempt to be too precise in aiming, to look for a perfect sight picture (aligned sights immobile on an aiming point). This attempt at perfection is self-defeating unless the shot goes off at *the moment* of perfection, because the natural movement of the shooter's arm will change this pretty picture.

The fault is that most shooters move their guns *away* from this perfect position by trying to make the gun fire before it moves off its aiming point.

The fear of shooting a poor score or the motivation to shoot better is always present. It never leaves the mind of a shooter on the range or in the field. Therefore, the corrective action that safeguards a shooter from falling into the bad habit of framing must be thought about as each and every shot is aimed; otherwise the shooter begins to think he or she is better than the rest of us and can make the gun go off exactly when it is hanging on an aiming point.

A secondary, and fairly common, fault is that shooters fail to realize that aiming errors do not ruin accuracy as long as the sights are kept in alignment. What appears to be a poor shot does not go out to the edges of a target but will hit where aimed — usually in and about the aiming area. (See Fig. 6-2). On the other hand, faulty sight alignment will move the point of impact to the target's outer area or beyond.

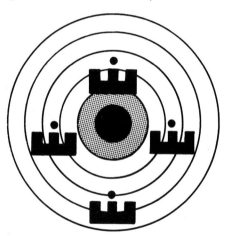

Figure 6-2. Common faults in aiming. Despite position of aligned sights, shots strike where aimed.

A common fault in directed fire from the hip or shoulder level is lack of visual concentration on the target. The pointing factor that makes directed fire reasonably accurate at short range is a response to this visual cue.

Summary

Shooters have to accept that their shiver-and-shake area when aiming will be quite large during the first sessions of aiming practice. However, and this is the important factor in accepting the concept of area aiming, shots fired with the sights correctly aligned will strike this shiver-and-shake area. Later, with practice, this area will diminish and the shots will be grouped closer together. Shots fired when the gun moves out of the aiming area are not as far out as shots fired when the sights are not aligned properly.

The sights of a handgun should be adjusted (fixed sights may require the services of a gunsmith) to hit where aimed at twenty-five yards. At longer ranges, shooters can compensate for bullet drop by using an aiming area just above where they want to hit the target.

Shots can be fired without using the handgun's sights to aim. This is directed fire from hip or shoulder level. Its accuracy is adequate for defensive shooting at short range, but depends on a shooter learning to look at a target — and then point the gun where looking.

Chapter 7

TRIGGER FINGER MOTION

Effective trigger finger motion should be imperceptible, impart steadily increasing pressure to the trigger, and be independent of grip pressure. It is a *smooth* motion without any sudden movement.

Imperceptibility — not knowing the handgun is about to go off — is an absolute necessity to pistol-shooting skill. A steadily increasing trigger pressure achieves a necessary awareness as to just when a handgun is about to fire, and an independent trigger pressure guards against jerking the trigger.

Imperceptibility

Imperceptibility in trigger finger motion does not come about by chance; it is the result of both determination and concentration. First, the shooter must be determined that he or she will not make the gun go off, not be baited by the lure of an aiming point and the apparently possible chance to precision-point aim. Second, shooters must subordinate the desire or wish to fire the shot when it is hanging on a point on the target (framing it) and must make every effort to achieve a steadily increasing trigger pressure, pressure that will release the hammer without the shooter becoming aware of the fact that it is about to be released and will fire the shot. Surprise when the shot goes off is the key idea. Many expert handgunners say imperceptibility results from "wishing" a shot off.

It is imperceptibility in trigger pressure that makes it possible for a shooter to hold the sights of a handgun in alignment with each other without flinching or otherwise moving the gun at the vital moment when the gun is fired and the bullet leaves the barrel.

Steadily Increasing Trigger Pressure

A steadily increasing pressure upon the trigger means a

trigger finger motion that starts and *keeps going* until the shot is fired, without any pause or hesitancy of any kind. It can be rapid or slow, but it is a continuing motion.

Years ago, the old stop-and-go trigger pressure actually built up a marked tendency to jerk the trigger and, of course, to flinch. The old idea of trigger motion was to *stop* the trigger pressure when the handgun moved away from the aiming point — to hold the pressure at the existing level — and then to "go" with a little more pressure when the gun moved back on its aiming point. Sounds good, and it can be accomplished most of the time, but not all of the time. Stop-and-go trigger motion results in a tight group plus several flyers: shots low and left on the target (jerking or flinching) or high and to the right (lunging forward in a healing motion to meet the expected recoil).

Stop-and-go trigger finger motion could be made to pay off in good scores on the paper target range, but it would be worse than useless in combat or hunting, when speed is required in firing the shot and *every* shot must be equally accurate. A stop-and-go trigger pressure takes time, and in combat or in hunting, time is something precious. An attacking criminal or a charging animal would upset any sequence of stop-and-go trigger finger notion. Also, the one or two flyers common with this trigger pressure may be the misses that mean disaster.

A *steadily increasing* trigger motion results in top accuracy with the pistol or revolver for *every* shot fired. Many shooters are often surprised to find out that their time-fire and rapid-fire scores surpass their slow-fire scores. In time and rapid fire, a shooter fires five shots within a stated time limit, usually twenty seconds for time fire and ten seconds for rapid fire. Shooter after shooter has been amazed at the tightness of a group of ten shots fired when there was just no time for stop-and-go trigger finger motion, and when the rapidity of fire demanded a steadily increasing trigger finger motion. It is in this characteristic of time- and rapid-fire shooting that effectiveness of the theory of a steadily increasing trigger motion was born and proved.

Straight-to-the-Rear Trigger Motion

Effective trigger motion demands that the trigger finger move straight to the rear. The viselike grip of the remaining fingers remains constant with no increase or decrease in grip pressure, and there is no pressure away from this straight-to-the-rear motion.

Trigger finger pressure to one side often develops. This may be detected by a creep or unevenness in the trigger motion that results from the trigger being pressed sideways against the uneven surfaces of its housing within the frame of the pistol or revolver. This is readily differentiated from a mechanical defect as it occurs only occasionally, when side pressure is exerted on the trigger.

The best method of controlling any tendency to putting side pressure on the trigger is to concentrate on straight-to-the-rear trigger pressure. Think of a spot on the palm of the shooting hand, just to the rear of the index finger's contact point on the trigger and try to touch this spot at the end of the trigger finger motion. This helps to direct trigger movement toward a point straight to the rear of the inital trigger pressure. (See 7-1.)

Sights may be held in alignment with a slight pressure to either right or left upon the trigger with the index finger. This will ruin accuracy as it flips the gun in a reaction to this pressure during the trigger backslap period just as the hammer

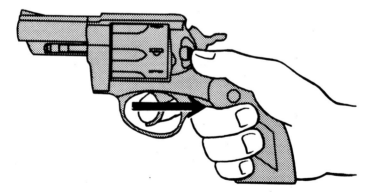

Figure 7-1. Straight-to-the-rear trigger motion.

falls and before the weapon fires, a vital moment for accuracy. Test for this side pressure by lining up the sights a few times. Let them drift out of alignment slightly, then bring them back with a pressure of the index finger to one side or the other on the trigger. Note that it can be done, but now quickly release the side pressure on the trigger while watching the sight alignment. The sights will flip back into misalignment — this is exactly what happens when a gun is fired. Avoid side pressure on the trigger when aligning the sights.

Pacing Trigger Motion

A long time span in applying trigger finger motion enhances the possibility of a shooter becoming impatient and backsliding into making the gun go off with a sudden trigger finger pressure.

Once the ability to fire one shot in slow fire has been achieved, the gun should be held out at arm's length for a second shot. The first effort after recovering from the recoil of the preceding shot is to fight to bring the gun back down on the target. If a revolver is being fired single action, this is when the hammer is cocked. As the gun settles down on the line of sight, the shooter draws the front sight into alignment with the rear sight *anywhere on the target,* and *at the same time* moves the entire gun and hastily aligned sights over and into the aiming area. The initial pressure is placed upon the trigger as the sights fall into proper alignment with each other. Trigger pressure is steadily increased as the sights are more carefully aligned and aimed until the weapon fires without any perception on the part of the shooter — except attention to a continuing of the trigger pressure.

Learning how to recover the aiming picture promptly and using it to pace the time of trigger finger motion are important for all shooting, even slow fire. This is based upon the idea that a concentration upon one task will lead to a conditioning to perform a necessary accompanying and related task.

Actually it is these second shots during initial practice sessions that lead to proper timing for the first shot, or any slow-fire shot. Aiming may be slightly slower on the first shot because the gun must be extended up and into the line of sight, rather than just bounced back after recoil at arm's length. However, the time span in the trigger finger motion of second shots is soon carried over into pacing trigger motion for the first shot.

Speeding up trigger finger motion does *not* mean hurrying a shot. It does mean that the sight alignment must be achieved rapidly, the gun moved quickly into the aiming area and fired without loss of time. However, it is still a careful shot.

A fast-paced trigger motion is invaluable when shooting against the time limits of rapid and time fire, in attempting to knock down an animal in the hunting field, or against the time limit inherent in confrontations with an armed opponent. This learning to time trigger finger motion with the recovery of the aiming picture will also be invaluable in achieving a *cadence* of equal time between shots: the same amount of time to sight and aim each shot — almost a guarantee of shot-to-shot accuracy.

Double-Action Trigger Motion

Trigger motion in double action revolver shooting involves a sweeping movement of the trigger finger to the rear. This may be a straight-through trigger motion, or it can be broken up into two stages.

Shooters using a straight-through trigger control must learn to hold their sights in alignment in an aiming area during *all* of this double-action trigger motion. This requires practice with the empty gun. It is a simple exercise and is nothing more than releasing the trigger finger forward with the same timing in which the trigger had been moved to the rear. It is a matter of lining up the sights, keeping them in alignment while putting on the pressure until the hammer falls, *and holding them in alignment as the trigger is released to its forward position.* Keep the sights in alignment throughout the entire process of putting pressure toward the rear on the trigger to fire the shot, and then releasing the trigger pressure with a forward motion of the trigger finger. This exercise develops a difficult-to-learn ability to hold the sights in alignment despite any slight bump at the moment of hammer release and cartridge ignition.

This bumping motion results from putting about fifteen pounds of pressure on the trigger to cock and release it. Any bump moves the aimed sights just as the gun is about to be fired. Muscular control can be developed to hold this pressure as long as the trigger pressure is straight to the rear and the sights are held in alignment at the moment of hammer release.

Shooters utilizing a two-stage trigger motion take up most of the apparent motion and weight of the trigger in the first motion of the two-stage trigger pull. (See Fig. 7-2.) The second stage of this trigger pressure is very similar to any single-action trigger motion. A slight pressure releases the hammer.

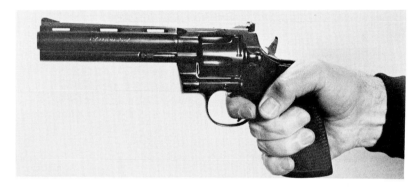

Figure 7-2. Two-stage, double-action trigger finger motion. Hammer is almost at full cock and tip of trigger finger touches pressure point (rear of trigger guard). Gun shown is a Colt Python worked over for double-action: hammer spur cut off and trigger mechanism smoothed and shortened slightly.

Most shooters utilize a "pressure point" to locate the end point of the first stage of this type of trigger pressure. This is a point the tip of the trigger finger touches when it is about two-thirds of the way through this trigger motion. It may be the rear edge of the trigger guard, the frame of the gun just above the rear of the trigger guard, the edge of a built-up grip, or even the tip of the shooter's thumb as it grips the gun. The contact of trigger fingertip with the pressure point serves to warn the shooter to hold the sweeping-back motion, and to start a trigger pressure that will ease into a smooth let-off with the same imperceptibility as in single-action and automatic pistol shooting.

The pressure point also serves to cushion trigger finger pressure at the time the hammer is released and a cartridge is fired. The shooter continues the trigger pressure when the tip of the trigger finger touches the pressure point, allowing the tip of this finger to slide along the pressure point as final pressure is placed upon the trigger. This cushioning of trigger-finger pressure in the second stage of two-stage double-action shooting prevents "bumping" from destroying the aim of the weapon at the vital moment of firing.

A straight-through trigger pressure in double-action revolver shooting may appear to be more difficult than two-stage trigger pressure at first, but it also can be mastered with the same tools: work and concentration. Again, it is a case of developing strength and some discrimination in the trigger finger. The apparent lack of control in the straight-through trigger pressure forces the marksman to work hard in developing a trigger finger motion that will not move the sights out of alignment, either while pressure is being exerted upon the trigger or at the vital moment of hammer release, when the bullet is about to leave the weapon.

Trigger Finger Placement

After the shooter has worked at fitting the gun into his or her hand a few times, place the index finger on the trigger. There are several options: shoving it in so that the base of the finger rests against the side of the gun; bending it outward so that the base of the finger rests upon the trigger; or splitting the difference. It is a matter of preference, but again uniformity is essential. For shot-to-shot accuracy, try to place the same portion of the index finger on the trigger for each shot. The proper placing of the index finger on the trigger is part of a good grip.

There should also be a reaching-down of the index finger as it is placed upon the trigger of a revolver. These triggers are pinned in their upper portion and swivel to the rear. Therefore, the index finger should be placed upon the trigger in a reasonable adjustment to the curve of most revolver triggers, and tending toward the bottom of the curved trigger. In single-action shooting, the proper placement is to use any portion of the first joint of the trigger finger to put pressure on the trigger, with many shooters bending the finger outward to place no more than the tip of the finger in contact with the trigger. In double-action shooting, the tip of the trigger finger can be used, but usually the trigger finger is pushed into the trigger guard and the trigger contacted at about the end of the first joint of the trigger finger.

Trigger Motion: Mechanical Defects

Three common forms of apparent trigger motion exist, and they are all detrimental to achieving effective trigger motion in pistol and revolver shooting. These are mechanical defects that roadblock attempts of a shooter to develop an imperceptible, steadily increasing, and independent trigger motion: (1) slack, (2) creep, and (3) backslap.

TRIGGER SLACK. This is the initial movement of the trigger before pressure is exerted upon the firing mechanism — the "free" movement of the trigger before it actually starts to function. Slack is not usually encountered when shooting a revolver, but it may be found on military-type handguns, such as the Colt .45 automatic pistol. Trigger slack must be taken up promptly and firmly before the actual trigger pressure.

TRIGGER Creep. Any easily perceptible trigger movement is usually termed a creep in the trigger. It may be a slight unevenness in the trigger movement due to roughness of the moving parts of the gun activating the firing mechanism; a definite grinding motion that occurs when minute pieces of grit find their way between these moving metal surfaces; or it may be a skipping motion that occurs when these surfaces become rounded. Any kind of creep makes it almost impossible to achieve the necessary *imperceptibility* of the trigger finger motion.

A trigger creep makes it difficult to hold the sights in alignment, destroys a shooter's ability to concentrate on alignment and trigger motion, and leads to a habit of sudden trigger pressures by the unevenness of its motion.

TRIGGER BACKSLAP. Gunsmiths can correct backslap or excessive trigger movement after the hammer or firing pin is released. Test for backslap by holding the empty gun at "Raise Pistol" position with the thumb of the nonshooting hand holding some pressure on the hammer spur. This pressure is just enough to let the hammer move forward when the trigger releases it, but firm enough to hold it in the just-released position. When the hammer is released, hold it *at that point* with the thumb pressure, and swing back on the trigger. Carefully observe if there is any motion to the trigger *after* it has released the hammer. If more motion than is necessary to release the firing mechanism is detected, the gun has backslap. Excessive backslap has a tendency to speed up trigger finger motion so that a "bump" occurs when the trigger stops its motion. The longer the trigger movement in this backslap, the greater the slapping motion against the gun — and the greater the possibility of disturbing the sight alignment and the aim of the gun at the really vital moment when the bullet is about to leave the barrel.

Common Faults

Applying the correct trigger finger motion is a problem for most novice shooters. The common faults are (1) jerking, (2) flinching, and (3) milking the trigger.

JERKING is the application of sudden pressure to fire the aimed gun. It can happen in single-action revolver shooting, in firing the automatic pistol, or in the final stage of the trigger motion in double-action shooting. This may only be a slight pressure at the end of the trigger motion, but it is usually sufficient to move the aimed pistol or revolver *away* from the aiming area.

Jerking the trigger is a deliberate and intentional act. Instead of a trigger finger motion that steadily increases the pressure until firing occurs, the jerk is a sudden pull on the trigger to *make the gun fire* at the split-second the shooter wants it to fire. This is opposed to the instructional doctrine of wishing them off: put on the pressure, faster or slower but not suddenly, and wait — and be really surprised at the moment the gun fires.

Jerking originates in framing a good sight picture (aligned sights on an aiming point) or in a grip pressure that squeezes the grip as the attempt is made to apply trigger pressure. As explained in Chapter 6, "framing" is an attempt to be too precise and to *make* the gun go off when the shooter thinks best, rather than waiting for the trigger finger motion to be completed. *Freezing* on a trigger describes the plight of a shooter who cannot seem to exert sufficient pressure upon the trigger of a handgun to fire the shot because of misdirecting pressure to the grip. This unfortunate shooter fights against an apparently heavy and abnormal trigger pressure: the trigger seems to require apparent pressures of 20 to 100 pounds. The shooter squeezes the grip with pounds and pounds of pressure, but the trigger finger is immobile. That is, it is motionless until the shooter becomes desperate at the great weight of the trigger and his or her inability to fire the gun, and exerts a sudden and convulsive trigger motion to fire it.

FLINCHING is a punching forward of the shooting hand and arm and the shoulder to meet the expected recoil when a trigger has been jerked. It will move the aimed gun away from where it was aimed a greater distance than jerking. The shooter, in jerking the trigger, is aware the gun will fire and pushes forward to meet the expected recoil. It is a natural human reaction. When the shooter is really surprised at the exact moment of firing, the recoil is over before a shooter can respond by flinching.

One of the problems of using small caliber handguns (.22 caliber) for range firing is that shooters can jerk the trigger and disturb their aim only slightly because the minor recoil of these weapons does not always lead to flinching. However, when these shooters move to the larger centerfire handguns (.38 caliber and up), jerking the trigger leads to flinching to meet the expected heavier recoil.

MILKING the trigger combines sudden trigger pressure with flinching. It is a convulsive tightening on the grip of the gun in double-action shooting at the time of trigger motion. It is often accompanied with an inexplicable throwing down of the gun. Strangely, it is not unlike the movement of the hand used by dairy farmers, or the motion seen in modern milking machines in cow barns. The time of firing a handgun can be perceived quite readily by a shooter milking a trigger in double action, and the strange throwing-down motion is probably a combined punching forward to meet the expected recoil plus some movement from the suddenly increased grip pressure. Milking is more common with the straight-through trigger motion than it is with two-stage trigger motion.

Summary

Trigger finger motion can be slow or rapid, but it should be imperceptible, i.e. give no indication the hammer is about to be released. Contributing to this no-notice factor is the lack of apparent trigger motion in single-action revolver or automatic pistol shooting and, in double-action revolver shooting (despite apparent trigger motion), no indication the hammer is about to be released. Trigger slack is not part of the trigger motion. There is too much apparent motion. Trigger creep or backslap must be corrected as these mechanical faults are apparent in trigger motion. A smooth trigger finger motion demands mechanical perfection of the trigger-hammer mechanism.

Trigger-finger motion must also be steadily increased (as opposed to stop-and-go), independent of grip pressure (no squeezing of the grip as pressure is applied to the trigger), and straight to the rear (avoiding any pressure to one side or the other).

Common faults linked to single-action revolver, automatic pistol, or two-stage double-action trigger-finger motions are jerking and flinching. An equally common fault of the straight-through double-action trigger-finger motion is milking the trigger. These faults move the gun, at the moment of firing, away from where it had been aimed.

Effective trigger finger motion is achieved when the shooter can increase trigger pressure steadily at a slow or fast pace and hold the aligned sights in the aiming area while *waiting* for the gun to fire.

Chapter 8

SELF-STUDY

$\mathbf{A}$NY handgun shooting fault can be corrected. Therefore, any shooter can improve his skill with the pistol or revolver. Corrective action, however, depends upon a shooter's personal skill at the diagnosis of shooting faults. No one can correct a nebulous fault; the cause of poor shooting must be discovered before any attempt to correct or remove the cause is at all possible.

Diagnosis starts with the point of impact of each bullet fired. Targets can be read. They are the communication media by which a shooter learns his or her faults. Each bullet hole will tell its story to the knowledgeable shooter.

Calling Shots

The concept of never firing a *careless* shot must be learned early, when slow fire is attempted for the first time. Care in shooting is learned from calling the shot. To call a shot is to note mentally just where the sights happened to be on target at the moment the weapon fired. Shots are naturally expected to hit the target where aimed, and something is wrong when there is any deviation from the expected point of impact.

The purpose of this system of locating shots on a target is to alert the shooter when bullets are striking *away* from where he or she believed they were aimed at the moment the handgun fired, the spot on target at the last visual image before the shock of recoil disturbed the position of the gun.

For the purpose of calling shots, the target is divided into pie-shaped segments in accordance with the positions of the hours on a clock face. The top segment in the center is known as twelve o'clock, the bottom as six o'clock, and the mid-positions at either side as three and nine o'clock. Finer distinctions can be made by the position of the intervening hours. The second coordinate to position the point of impact of a bullet upon a target in calling shots is the distance away from the center. This can be achieved by using standard measurements, or the scoring rings of the bull's-eye target can be utilized. At hit at three o'clock can either be "2 inches" out, or "8 at three o'clock." (See Fig. 8-1.)

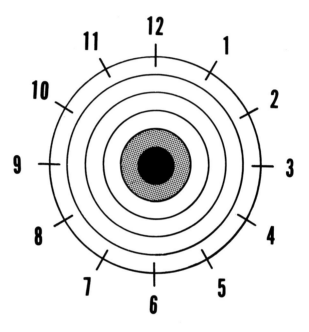

Figure 8-1. Locating point of impact of bullets on target. Clockface figures around target identify target area: high: 12 o'clock, low: 6 o'clock, other areas as indicated.

To call a shot, the shooter notes the expected point of impact immediately after firing a shot or tells a companion, shooting partner, or coach "A 7 at four o'clock" or "Probably a 10 or a 9, just out, at six o'clock." A small replica of a target can be marked with points of impact and the target checked after firing five or ten shots. Scoping — the use of a spotting scope after each shot is fired — simplifies this procedure. The bullet holes are readily visible, and the shooter need not make any written record. This is also true of big-bore handguns as the size of the bullet hole is usually visible without a scope at short handgun ranges.

In any event, if the bullet does strike where the shooter

thought it was aimed at the moment of firing — or within two or three inches of expectations — go to the next shot, attempting to repeat the procedure that made the called shot strike where you called it. On the other hand, if the bullet did not strike in its expected location, an analysis must be made of the causes of failure. First, mentally check out your last sight relationship. Was the front sight squarely in the middle of the rear sight? What was your last visual impression of the lines of white and of the relationship between the tops of the two sights? If your considered review is good, then the fault must rest with trigger finger motion: jerky, aware-of-when-the-gun-was-about-to-fire trigger finger motion.

There can be no other explanation if the shooter has been *careful* and sights are held in good alignment with each other, with a constant grip and tension-free position maintained. The only reasonable conclusion justified is that a sudden pressure on the trigger and possibly flinching, or both, moved the gun away from where it had been aimed. This is the reason for calling the shot: to determine when the shot does not hit where expected.

Shots can be called in time and rapid fire despite the number of shots fired. It is a technique of differentiating between mostly good shots and those that were in the outer limits of a shooter's aiming area when fired. At the end of each string of shots fired, a shooter checks the call for his bad shots. These should be the only shots in the edges of the aiming area.

Shots called good and found to be low on the target result from flinching, a punching forward to meet the expected recoil motion of the handgun. When right-handed shooters flinch, their shots are low and left on the target; left-handed shooters who flinch will push their shots low and to the right.

Shots called good and found to be high on the target are an indication of pushing forward to meet the recoil of the handgun. This flinching motion is termed *heeling* as it results from an awareness the weapon is about to fire, and the shooter pushes forward with the base of the shooting hand's thumb to meet it. Right-handed shooters will heel their shots high and to the right; left-handed shooters high and left.

A good call means that a shooter did observe where the sights were aimed at the moment of firing. This does not mean the call is for a shot in the center of the target, only that the shooter was satisfied he or she did not disturb the aiming process by jerking the trigger and can identify the section of the target where the sights were at the moment of firing.

"Reading the target" allows a shooter to determine if the fault was flinching or heeling. When a good call is made and the point of impact is elsewhere than in the flinching or heeling areas, or the shooter is certain he or she did not jerk the trigger, the fault may be in aligning the sights or "losing" the sight alignment by focusing vision on the target rather than the sights.

The Sixth-Shot Warning

The sixth-shot warning is available only to revolver shooters. It was discovered accidentally. Range practice on bull's-eye targets was common in many police departments. Ten shots were fired at these targets, and since the highest value of one shot was 10, the possible was 100. Shooters were instructed to load five rounds (leaving one chamber empty). In the stress of range firing many police officers lost count of shots fired and continued until the hammer fell on the empty chamber of their revolvers.

Instructors at these ranges found that the action of the shooter in firing this sixth shot was an excellent opportunity to ascertain how the trigger pressure had been applied: whether or not the front sight dipped or flipped at the moment the hammer fell. This noting of sight movements (or movement of the entire gun) when the sixth shot is fired is an alert that the shooter has faulty trigger finger motion and this has resulted in apparent flinching.

The shock of both the "whoom" of firing and the accompanying smack of recoil makes it impossible to distinguish sight (or gun) movements as the revolver is fired. The effect of noise and blast covers up any discernible movement. However, when the hammer falls unexpectedly on an empty chamber, any fault in trigger finger motion is displayed publicly.

The sixth-shot warning is invaluable in detecting jerking and flinching. For this reason, many shooting instructors load a "suspect" shooter's revolver with a mixture of live cartridges

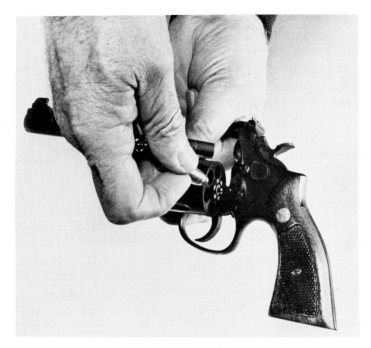

Figure 8-2. "Swiss" loading. Coach or fellow shooter loads revolver with a mixture of live cartridges and empty cases to provide "suspect" shooters with a means of finding out if they are jerking the trigger (hammer falls unexpectedly on empty case as shooter is not aware of the arrangement of live and empty shells; trigger jerking is revealed by sudden movement of gun when hammer fails).

and empty cases. (See Fig. 8-2.)

This actual "Swiss" loading (so-called because the empty cases are holes in the gun's firing pattern) is blocked from the shooter by the instructor's body. The revolver is then handed to the shooter with instruction to aim and fire. The sixth-shot warning occurs whenever the hammer falls on one of the empty cases instead of a live cartridge. The value of this sixth-shot warning is that it is the ultimate in self-study.

The Area Aiming Target

Shooters having problems in detecting and identifying their

faults may find blank targets (no aiming point such as a bull's-eye or x-ring of a silhouette target) helpful. Shooting at a target without any apparent aiming point places emphasis upon focusing on the sights and holding them in alignment and removes the tendency to frame shots when the sights hang on a selected aiming point.

A blank target can be made an area-aiming target by marking out a seven- or eight-inch square with a line of black target pasters or heavy marking pen. This seven- or eight-inch marking sets out the aiming area.

When a shooter can fire all shots into this aiming area, calling each one correctly as to their location, then firing can be resumed on the bull's-eye or silhouette target.

Dry Shooting

Simulated firing using the empty gun has justly earned the term of dry shooting. It is difficult to maintain interest in any activity in which nothing happens. Dry shooting can be interesting if it is planned as a drill in the basic techniques of aiming and of trigger finger motion. Interest can also be heightened if a definite schedule of practice is worked out for each dry-shooting session, and if this routine includes varied forms of shooting: slow, time, and rapid-fire; both types of trigger motion, single- and double-action; both basic and combat positions; and weak-hand practice as well as practice with the strong hand.

If a routine of dry shooting is nothing more than arm exercises, then only the muscular system is developed, but if intelligent attempts are made to diagnose faults as they occur in dry shooting, this practice can be invaluable.

Dry shooting can be made to yield these dividends only when the student-shooter constantly searches for faulty procedures. Both grip and position are checked frequently, and area aiming and trigger finger motion are reviewed every time the handgun is aimed and the trigger is actuated.

Every shot in dry shooting can be a sixth shot for the purpose of checking trigger-finger motion. Did the sights or the gun move *as the hammer fell?* They do move when the trigger is jerked.

Dry shooting practice should be on a 3:1 ratio with range practice: three times the number of shots fired in range practice is the normal limit of a dry-shooting session during the same period. Do not dry shoot too much. Unless dry shooting is checked against range firing to detect the possibility of newly acquired bad habits, it is worthless.

Diagnosing Scores

A beginning shooter must show improvement. Strangely, lack of improvement generally means a regression — lower and lower scores, poorer and poorer marksmanship. It definitely means less enjoyment of shooting sessions.

In keeping track of scores, the student-shooter has a fine opportunity for continual self-evaluation. Just as the precept of never firing a *careless* shot implies continual care in the digital dexterity of handgunning, so too will score-keeping afford a continual scanning of every shot fired.

Keep a record of *all* scores fired. Average weekly and monthly shooting scores. Make an analysis of these averages. Is the general trend upward or downward? What is the relationship of scores fired during slow fire without any time limit to scores fired under the pressure of a time limit? Scores and their trends over a week or more of shooting are symptomatic: good shooting procedures, high scores; poor procedures, low scores.

Coach and Pupil

Two shooters can aid each other in self-study. This is the traditional "coach and pupil" form of instruction. As one of the team shoots (or even dry shoots), the other observes and reports on this observation. They then reverse roles.

By having faults identified, a shooter can correct them. More important, however, is the fact that coaching develops a new awareness in both shooters of their own shooting procedure and possible faults.

The coach's position is not that of spectator; it is to the rear of the shooter, in a position to observe and diagnose shooting faults. It should be behind the shooter, but sufficiently close for safety — to grasp the shooter's elbow and prevent turning, which might move the shooter's gun muzzle from the correct downrange position. Coaches can move up alongside a shooter to "Swiss" load a revolver, but otherwise their position is safely to the rear.

In this position, the shooter can be alerted to a fault between shots. Coaches do not speak to shooters, or move about, while a shooter is aiming and firing.

A particular task of the coach is to outline the pupil's handgun against a reference point and note if the weapon moves when the hammer falls on an empty chamber (sixth shot, or when revolver is loaded partly with empties to facilitate this observation).

When shooters move downrange to examine and score targets, the coach and pupil discuss possible faults as they view and paste the holes in each target.

Common Faults

The major problem in self-study is the tendency to overlook certain faults:

1. shooting without calling shots
2. failing to recognize the sixth-shot warning
3. failing to "read the target"
4. improper "dry shooting" practice
5. poor score-keeping habits.

Failing to utilize the coach and pupil approach to self-study is not a fault, unless failing to utilize available help can be considered a fault. In fact, shooters guilty of the common faults listed above are in desperate need of a coach.

Summary

Shooters must distinguish between bullets that hit where they are called and those that do not. Shots striking where they are called are an indication that a shooter has mastered the concepts of area aiming and trigger finger motion and can move on to remedial action directed at reducing the size of the aiming area. Shots striking *away* from where they have been called indicate the shooter's remedial action must be directed at faults in sight alignment, aiming, or trigger pressure or some combination of such faults.

The sixth-shot warning, area-aiming targets, dry shooting, diagnosing scores, and the coach and pupil method of observation and fault finding are all effective measures to detect improper procedures that ruin the accuracy of shots fired.

Chapter 9

BREATHING

Holding the breath without strain while shooting the handgun is essential to accuracy. At one time many shooters believed the how-to of breathing was immaterial as long as it did not lead to near-strangulation. More recently, emphasis has been on the mechanics of breathing as related to aiming and trigger finger motion.

Breath Adjustment

A handgunner should hold his or her breath without muscular tension when shooting. Adjustment of breathing must be accomplished without any tension in the diaphragm (the partition of muscles and tendons between the chest cavity and the abdominal cavity). Breathing at both inspiration and expiration involves movements of the diaphragm, the rib cage, and the muscles supporting the abdomen. Diaphragmatic tension, however, can be relaxed at expiration.

Take a couple of heavy or deep breaths, and a few light or shallow breaths. Note the considerable tension at inspiration during heavy breathing, how the entire chest-abdomen area seems tight when the lungs are bursting-full of air. Note the completely opposite picture, the fine feeling of relaxation, at expiration.

Now take a normal or slightly deeper than normal breath. Exhale about half of the air taken in and relax the chest and abdominal area. This is the breathing adjustment most helpful to shooting. (See Fig. 9-1.)

Shooters can practice this breath adjustment by taking a few deep breaths in which they "drop" the diaphragm at full exhalation. There is a feel to relaxation in the chest-abdominal area and shooters must learn how to achieve and recognize it.

A studied attempt at breath adjustment must be made when learning to shoot a pistol or revolver. It is somewhat like

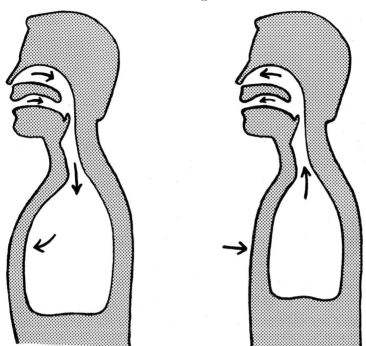

Figure 9-1. Breath control. Left: inhalation. Right: exhalation. Arrows inside body show movement of breath; arrow on outside of body (right figure) indicates chest-stomach area around diaphragm that must be relaxed upon exhalation. Note that about half of the breath is exhaled, the remainder held while the handgun is aimed and fired (one or more times).

learning proper breathing for swimming. It must be timed to coincide with the aiming-and-firing cycle, just as in swimming it must be timed with the swimming stroke. However, in either case, once learned it is nothing more than a conditioned reflex, something that is done without conscious thinking.

When to hold the breath is of great importance. It should be timed to the pace of the trigger finger motion. Take the empty gun in your hand, slip into the basic shooting position, and come to "Raise Pistol." Establish a line of sight with the head erect and body without tension, take a few normal to deep breaths, hold one breath at half capacity, and time it with the extension of the gun arm into the line of sight to the aiming position. When aiming becomes uncomfortable, expel the air and return to the "Raise Pistol" position.

Novice shooters are always surprised by the length of time a handgun can be aimed before any need to "fight" for air is apparent. The less air held in the lungs (below 50 percent) the greater the span of comfortable aiming.

Once a shooter is aware of just how long a half-breath can be held without tension in the diaphragm area, breathing can be adjusted to the pace of the trigger finger motion:

1. slow fire — as necessary for each shot fired
2. time or rapid fire — as necessary to the number of shots that are to be fired without reloading (five or six shots are usually fired in both time and rapid fire on standard courses).

Aiming longer than necessary in slow fire puts a strain on the body's ability to hold the handgun within an aiming area, as well as on the ability to hold the breath. Because of the association of most handgunning with combat shooting, lengthy periods of aiming have always been discouraged.

Once breathing control is mastered, a shooter knows he or she can adjust their breathing to fire as many shots as required in a similar time limit — or in combat.

Concentration on Aiming and Firing

The key to the control of breathing in handgunning is a subordination of breath control to concentration upon aiming, and trigger finger motion.

As the breath is held, during the moments leading up to the firing of a handgun, it is very appropriate to stress the importance of the sights and the trigger motion.

This sights-trigger concentration at this critical time contributes to the general relaxation of the shooter's body and mind. A shooter should not go limp, but he or she should relax all muscles other than those necessary to the primary activity of aiming and firing. While a shooter's mind does not blank out, there is a deliberate concentration on the sights and the trigger that excludes other mental activity. This is no more than a concentration of muscular and neural energy.

"Psyching" is an effective method for controlling breathing and gaining relaxation by concentrating on sighting and firing. It is the use of suggestion to direct and control a shooter's physical and mental activity. Each time the shooter takes a breath and aims, he or she thinks of a commanding voice repeating over and over: "Watch the sights, easy on the trigger . . . sights . . . trigger . . . sights . . . trigger."

Only when the shot is fired or a string of shots completed does the shooter exhale and stop this self-communication.

Common Faults

The common faults of breath adjustment for handgunners follow:

1. holding breath before gun is in aiming position
2. trying to retain too much air while aiming and firing
3. "fighting" for air due to long periods of aiming
4. thinking about breath control (or other problems).

Breathing must be timed to aiming and firing. The breath should be taken and held as recommended (inhalation of a normal to heavy breath, exhalation of at least 50 percent of it, and a conscious relaxation of the diaphragm at time of exhalation); the shooter's concentration at the time must be on the sights and trigger finger motion.

Summary

Normal breathing must be suspended while a handgun is aimed and fired; breathing while aiming causes the shooter's arm to rise and fall. The breath is held during aiming and firing by the inhalation of normal to heavy breath, the exhalation of at least 50 percent of this air, and the conscious relaxing of the muscles of the diaphragm. Shooters can "psych" themselves to avoid thinking about breath control or other problems while aiming and firing. This involves some self-communication ("sights . . . trigger . . . sights . . . trigger") to force concentration on the primary activity of sighting and aiming and relaxing the muscles and mind of the shooter.

Chapter 10

PLANNED PRACTICE

PISTOL and revolver shooting requires a three-month program of practice to develop basic skills. The first thirty days offer nothing more than an opportunity for a student-shooter to learn the mechanics of shooting. The next month is a period of trial and error, of diagnosis and correction. The final thirty days is a polishing-up time, a period of systematic review of handgunning and its component parts: position, grip, sighting, aiming, and trigger finger motion.

This ninety day program in handgunning will teach muscular control as well as knowledge and understanding of theory. It is not enough that a shooter develop the muscular structure to hold the weight of a gun at arm's length without tension, nor merely gain the facts about shooting theory. It is vitally necessary that the student-shooter understand the reasons for the shooting theory outlined in this text, particularly the concepts of area aiming and trigger finger motion. In addition, any learning program must provide time to do things wrong and to make mistakes. A ninety day period is usually sufficient for most shooters.

There is a time lag to real development in learning any skill or sport while the learner develops the combination of understanding and determination necessary for learning.

Possibly 10 percent of all beginning shooters can learn to line up the sights, aim correctly, and shoot with the proper trigger pressure. The remaining more average individuals ruin their aim by concentrating on the "hold" in relation to the bull's-eye or other aiming point, and become trigger "jerks."

A program for effective shooting, therefore, must consider the difficulty the great majority of people have in overcoming this psychological barrier. It must provide a drill in the basic concepts at the same time it is providing for range practice that will permit the shooter-student to test his or her own shortcuts to shooting skill. The program of instruction must also put greater and greater demands upon the learning shooter to force a more rapid discovery of faults and the need for corrective action. It must build to the day when skill is achieved: *the day the shooter learns to control trigger pressure.*

Muscle Building

Extensive physical conditioning of the muscles that control the hand and support the arm is absolutely necessary for all students of shooting. Handgun shooting places an unusual demand upon the muscular system of a shooter: an unusual load at the end of the arm. In addition, this load (pistol or revolver) must be held without muscular effort or tension to achieve the steadiness necessary for effective shooting. Exercise equipment aids in building the muscles necessary for the tasks of handgunning. (See Figure 10-1.)

Exercise with a weight at the end of the arm will help to lessen the area in which movement occurs during the aiming-

Figure 10-1. Exercise equipment: exercise bicycle to strengthen legs of shooter; hand exerciser for grip development; and dumbbell for arm-shoulder-back exercises.

and-firing cycle. Dumbbells (4 to 6 pounds) are excellent. An electric iron is a fine weight for such practice. An electric drill can be utilized, and some of them even have "pistol" grips. A milk bottle filled with water can be grasped by its neck.

Pick up the weight selected and grasp it firmly. Take the "Raise Pistol" position; extend the weight out at arm's length. Sight along its top and try to hold it within the target aiming area, or at least *up* to it. Return to "Raise Pistol" position when fired, and repeat — and repeat and repeat.

These arm-shoulder-back exercise sessions can also be tied in with correct breath adjustment. The objective is to hold the small amount of breath necessary for the aiming-and-firing cycle without tension of any kind. Remember, this must be done without conscious thinking. Tie breathing in with the extension of the arm into shooting position.

Rest sessions between arm-shoulder-back exercises can be utilized for exercising each hand. A rubber or spring grip exerciser, or a hard rubber ball (handball, racketball) is an excellent device to strengthen the muscles used in grasping the handgun when shooting.

An exercise bicycle is the necessary indoor equipment to strengthen the legs. Of course, "bike" riding outdoors is a more enjoyable substitute.

A diminishing aiming area can be speeded up through exercises. Muscular development means the pistol or revolver can be held out at arm's length without any feeling of tension or tiredness. Since the "away" theory proves shots cannot be "horsed" into the center of a target with any regularity, then the way to reduce the normal shiver-and-shake area is through exercise.

The amount of exercise necessary for muscle building depends upon the physical condition of a shooter. Most novice shooters require considerable regular exercise to adequately handle the tasks of aiming and firing and to develop a stable shooting platform in both the basic standing position and in all of the combat positions.

In any planned practice program the physical condition and good health of a shooter is of major importance.

Weak-Hand Practice

The weak hand of right-handed shooters is the left hand, and vice-versa for left-handers. At some stages of combat shooting, shooters must load their weapons, transfer them to their weak hand, and fire at the target. The rationale for weak-hand shooting is that injury or restraint may render the strong hand/arm of a shooter useless and the only alternative is to use the other hand to shoot.

In the initial stages of a planned shooting program, a considerable amount of exercise and dry shooting should be aimed at learning how to hold, aim and fire with the weak hand. This involves primarily a general reversal of position and grip. The concepts of area aiming and trigger finger motion are the same and still dominant.

Range Practice

It is on the pistol range that the shooter tests his or her skills. Firing sessions on the range are the occasion for shooters to panic suddenly and to forget everything they have learned about area aiming and a steadily increasing trigger finger motion.

There is a high interest potential in range practice: either the achievement of good shooting or a failure to shoot well is immediately known. Unlike dry shooting, shooters will find their faults on display: (1) movement of gun on the sixth shot, (2) "away" bullet holes in the target due to jerking and flinching.

Ninety Day Planned Practice Program

The first four week period of shooting builds up the slow-fire skills of the shooter and leads him or her into the time fire (five shots in twenty seconds) stage of pistol and revolver shooting. An outline for the ninety days of planned shooting follows.

FIRST WEEK. Shoot two targets (bull's-eye) at twenty-five yards to ten shots each for a total of twenty shots, no more. This is slow fire, shooter's arm returning to rest ("Raise Pistol") between shots. Concentrate on sight alignment and a steadily increasing trigger pressure. Think about every shot fired. This is the reason for the twenty-shot limitation. Shooting a great number of cartridges leads to a blurring of the memory in regard to the poor shots. A sort of mental sugar-coating occurs. The student shoots and shoots, blasting out of his or her immediate recall all of the hits except those he or she wants to remember — the good shots.

SECOND WEEK. Shoot three ten-shot targets (bull's-eye) at twenty-five yards for a total of thirty shots, no more. Think about every shot fired. Read every target. Watch the sight and gun for movement on the sixth shot. This is slow fire for automatic pistol shooters, and a modified slow fire for revolver shooters. Fire two shots before resting ("Raise Pistol"), keeping the arm fully extended from shot to shot. Single-action shooters must be careful not to thumb the gun, to let the hammer slip from under the thumb. In cocking the gun, in single- or double-action, keep the sights as close to alignment as possible and avoid unnecessary gun movement.

At this range session, practice lowering the hammer — for instances when a revolver is cocked in single action and it is decided not to fire it. Remember, use care, let the hammer down halfway, then take the finger off the trigger and lower the hammer slowly with the thumb.

THIRD WEEK. Shoot thirty shots at twenty-five yards slow-fire, and ten shots time fire (20 seconds) on the bull's-eye target for a total of forty rounds. Work at self-diagnosis and correction. Seek cadence (even pacing of trigger finger motion for each shot) in time fire. Two range sessions in this week are desirable (Monday/Thursday; Tuesday/Friday; Saturday/Wednesday).

FOURTH WEEK. Repeat third-week program, and fire ten shots of "first shot" practice on a bull's-eye target at twenty-five yards. This is slow fire in which the arm is extended for every shot and returned to the "Raise Pistol" position between shots. Trigger finger motion is paced as in the initial shot of a time fire string. The shot is not hurried nor is it timed, but no time can be lost. This fifty-shot session can be repeated once or twice this week.

FIFTH WEEK. Work on known faults. Allow up to thirty cartridges for corrective practice on the pistol range during each firing session. Use a blank (area aiming) target in order to fight against the habit of framing the shot. In this blank target practice, be certain not to look through the sights, and be sure to let the gun swing naturally within the aiming area in which you can hold the gun. Possibly another check-up device may be useful for revolver shooters. This is "Swiss-loading". Ask a fellow shooter to work with you.

Note: Revolver shooters should start with single-action shooting in the third week; and then mix both styles during the fourth and fifth weeks.

Finish up this firing session with thirty shots fired: two or three shots without coming back to a position of rest; then after rest, fire two or three more shots until the handgun is emptied. Try for a cadence of time fire (5 shots in 20 seconds), but do not hurry any shot. (Remember, never fire a *careless* shot. If hurrying a shot off tends to make a shooter careless, it is best not to hurry — just make every effort to concentrate on following shots: forget the shot just fired, concentrate on sights and trigger and firing the coming shot.)

SIXTH AND SEVENTH WEEKS. Shoot ten shots in slow fire. Take *care* with each shot. Call it; check the call. Rest at "Raise Pistol" between each shot fired. Come back to "Raise Pistol" position if you do not fire the shot in a reasonable time (shiver-and-shake increases with the length of time the gun is aimed). Do not hurry any shot. Use the bull's-eye target.

Shoot twenty shots in time fire (20 seconds for each 5 shots) on the bull's-eye target. The arm is fully extended for all five shots and the shooter attempts a regular cadence in pacing trigger finger motion for each shot. Be generous in timing this shooting; it is better to go overtime than it is to hurry a shot and jerk or fire when the sights are not properly aligned.

Shoot another thirty cartridges in the type of fire in which more shooting appears to be necessary. One or two lengthy sessions a week is sufficient at this time. Reflect on past shooting sessions.

EIGHTH WEEK. Range practice during the eighth week is

limited to two shooting sessions. This should be sessions in which the shooter fires on the silhouette target and uses the combat positions for the first time. Emphasis should be on aimed-fire positions: two-hand standing (25 yards), sitting (25 yards), and prone (50 yards). Revolver shooters should fire double-action. This is a think-and-shoot session in which aiming areas on this target are developed, and the problems of selected combat positions are explored. A total of sixty to one hundred cartridges should be fired.

NINTH WEEK. Fire on the silhouette target using all combat positions. Emphasis should be on directed-fire positions: hip (7 yards) and point-shoulder (15 yards). Try the Weaver position. Revolver shooters should fire double-action. Two or three firing sessions on the range are recommended for this week, and 100 to 120 cartridges should be fired.

TENTH WEEK. Fire on silhouette targets using all combat positions. Shoot no less than 120 cartridges, and shoot at least twice this week. Revolver shooters should fire double-action and use a speed loader each time the gun is loaded. They may fire single-action from the sitting and prone positions, and — when barricades are available — fire from the two-hand standing position, resting the hand(s) on the edge of the barricade. In actual combat, this position would depend on the type of rest available (tree, pole, fence, car hood or top) and whether it afforded protection for the shooter. There is an assumption that protection is inherent in this position, and shooters should not expose any portion of their body not required by the act of aiming and firing.

ELEVENTH WEEK. Prior to firing in this week, a shooter should decide which of the combat shooting positions are best suited to his or her self-defense needs and from which they can deliver the most accurate fire. Fire between 100 and 120 shots, using the silhouette target for all firing. In this session, shooters should concentrate on three major distances: seven, fifteen, and twenty-five yards. Try the Weaver position for two-hand standing aimed fire. Experiment at twenty-five yards with the two-hand standing position and the sitting position, using no rest and various types of rests such as the barricade. Shoot three times this week, if possible, and in the final session concentrate on the two or three positions selected as the "best" positions at seven, fifteen, and twenty-five yards. Revolver shooters must fire double-action and use a speedloader.

FINAL WEEK. This is a week of testing, of examining the progressively successful nature of regular, planned practice. Fire the following program in each session, and try to shoot twice this week.

1. Bull's-eye Target: Shoot ten shots slow fire, no time limit, and twenty shots time fire (5 shots in 20 seconds). Revolver shooters may shoot single-action or double-action.
2. Silhouette Target: Shoot six shots at seven yards from the position most suited to the shooter and this range. This is directed fire from hip, chest, or shoulder levels. Trigger pacing should be rapid and the six shots fired in a regular cadence without rest. Shoot six shots at fifteen yards from the point-shoulder position, two-hand standing position, no rest, and six shots from the sitting position — all at twenty-five yards. Trigger pacing is slower than at seven or fifteen yards but should be no less than the pacing of time fire on the bull's-eye target: five shots in twenty seconds. Revolver shooters must use double-action at all positions.

The average of all shots fired during this week is the final examination. It should average 80 percent or more of the possible total on each target.

Note: The combat shooting in this program is to hone the aiming and firing skills of shooters. Any practice in drawing from holster or in combat-ready stances should be postponed until this program is completed.

The last week should conclude with a final examination. (See Fig. 10-2.) This can be a test of slow, time, or rapid fire on the bull's-eye target; or some combination of combat shooting on the silhouette. A "passing" grade should be the satisfaction of knowing that life saving accuracy can be achieved. This is not a specified percentage of the possible that could be scored on the target selected but rather is the conclusion that the difficult skill of handgunning has been learned.

Follow-up Practice

Handgunning is one of the most rewarding sports. No matter

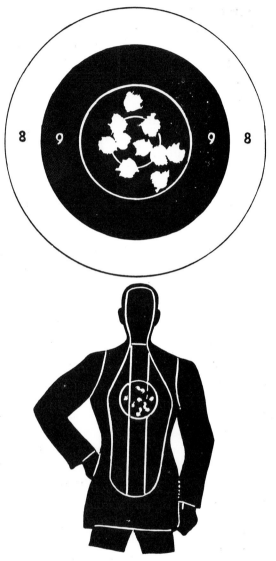

Figure 10-2. Final test: a group of shots centered on target.

what the skill level of the shooter, there is a test situation. The
target — on the range, in the hunting field, or in combat — is
both a confrontation and a challenge. The paper target on the
range returns a blank stare to the shooter, saying in effect

"Let's see how good you are," and then displays the shooter's response visually. The charging animal or the armed opponent states the same proposition but the shooter may be in the hospital or the morgue if the challenge is not met and overcome.

A basic skill level can be achieved as a result of the foregoing ninety day planned practice, but this skill level can only be maintained by follow-up practice. It can be improved, of course, by regular practice; lack of regular practice is most likely to reduce any skill level attained.

Regular follow-up practice can improve skill levels; some follow-up practice can maintain skill levels previously achieved; lack of any contemporary follow-up shooting will seriously diminish any skill level of the past.

The skills of handgunning must be learned and must be practiced to be maintained. Learning handgunning and holding achieved skills can be worthwhile. It is one of the few sports that provides an extra dividend: it may someday save your life.

Police and other law enforcement officers should practice shooting in dim light or at night. Safety should be emphasized, particularly not firing when the pistol or revolver cannot be pointed or aimed or the target adequately identified. The nighttime sessions can be illuminated by flashlight or the use of the lights of one or more automobiles — as is common in some combat shooting situations in real life.

These shooters, and others interested in self-defense shooting, can experiment with exertion or physical stress shooting. This does not mean shooting while running, but it does mean shooting after running. This type of practice produces an awareness by shooters of the impact of an increase in heart and respiratory rates upon the ability to aim and fire a handgun. While some physical exertion is necessary on the firing range to raise the body's response to stress, it may be present without any physical activity in a real-life combat situation as the human body-alarm reaction (fight or flight) does the same job.

Common Faults

The two most common faults of shooters in a planned prac-

tice program follow:
1. failure to follow program outline
2. failure to detect and diagnose faults, particularly in regard to aiming, trigger finger motion, and muscular tensions

Shooting less than programmed is less harmful than shooting too much in any one range session, or shooting too often — one day after the other in the first two months.

Shooting without thinking of the mechanics and concepts of shooting is a waste of time and money. Progressive improvement results from intelligent practice: thinking and shooting. A loss of achieved skills is likely unless a schedule of regular follow-up shooting holds and improves achieved skills.

Summary

The ninety day planned practice program includes exercises to develop the muscles of a shooter for the task of holding a pistol or revolver at arm's length with some steadiness and little effort or fatigue. Particular stress is on developing the weak hand of a shooter. Combat shooting requires shooting with this hand, as it may be necessary in combat if the strong hand normally used is injured or restrained.

Firing the handgun on a firing range tests the skill of a shooter, as it enhances the general learning environment by offering signs of effective or ineffective procedures. A ninety day program of progressively successful practice guides novice shooters through the first months of learning-by-doing. Follow-up practice keeps achieved skills and can lead to greater improvement.

BIBLIOGRAPHY

Agosta, Roy. *Manual of Basic Police Firearms Instruction and Safe Handling Practices.* Springfield, Ill.: Charles C Thomas, 1974.

Askins, Charles. *The Pistol Shooter's Book.* Harrisburg, Pa.: The Stackpole Co., 1961.

Bristow, Robert. *An Introduction to Modern Police Firearms.* Beverly Hills, Ca.: Glencoe Press, 1969.

Fisher, Morris. *Mastering the Pistol and the Revolver.* New York: G.P. Putman's Sons, 1940.

Gaylord, Chic. *Handgunner's Guide.* New York: Hastings House, 1960

Haven, Charles T. and Frank A. Belden. *A History of the Colt Revolver.* New York: Bonanza Books, 1940.

Jennings, Mike. *Instinct Shooting.* New York: Dodd, Mead & Co., 1968 (Original edition, 1959).

Koller, Larry (revised by Robert Elman). *How to Shoot.* Garden City, N.Y.: Doubleday & Co., 1976.

Logan, Herschel C. *Cartridges.* New York: Bonanza Books, 1959.

Mason, James D. *Combat Handgun Shooting.* Springfield, Ill.: Charles C Thomas, 1976.

McGivern, Ed. *Fast and Fancy Revolver Shooting* (Anniversary Edition). Chicago, Ill.: Follett Publishing Company, 1975.

Parsons, John E. *Smith and Wesson Revolvers.* New York: William Morrow & Co., 1957.

Reichenbach, William. *Sixguns and Bullseyes.* Onslow County, North Carolina: Small-arms Technical Publishing Company (Samworth), 1936.

Roper, Walter. *Pistol and Revolver Shooting.* New York: the Macmillan Company, 1946.

Taylorson, A.W.F. *Revolving Arms.* New York: Walker & Co., 1967.

Weston, Paul B. *Combat Shooting For Police.* (2nd Ed.) Springfield, Ill.: Charles C Thomas, 1978.

Weston, Paul B. *Target Shooting Today.* New York: Greenberg, 1950.

INDEX

101